'I am Lady

'Forgive me f...
he said, 'but ...
assure you, La...
year, construct...
be the strongest man in the whole of Mayfair.
I should know, for she is my granddam.'

'You are such a quiz, my lord,' she said. 'Of course I am not *that* Lady Kirkham. I am the other Lady Kirkham. I am your wife.'

Dear Reader

We complete Paula Marshall's trilogy this month, moving outside our usual limits to the restless world of 1920. Kate's son has discovered his true origins and is a changed man. Elizabeth Lowther gives us a sparkling Regency where Lord Kirkham finds himself saddled with an unwanted wife!

In our American books, Caryn Cameron charts the brink of the Civil War, and Elisabeth MacDonald looks at how differently the Spanish and the English dealt with California in the 1870s.

Absorbing reads for your pleasure!

The Editor

Recent titles by the same author:

BREATH OF SCANDAL
LOVE'S PAROLE
THE RANSOMED BRIDE

GAMBLER'S WEDDING

Elizabeth Lowther

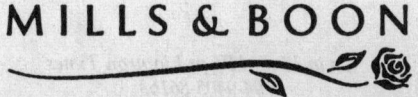

MILLS & BOON LIMITED
ETON HOUSE, 18–24 PARADISE ROAD
RICHMOND, SURREY, TW9 1SR

DID YOU PURCHASE THIS BOOK WITHOUT A COVER?

If you did, you should be aware it is **stolen property** as it was reported *unsold and destroyed* by a retailer. Neither the Author nor the publisher has received any payment for this book.

All the characters in this book have no existence outside the imagination of the Author, and have no relation whatsoever to anyone bearing the same name or names. They are not even distantly inspired by any individual known or unknown to the Author, and all the incidents are pure invention.

All Rights Reserved. The text of this publication or any part thereof may not be reproduced or transmitted in any form or by any means, electronic or mechanical, including photocopying, recording, storage in an information retrieval system, or otherwise, without the written permission of the publisher.

This book is sold subject to the condition that it shall not, by way of trade or otherwise, be lent, resold, hired out or otherwise circulated without the prior consent of the publisher in any form of binding or cover other than that in which it is published and without a similar condition including this condition being imposed on the subsequent purchaser.

First published in Great Britain 1994 by Mills & Boon Limited

© Elizabeth Lowther 1994

Australian copyright 1994   Philippine copyright 1994
This edition 1994

ISBN 0 263 78251 4

Set in 10 on 11½ pt Linotron Times
04-9405-86163

Typeset in Great Britain by Centracet, Cambridge
Printed and bound in Great Britain by
BPCC Paperbacks Ltd
Member of BPCC Ltd

CHAPTER ONE

JOHN EDWARD ST CLAIR EVELEIGH, the tenth Lord Kirkham, awoke very carefully. The reason for such caution was his conviction that a hundred vindictive demons were pounding at the inside of his skull with sledge-hammers. The previous night's merrymaking must have been something out of the ordinary to have reduced him to this state. It was a pity he could not remember anything about it. He waited for the demons to reduce their activities to more human proportions.

Outside, the fashionable folk of Hanover Square were going about their daily affairs. Boots stamped, horses' hooves clattered, iron-shod carriage-wheels rumbled over cobbles. If his servants had had any consideration they would have laid down straw outside the house to muffle the sounds of the traffic, as one did for the gravely ill or dying. He was not dying, though judging by his physical state it was a close-run thing. He decided to concentrate upon remaining very, very still.

It was while he was lying thus, with his long, lean body in a prone position, that he made an interesting discovery. He was not alone in bed. Intrigued, he stretched out an exploratory hand and encountered a leg. It was slender and rounded, and undeniably feminine, causing curiosity to overcome his agony. With an effort he forced open an eyelid for the merest second, then let it close again. In one brief glimpse he had taken in the relevant details.

His companion was sitting up in bed sipping a cup of

chocolate. For the sake of his turbulent stomach he preferred to ignore this activity, but everything else about her was perfection. Long curling strands of golden hair escaping from a muslin nightcap, a complexion delicate enough to send any wild rose into paroxysms of envy, and eyes of so deep a blue he wondered if they might be closer to violet. Yes, perfection was the only word to describe her.

Lord Kirkham gave a self-satisfied sigh. It was gratifying to know that, even when completely foxed, one's taste was impeccable. There was only one snag. For the life of him he could not think who she was! This was an omission he decided to rectify immediately. With eyes still closed he gave the rounded thigh an appreciative pat and said, 'Good morning, my dear. Did you sleep well?'

'Yes, thank you, my lord. Did you?'

The voice was as delightful as the rest of her; soft, low, well-modulated.

'Tolerably, my dear, tolerably,' he replied, preferring to ignore the fact that his recent state of unconsciousness might have raised the hopes of any enterprising undertaker.

'Would you care for some chocolate?' she enquired. 'It's quite delicious, and there's lots here, still piping hot. Shall I ring for another cup?'

It was not a happy suggestion, though it showed a kind heart. Another asset of this vision of loveliness. For a few minutes Kirkham was forced to concentrate on a rebellious stomach. Only when he had succeeded in quelling his mutinous digestion did he manage to answer, 'Thank you, but no.'

'You sound quite frail, my lord. Can it be that you are not quite the thing this morning?' The concern in her soft voice was delightful to hear.

'I fear you are right. I fancy there was something wrong with that last bottle of claret.' He could not remember any last bottle of claret, but there was bound to have been one.

'The last bottle, was it, my lord? Are you sure it was not the one before, or the one before that?'

Did he detect a strange edge to her voice? No, he must have been mistaken, for there came the chink of delicate porcelain as she put down her cup, the soft cool fingers stroked his dark hair away from his forehead. Those fingers began gently caressing his tortured brow.

'There, is that not better?' she asked softly.

'Much, much better,' he murmured.

He accepted the softness of her touch until her caresses had soothed the demons in his head into near submission. Beautiful, gentle, kind, soft-voiced, she was all he had ever wanted in a woman; but he still did not know who she was. He gave the rounded thigh another pat.

'You are such a beautiful creature, it is a joy to have your company, truly it is,' he began. 'However, I must make a confession. The blame can no doubt be given to that rancid claret, it has certainly addled my wits, but I have to admit I cannot remember your name.'

The soothing fingers ceased their caressing, as the Beautiful Creature gave a little laugh. It was a delightful laugh, with no hint of harshness, just the sort of laugh he would have expected from her. She laughed again.

'Surely you cannot have forgotten, my lord. I am Lady Kirkham.'

He was almost taken aback by her reply, but not quite. If there was one thing he liked it was a pretty woman with a sense of humour.

'Forgive me for contradicting you, my dear,' he said,

as jokingly as his condition would allow, 'but you are not Lady Kirkham. I assure you, Lady Kirkham is in her seventieth year, constructed of solid granite, and said to be the strongest man in the whole of Mayfair. No, you are not at all like Lady Kirkham. I should know, for she is my granddam.'

The Beautiful Creature gave another trilling laugh, during which she gently but firmly removed his hand from her thigh.

'You are such a quiz, my lord,' she said. 'Of course I am not *that* Lady Kirkham. I am the other Lady Kirkham. I am your wife.'

Now he really was taken aback. He liked a joke as well as the next man, but for the life of him he could not see where this was leading.

'I am going to have to contradict you yet again, with your permission,' he said. 'You see, I am not married. I have no wife. The last I recall, my bachelorhood was complete and beyond any doubt.'

'The last you recall, you say, my lord? You have no recollection? Then clearly it is my happy duty to inform you that you are now a married man.'

'It distresses me to keep insisting to a beautiful woman that she is wrong, but I fear I have no alternative. I am not married. I have no wife.' He was beginning to find this joke bewildering. His brain was in no fit state for conundrums. However, never let it be said that Kirkham ever spoiled a good jape. Determined to maintain his reputation as one of the liveliest, most amusing young men about town, he rallied his foggy wits and replied lightly, 'I must admit that several attempts have been made to steer me to the altar. I suppose I must take the trip some day — my duty as the last of the Kirkhams and all that — and in fact one mama has almost got my foot in the church door. She is a terrible dragon, but her daughter is a pleasant enough little thing, if one likes mice. And she does happen to be an extremely wealthy mouse, so I suppose she will do as well as any other. Therefore you see, my dear, you cannot possibly be married to me.'

'But I am. Poor mouse and poor dragon, they will have to look elsewhere for a bridegroom, because you are mine!'

Kirkham was becoming irritated by her teasing. Manfully, though, he made one last attempt to keep the conversation light.

'Oh, yes? And when were we married? And where? St George's, I suppose? It's handy enough, being just across the square.'

'Of course not. We were married at St Willibrod's. Don't you remember? Such an ancient little church in the City. And we were married last night. Don't you recall that, either? It was so romantic, an evening wedding. Making our vows by candlelight. The only thing lacking was music, but then one can't have everything. All else was perfection.'

'No, it was not,' retorted Kirkham, his patience at an end, 'because it never took place. There was no wedding, no church, and no candles!' He said the words with conviction. The trouble was that from the dimmer recesses of his mind came a disturbing tableau. It was night, and by the light of flickering candles a spare nervous figure dressed in a clerical surplice and grubby nightcap was intoning the marriage service. In an effort to brush away this distressing vision he snapped, 'Now let's stop all this nonsense. Tell me what you are up to, and what your name is. Your real name, not this idiotic Lady Kirkham nonsense,' he added, as the Beautiful Creature opened her mouth to reply.

His eyes were wide open, and now he looked at her

properly there was a determined set to her jaw and a firmness about her mouth he had not noticed in his first brief glimpse. She was as pretty as ever, but she was no empty-headed bit of muslin, he could see that. There was a certain steeliness in those dark blue eyes as they regarded him unflinchingly which reminded him incongruously of his grandmother, the other Lady Kirkham—no, dash it! The *only* Lady Kirkham!

'I'm not *up to* anything, as you put it,' she replied, 'save being a good and dutiful wife to you. And my name, before our marriage, was Daubenay. Miss Melissa Daubenay, now become Melissa Eveleigh, Lady Kirkham.'

'Ha!' he snorted scornfully. 'Ha!' He wished he could think of a more cutting response, but that name, Daubenay, had struck an uncomfortable chord in his memory. Somehow he associated it with a gaming-house, and a young man glaring across the card-table at him with all the intense desperation of one who had lost far more than he could ever repay. That desperation shone out of dark blue eyes which were annoyingly familiar. Once more he shut out the nightmare. 'Ha!' he said again. 'Ha!'

'Is that all you are going to say, my lord? If so I must confess I find your conversation a mite tedious.'

'Tedious, is it?' he cried indignantly. 'If that is your reaction there is nothing stopping you from leaving. Pray do not let me detain you!'

'But you do, my lord. My concern for your family reputation forces me to stay.'

'How so?'

'The suddenness of our marriage, and the—er—unconventional circumstances of our union are both enough to have tongues wagging. If Lord Kirkham's bride were to leave him immediately after the wedding—

night—my word, every club and coffee-house in London would be alight with the scandal.'

'Oh, so that's your game, is it? Trying to extort money out of me to prevent some fictitious scandal. Well, it won't work because you are not my bride. If you are what you claim, then prove it. Go on! Where's the proof?'

Melissa gave a patient sigh. 'I knew you would be difficult, and so I made provision accordingly.' She rummaged beneath her pillow and, producing a piece of paper, handed it to him. 'Our marriage lines, my lord.'

Kirkham gave them the briefest scrutiny. They looked alarmingly official, but he refused to be daunted. With a cry of, 'Fake!' he tore the document into tiny pieces and tossed them disparagingly into the air.

'Just the sort of thing I expected you to do,' Melissa said complacently. 'Fortunately it was only a copy. The original I have in a safe place, you may be sure of it.'

'You fancy you know my character, do you? How long have we been acquainted?' If he kept cross-questioning her then surely she would eventually betray what game she was playing?

She gazed towards the French clock on the mantelshelf.

'Approximately four-and-twenty hours,' she said.

Temporarily he was nonplussed. Surely he had not been drunk for that length of time? Not he, whose ability to hold his liquor was a legend the length and breadth of St James's?

'One day scarcely seems enough time in which to sum up a man,' he replied, returning to the attack.

'Believe me, that was quite long enough to determine what sort of a creature you are!' It was strange how her soft, well-modulated voice had suddenly assumed a stony quality.

'Oh, yes? Then tell me, what sort of a creature am I?' he taunted her.

'You are a drunkard, and a rake. Fortunately for you you were born into the peerage and into wealth. In any other walk of life you would be labelled a rogue and a ne'er-do-well. Worst of all, though, you are a gambler! One who cares not how many lives he ruins, nor fortunes he brings down, just so long as he has the thrill of turning over the cards. In short, you are despicable!'

'Having such a bad opinion of me, I wonder you married me!' he cried, incensed by such an unflattering description.

'You admit it at last! You admit that I am your wife, do you, Kirkham?' she crowed triumphantly.

'No, I do not!' he retorted, annoyed at his temporary slip. 'And I did not give you leave to address me in so familiar a fashion.'

'I am your wife, and I will address you in any fashion I choose!' was the furious response.

'Then show me proof! All I've seen so far is a paltry scrap of paper that you doubtless wrote yourself.'

'Oh, Kirkham, won't you even recognise your ring, put on my finger by you?' Suddenly her voice had gone soft once more, almost winsome, as she held up her left hand.

There, sure enough, on the third finger, was his signet-ring. Startled, he gazed down at his own hand. It was bare.

'What is that. . .? How did that. . .?' he spluttered in puzzled rage. It was not an easy ring to remove. He had always worn it on his little finger because it was rather too small. A sentimental streak in him had refused to have it enlarged; he preferred to keep it in the ... state in which his late, adoring mother had given it to him. Now this female was flaunting it under his nose. He looked again at his own unblemished hand. The ring could not have been forced from his finger while he was unconscious or there would have been bruising. Only he could remove it painlessly. It was most bewildering.

'Of course, it is a little large for me,' Melissa stated, wiggling her slender fingers. 'But do not fear that I'll lose it. Look, I've bound wool round it to make it fit.'

Kirkham gave a growl of rage. It took all of his self-control not to snatch the ring back. Never had he been in a situation like this, not in all his six-and-twenty years of scrape-filled existence.

It occured to him that it was eccentric, not to say bizarre, to be carrying out such an acrimonious conversation while still in bed with the other protagonist, particularly since the other protagonist was a complete stranger. She looked very settled, reclining against the monogrammed pillows in her frilled cambric bedgown, so it was up to him to end this ridiculous situation. What he should do was to leap to his feet, then, towering over this female in a dominant manner suited to his nobility and station in life, order her to leave. That was what he should do. The problem was that the merest thought of standing up caused his entire physical being to quail. Then he had a flash of inspiration.

'Pentecost!' he cried. 'My manservant! He knows all my business. He must have put me to bed last night. He will identify you for the charlatan you are!'

If he expected Melissa to be anxious he was disappointed. She merely settled herself more comfortably against the pillows and said, 'By all means ring for your man if you wish. He can take away my pot of chocolate. It has grown quite cold.'

Although it cost him much, for the demons had resumed their pounding on his brain, he sat up and tugged forcefully on the bell-pull.

Pentecost's entry was slow and stately; but then all his movements were slow and stately. His portly form approached the bed.

'You rang, my lord?' he enquired.

'Yes, I rang! Pentecost, there is a female in bed with me. Have a good look at her and tell me who she is.'

'Very good, my lord. I will ascertain the lady's identity.'

With head held high, Pentecost made his measured progress round the huge bed, and bowed to Melissa with a, 'By your leave, my lady.'

'Certainly, Pentecost, go right ahead and identify me,' said Melissa, quite unperturbed. 'Above all things you must obey your master's commands.'

'Thank you, my lady. It is very kind of you, my lady.'

With a flourish of one hand Pentecost hooked the heavy damask bed curtain further back, scrutinised Melissa's face, then, with another bow, withdrew to plod serenely back to Kirkham's side of the bed.

'Well?' demanded his master.

'To the best of my knowledge, my lord, I believe the lady to be Lady Kirkham.'

'What? She can't be!'

'By your leave, my lord, you introduced the lady as such. "Congratulate me, Pentecost, and greet your mistress, the new Lady Kirkham.". Those were your very words, my lord.'

'No. . . When did this happen?'

'Last night, at about midnight, my lord. When you returned home.'

'Returned home? Where had I been?'

'I understand you were at your wedding, my lord,' said Pentecost.

'No I wasn't! Because there was no wedding!' snapped Kirkham irritably. 'Who else knows about this business?'

'The entire domestic staff, my lord. You had them all summoned to be presented to Lady Kirkham. Then, at Mr O'Gallagher's suggestion, we drank a toast to your wedded bliss and future happiness.'

At the sound of that name Kirkham felt himself relax. There was not a greater practical joker in the whole of London than his good friend, O'Gallagher. If Shaun were involved then this had to be some sort of foolery. More subtle than his usual efforts, but foolery none the less. Thank goodness! He gave a sigh of relief.

'Mr O'Gallagher was present?' he said, beginning to smile.

'Yes, my lord, and another gentleman, a Mr Daubenay. They accompanied you home.'

Daubeney! That name again! The smile went from Kirkham's face. Somehow his hope that this might be a joke faded. It was beginning to look much more sinister.

'Did they say anything? Give any details?' he demanded.

'No, my lord, though Mr O'Gallagher's coachman informed me that the ceremony took place at St Willibrod's.'

'No, it didn't!' cried Kirkham, angry once more, 'because there was no ceremony, no church, no St Willibrod. Who ever heard of such a saint?'

Pentecost coughed politely. 'I believe he was one of the lesser known Saxon saints, my lord. A nephew of St Boniface——'

'I do not care whose nephew he was!' snapped

Kirkham. 'I was never married in any church dedicated to him.'

'If you say so, my lord.'

'I do say so! Oh, get out!'

Melissa had been listening quietly to the conversation. Now she roused herself.

'Pentecost, be kind enough to remove my chocolate-tray, if you please,' she said.

'Very good, my lady.'

'She is not your lady!' declared Kirkham, angrily. 'She is not my lady! She is not anybody's lady! Now get out, you fool!'

The manservant somehow managed to leave the room with as much dignity as he had entered it. Not even having to side-step the slipper thrown at his head by his employer caused him to falter in his serene exit nor occasioned the least clatter of china as he carried away the tray.

'You should not get so angry. It will do you no good at all,' said Melissa.

'Now you are telling me how to behave, are you? Is that part of your trickery too?'

'It's part of my wifely concern for you, Kirkham, dear,' she said in a soothing voice. 'You are not at all the thing this morning, you have already admitted it. You'll only make your headache worse.'

'It can't get worse.' He clasped at his temples. 'It's at the peak of its strength now! For pity's sake tell me what all this is about, then leave. . . And don't call me Kirkham!' he added belatedly.

'I think it is somewhat early in our relationship to call you John. When we've been married a little longer, perhaps.'

He buried his head further in his hands.

'That's enough,' he groaned. 'I can't take any more

of this. Get dressed and leave, before I have you thrown out.'

'I am surprised you haven't threatened that before now,' remarked Melissa with astonishing calm.

'I try to avoid being discourteous to females, even females of your sort,' he retorted.

'That's not the true reason, is it?' she persisted. 'The real reason why you haven't had me dragged from this room is that you are afraid that what I say is true.'

'Of course not,' he declared. But she was right. There was something he should remember. Something kept evading him. Something which caused an uncomfortable coldness to settle in the pit of his stomach.

He opened his eyes to find Melissa regarding him steadily. The expression in her gaze could only be described as intense dislike. This female was tenacious, he could see it in every line of her beautiful face. He feared she was going to be hard to shake off. Then anger took hold of him, and a determination not to be beaten by this creature, no matter how lovely she might be.

'There never was any wedding ceremony!' he stated grimly.

'Yes, there was!' she retorted with equal vehemence. 'If you search in that alcoholic fog of a brain of yours you will recall it. A perfectly legal wedding.'

'No!' he bellowed. 'There was not! We are not married, do you hear?'

'I hear, and so does half of London,' Melissa answered tartly. 'But denying something at the top of your voice like a costermonger does not make it so. We are man and wife!'

'Never! I repeat, you are no wife of mine. But, by

Harry, when you go on at a fellow in such a way you certainly sound like one!'

So saying, he rose and strode swiftly from the bedchamber with as much dignity as any man could when still clad in his nightshirt. Angrily he slammed the door after him. It was not a wise action for someone with a head in such a fragile condition. His yelp of anguish was clearly audible in the room he had just left.

After he had gone Melissa slumped back against the pillows. To her annoyance she found that she was trembling. The enormity of what she had done gnawed at her, but how else *could* she have acted? There had been no alternative but to marry Lord Kirkham—at least none that she would tolerate. Not that she considered being the wife of Kirkham a happy prospect; he was exactly the sort of man she despised. Still, the die was cast. There was no going back now. She permitted herself a bitter smile. It was ironic that she, who hated gambling above all things, should have married one of the most ardent gamblers in London.

There was a tap at the door and she sat bolt upright, only to relax as the familiar figure of Polly entered.

'And how does his lordship like married life?' Polly asked.

'Not much,' admitted Melissa. 'He has spent a deal of time protesting that he is still a bachelor.'

'He won't be the only married man who's done that.' Polly's teeth gleamed a dazzling white against the rich coffee colour of her skin. Then her smile faded. 'Does he remember nothing of the ceremony?'

'He says not, but I fancy he does have some recollection.'

'No doubt it will all come back to him in time, when he is feeling more like himself.'

'You mean when he has sobered up,' said Melissa tartly, then she sighed. 'I fancy it will not make things any easier if he does remember.'

'You've no call to sound worried. Things'll work out, don't you fret.'

'I am not worried for myself alone, Polly, I am anxious for you. I know we did everything to make things legal and proper, but there is bound to be terrible trouble. When it comes there is no need for you to be involved. Go now, while there is still time.'

'And where d'you propose I go? No, I belong to you now. I'm staying.'

'You do not belong to me,' protested Melissa. 'How many times do I have to tell you? There is no slavery in this country any more. You are free to find work wherever you choose.'

'If there's no slavery any more, why did you buy me from my last owner?'

'He didn't own you, either. He was a rogue and a villain. No wonder you ran away from him. To pay him off was the only way to stop him hounding you.'

'You sold your last piece of jewellery, your mother's cameo, to get rid of him. If that doesn't make me belong to you I don't know what does.'

'Polly, I beg you to go,' pleaded Melissa. 'You owe me nothing. You've been my good friend and help these last two years. I've never been able to pay you anything. Now you can find yourself a good situation and get on in the world.'

'I've got a good situation,' said Polly stubbornly. 'Yesterday I was general help to Miss Melissa Daubenay, who lived in an alley off Newgate Street and who hadn't two ha'pennies to rub together most of the time. Now I'm maid to Lady Kirkham of Hanover Square, wife of a genuine lord. That's quite enough getting on in the world for me. Besides,' she added, 'You need someone you can trust below stairs in this place. Else how will you know what's going on?'

Melissa could not repress a little pang of relief. The days to come were bound to be difficult. Having Polly's loyal friendship was going to be a great comfort. It had been a fortunate day for her when she had taken in the poor bedraggled West Indian girl and rescued her from the cruel rogue who had claimed to be her master.

'And what is going on below stairs?' she asked.

'A lot of tongue-wagging, you might be sure, though it stops when I come along.'

'I suppose that was only to be expected. The story of the wedding will be all over town by now. One more reason why I cannot back out of the situation, eh?' Melissa pushed back the bed covers and rose. The longer she stayed in bed, the more appalling seemed her problems. What she needed to dispel her anxieties was action. 'I think I had better begin my first day as Lady Kirkham now,' she said.

'Very good, my lady.'

It sounded odd to hear Polly's familiar voice address her thus, and she was forced to chuckle.

'That's better,' beamed Polly. 'You was looking too serious, and without cause, in my view. It'll all turn out well, you'll see. Now, does your ladyship want breakfast in here or downstairs?'

'Downstairs, please.' She may as well make an immediate start to her new life.

'Very good, I'll go and fetch your hot water. Which dress shall I lay out?'

'There's not much choice, is there? It must either be the grey stuff gown or the lilac merino. The lilac for this morning, I think.'

Old and shabby, it had been turned and redyed so

often Melissa had forgotten which was the original right side of the fabric; but it would have to do.

'That's not much of a gown for Lady Kirkham to wear,' commented Polly. 'But now, in your new station in life, you'll be able to buy fine silks and satins.'

'No!' said Melissa vehemently. 'One thing I am determined about! I will not make any financial gain from this marriage. Circumstances forced me to wed Lord Kirkham, but it is my intention to withdraw from his life and from Society at the first opportunity. He will never have cause to accuse me of being after his money.'

'If that is what you want,' said Polly with reluctance, holding up the limp, much-washed merino. 'Though in my opinion he'd never even notice the cost of a dress-length or two.'

'Probably not, but I have no intention of finding out.'

'He's a generous enough gentleman, judging from the talk below stairs.' Polly's voice came from the adjoining dressing-room. 'Very free with his money.'

'No doubt. He has enough of it. What a pity he does not realise that other people are not so fortunate!'

'Do not take against him too much. Being generous can be a good fault. And he's not unpleasant on the eye. Very fine shoulders, he's got, and as for his face, that's handsome enough to please anybody.'

'He does not please me,' Melissa said firmly. 'I am surprised at you, finding such good points in him. I thought you had more sense.'

'He's no angel, I never said that.' Polly's head appeared round the door. 'But have you thought? You might have found yourself in exactly this predicament, but with a man who was a tight-purse, and as ugly as an ape from Astley's Circus into the bargain. Things could be worse.'

They could, Melissa was forced to agree, but not much. Here she was married to a man she did not want, and who certainly did not want her. Ahead of her she could only see a tangle of legal and emotional difficulties. But first things must come first. With Polly's help she dressed, then leaving the security of the bedroom she headed for the dining-room. Before she faced the outside world she must tackle life at the house in Hanover Square. With head erect and back straight, ignoring the frankly curious eyes of the footmen, she swept down the curving staircase. For better or for worse she was Lady Kirkham, and she would let no one forget it!

CHAPTER TWO

BREAKFAST in the elegant dining-room promised to be a daunting affair. The vast table, set with gleaming silver and porcelain, seemed to stretch for ever. Standing discreetly at a distance, an army of bewigged and liveried footmen, under the eagle eye of the butler, attended upon Melissa's slightest wish. It was all a far cry from the cramped rooms off Newgate Street, where one minute chamber served as dining-room, parlour and kitchen.

Melissa felt her normally healthy appetite waver, but only for a brief moment. She was Lady Kirkham. She had every right to be here. She was not going to let the unusual circumstances come between her and a hearty breakfast. With determination she consumed coffee, hot rolls and butter. As she ate she had to admit that Lord Kirkham's absence had a lot to do with the enjoyment of her meal. A tentative enquiry informed her that he was not in the house. She would have to meet up with him again soon, she knew, and she was ready for the confrontation. In the meantime it was agreeable to finish breakfast without any contention.

She drained her coffee-cup and faced her next problem. What should she do now? Through the window the bright winter sunshine tempted her to go for a walk, but she decided that to leave the house would be folly. Her position as Lady Kirkham was very tenuous at the moment, and she would not do anything to jeopardise it. Kirkham clearly drew the line at actually throwing her out of the house; he might have fewer qualms about barring the door against her re-entry. No, a stroll in the park would have to wait. What would she have done under normal circumstances? she wondered. As a new wife surely she would set her household in order? Very well, domestic matters would be her immediate concern, as befitted her position as châtelaine of the house in Hanover Square.

'Fraser, remind me as to the housekeeper's name, if you please?' she said.

'She is Mrs Hawkins, my lady,' the butler informed her.

'Thank you. Would you be kind enough to inform her that I would like to see her in ten minutes.'

'Very good, my lady. Where will your ladyship be?'

Melissa was nonplussed. Her knowledge of the geography of the house was sketchy; she had only found the dining-room because one of the flunkeys had thrown open the door as she approached.

Seeing her dilemma, the butler said, 'May I venture to suggest the morning-room, my lady. It is very pleasant at this time of day and has an agreeable aspect on to the garden.'

'The morning-room it shall be, if someone will show me where it is.'

Fraser himself served as her escort, while a mere footman was dispatched to fetch the housekeeper. That Mrs Hawkins resented being so summoned was obvious from her demeanour as soon as she was ushered into the room. Melissa could almost hear the indignant rattling of whalebone beneath the layers of still bombasine.

'I hope your ladyship has no cause for complaint already,' the housekeeper said, after delivering the briefest of curtsies. It was the suspicious way she hesitated slightly as she said 'your ladyship' that put

Melissa on her guard. Here was someone out to question her position.

'Why do you ask? Do you fear you have been remiss in some duty, Mrs Hawkins?' she asked calmly.

'Certainly not, my lady.' The housekeeper's reply was just a little too prompt, bordering on the insolent.

'Good. In that case we can continue with the reasons why I sent for you. I wish to be shown around the house. Would eleven o'clock be convenient for you? I have no wish to disrupt your ordinary duties.'

'That will be quite convenient, thank you, my lady.'

'Good. Now, I think it is important for you and I to establish a good routine. To this end I suggest that you present your housekeeping-books — the accounts, your work-book and so on — to me every Friday morning.'

'Every Friday, my lady?' The suspicion in the housekeeper's voice changed to indignation.

'Yes, certainly. I know some ladies deal with housekeeping matters only once a month, but I prefer to tackle them once a week. After all, a month is a long time for an error to go unrectified, is it not?'

'An error, my lady?' The indignation in Mrs Hawkins's voice was growing. 'I promise you, I am not in the habit of making errors.'

'I am glad to hear it. In that case it will be no extra hardship for you to present me with your books every seven days. I think that is all for the moment, unless you wish to say something?'

'No, thank you, my lady.'

'Good, then we will meet again at eleven. In the meantime would you be kind enough to send the cook to me.'

'The cook, my lady?'

'Certainly. I wish to order the meals for the day.'

'But I always order the menus, my lady.'

'Then I will be glad to relieve you of one onerous duty.'

'It is not onerous, I assure you, my lady. I would prefer to do it, and I fancy his lordship would prefer it too.'

'Oh, you do, do you?' Melissa's voice was growing more steely at the persistent insolence in the housekeeper's manner.

'Yes, my lady. His lordship trusts my judgement implicitly.'

'I am sure he does,' said Melissa. 'However, we all have our little foibles, and mine is that I like to direct the household myself. You must appreciate that this is no longer a bachelor establishment. Be kind enough to send the cook to me.'

The atmosphere in the room was tense as two female wills battled silently for supremacy. But Melissa was not one to back down. She continued to regard the housekeeper with a stern, unwavering gaze.

Then Mrs Hawkins said, 'Very good, my lady.' Her voice was barely audible through her anger. She had made her bid for dominance in domestic matters, and she had lost. She closed the door behind her with exaggerated care.

Melissa could envisage life ahead as one perpetual battle with the housekeeper, and that was not a happy prospect. However, she was not one to make hasty judgements. No doubt the woman had had total control of the household until now; she would need time to adjust. That was only fair, since Lord Kirkham himself seemed to be having difficulties in adjusting to the new situation.

Thoughts of Kirkham caused an uncomfortable tightening in her stomach. Had she done the right thing in going ahead with the wedding? Had there really been no other way? Before doubts could totally beset her there was a respectful tap at the door and the cook entered. Not a plump rosy-cheeked woman, as Melissa had expected, but a long, thin man with an olive complexion. She should have anticipated that someone of Kirkham's standing would have a chef in charge of his kitchens, and a French one if her guess were correct. Oh, dear, was she going to have more servant problems, and foreign ones at that?

'Milady, I am Bertrand, *chef de cuisine extraordinaire*, and will you permit me to say how I anticipates the serving of so beautiful a lady with much, much *plaisir*.' As he spoke the chef gave a sweeping bow, accompanied by a flourish of his starched hat. His words might have been extravagant and his grammar inaccurate, but there was no mistaking the sincerity of his sentiments. His '*plaisir*' positively radiated from his long thin face.

'Monsieur Bertrand, I am glad to make your acquaintance. I fancy we will get to know one another well for, in future, I will be ordering the meals instead of Mrs Hawkins.'

The sigh of mingled triumph and delight that escaped from the Frenchman told its own story.

'You say it, milady, and I am glad. A housekeeper, what does she know of food, while you, milady, your taste will be *parfait*.'

'I am taking over because Mrs Hawkins has responsibilities enough, not because she is incompetent,' Melissa said firmly. She was determined not to add fuel to the feud in the kitchen.

'No, milady. Of course not, milady!' In spite of his assurances Bertrand's eyes still gleamed with satisfaction.

'Now, for tonight's dinner, what do you suggest?'

Evidently this was a chance for which the chef had long awaited, for he poured forth such a stream of suggestions — lobster patties, fricassees heavy with spice, meats dressed in rich sauces, creamy syllabubs — that Melissa was forced to hold up her hand.

'Stop, Monsieur Bertrand!' she laughed. 'You have given enough ideas for the most sumptuous of banquets. For tonight's dinner, however, I think Lord Kirkham might appreciate something — er — more easily digested.'

Bertrand's eyes twinkled with understanding.

'Of course, milady. How foolish of me! Dinner, it shall be light and sustaining, suitable for an ardent bridegroom, eh?'

This was not quite what Melissa had had in mind. She had not been considering bolstering Kirkham's libido, her concern had been more for the delicate state of his stomach, but she had no wish to enter into any arguments.

'A few plain dishes will be appropriate,' she said, picking up her pen. 'A nourishing soup to begin with, perhaps?'

Her interview with Bertrand eventually came to an end, her tour of the house with Mrs Hawkins was brief and hostile, then once more Melissa was left to her own devices. The place seemed unnaturally quiet, even the sounds from the street outside might have been from another world. She almost wished that Kirkham would return. There was so much more to be said between them, matters to be explained, arrangements to be made, and she longed to get it over and done with. The uncertainty of it all made her nerves taut as bowstrings. Not that she intended to show it. Exerting a firm control over her feelings, she selected a book from the library, and settled herself in the withdrawing-room. When

Kirkham entered the room some twenty minutes later he took one look at her and declared irritably, 'What, you are still here? You have certainly made yourself at home!'

'Naturally, for this is now my home. Had you forgotten, Kirkham, dear?' she said sweetly.

'Don't start all that "Kirkham, dear" nonsense again, do you hear? I won't stand for it! I had hoped you had gone, given up whatever foolish enterprise you had embarked upon. It will do you no good to stay. I will not pay you a penny piece!'

'Sadly your temper has not improved,' said Melissa. 'Are you still feeling unwell? A little seltzer is good for a disordered stomach. Shall I ring for Fraser——?'

'No, you shall not! It is not seltzer that will improve my digestion, it is your absence! Will you kindly collect your things, if you have got any, and leave this house?'

'And if I do not?'

'Then I will forget all my chivalrous instincts and have you thrown out.'

'And what a pretty story that would make. Already the news that Lord Kirkham has got himself a wife must be round half of London. The tale that he had his servants throw her out on to the streets would be round town in a fraction of that time.'

Kirkham sank into an armchair. He was feeling more robust than when he had left the house but he was far from being his usual spirited self. If only he had managed to find his friend O'Gallagher! O'Gallagher would know the truth of this sorry mess. But though he had tramped through London for hours he had found no sign of the Irishman.

'Tell me what you want and have done with it,' he said. 'What is this all about? What harm have I ever done you, that you must plague me so?'

'You really want to know?' Melissa laid aside her book and regarded her new and unwanted husband steadily.

It occurred to her that this was the first time she had seen him looking presentable. Unshaven, with a hangover, and wearing a crumpled nightshirt, he had not been particularly appealing last night; and at the wedding he had been far from his best. Now, though, she was forced to admit that Polly had been right, he was a handsome man. His dark hair fell easily and naturally into the waves that were fashionable at the moment, his broad shoulders, so admired by Polly, were accentuated by a superbly tailored coat in blue broadcloth. The jersey of his well-cut 'inexpressibles' betrayed—as was the intention—the fact that his legs were long and well-shaped. Yes, he was a fine-looking fellow—and she still disliked him intensely!

'Since your memory seems to have failed you so abysmally, perhaps I had better supply you with the relevant details,' she said. 'This miserable affair started two days ago——'

'It can't have! I refuse to believe I've been in a drunken stupor for two whole days——' he cried.

'Do not interrupt!' she snapped. 'Else I will leave you to remember the whole sordid mess yourself, by which time you would be the laughing-stock of the entire town.'

Kirkham's mouth tightened. 'Carry on,' he said grimly.

'Very well. The night before last you won me in a game of cards.'

'I did what?'

'Did I not speak clearly enough for you? You won me at cards!'

'Then for pity's sake tell me what game I was playing,

so that in future I can avoid. . .' His voice tailed away under the scorn in her dark blue eyes.

'Don't make things worse,' she stated. 'You come out of this very badly as it is. Let me refresh your memory. You were in a gaming-hell near Covent Garden, where you engaged to play against a young man. The stakes were high and your luck was in. Long before the night was over you had taken every penny he owned. Even then you did not stop. You played on and on, taking promissory note after promissory note until it must have been obvious to you, even in your drunken state, that he had not the least hope of ever repaying you. And still you egged him on——'

'One moment,' broke in Kirkham. 'Let me get one thing clear. I presume this young man was free to leave the gaming-table at any time he chose? I mean, he was not tied to his chair? I did not have Pentecost standing behind him with a pistol at his head, or anything of that nature? He could have got up and walked away?'

'He could have done, but he was too weak a character—— I will deal with him when I find him.'

'Ah,' said Kirkham. 'Mr Daubenay.'

'Yes, Mr Daubenay. My brother. I am not excusing his conduct. But he must wait. It is you I am dealing with now.'

'Carry on with your cock-and-bull story.' Kirkham waved an airy hand. He wished he could feel as confident. There was an assurance about this female that made her uncomfortably credible. Moreover he feared he had some recollection of a card-table strewn with more promissory notes than was usual, and an insistent voice pleading for just one more game. 'Give me a chance, my lord. My luck's changing, I can feel it. One last chance!' The words echoed in his head.

Though he could not identify the speaker, Kirkham had an uncomfortable idea who he would turn out to be.

'Having lost so disastrously to you, my brother then staked what he considered to be his one remaining asset — me!'

From the way Melissa spoke Kirkham decided he would sooner not be in her brother's shoes when she met up with him. In the meantime he had his own troubles to worry about.

'And I presumably won you,' he said. 'Such a thing is not unknown. It's happened before.'

'Not to me!' retorted Melissa.

'Very well, to you it was a novelty. May I point out that, like your brother, you were free to decline. He had the excuse of being a weak character, you have said so yourself. Although I have known you for only a brief time I would hesitate to hurl such an accusation in your direction, so I would be grateful to hear your excuse.'

Kirkham felt more at ease. He was on firmer ground now. The girl fancied she had a grievance, not without just cause, he was forced to admit. He would hear her out, agree to forget about her brother's debts, send her off with a hundred guineas in her pocket and that would be an end of it. No, he would make that two hundred gold 'uns, she was deuced pretty, and besides he would dine out on this adventure for months to come. He could hear himself now: 'And there she was, my dear fellows, this glorious creature in bed beside me, and me without the least idea who she was!' Yes, it would make a fine yarn — providing he got the upper hand in the end.

'My excuse is that, for all his faults, I love my brother dearly.' Melissa's voice broke into his thoughts. 'If I refused to co-operate then he would have welshed on a gambling debt. It would have meant social ruin. I could not do that to him.'

'Your sisterly affection does you credit. What I still do not understand is this marriage nonsense.'

'In what other capacity did you expect me to come to you? As a housemaid?'

'Oh, no,' replied Kirkham hurriedly. He was beginning to recognise that steely note in her voice all too well.

'As a companion to your grandmother?'

'No. . .well, probably not.'

'I think you mean certainly not!' Now she rounded on him angrily. 'I know exactly what you had in mind. I was to provide a few days' amusement for you, then be cast aside like a worn coat. Well, I had other ideas. Throughout years of poverty — caused, may I point out, by my late father's compulsive gambling — I have managed to retain my honour and my reputation. It has not been easy. Honour and reputation are luxuries usually denied to the impoverished. Poor or not, I was not going to relinquish them to you. I would honour my brother's debts, but on my terms. As your wife, not your strumpet!'

Kirkham was impressed by her fiery manner. This was a remarkable woman indeed. It was a pity she was so trying.

'Very commendable sentiments,' he said nonchalantly. 'Your efforts were quite wasted, though. I do not know what mock ceremony you dragged me through while I was — er — indisposed, but it won't wash, you know. My lawyer will have it declared null and void in a trice, and then where will your honour and reputation be?'

'Still intact, Kirkham, dear.' She said his name with derision. 'Your lawyer had better prepare himself for a hard struggle to get this marriage annulled. I made sure everything was legal and watertight—the special licence, the ceremony with a genuine man of the cloth to conduct it, adequate witnesses.'

'A special licence, the ceremony and the rest? Are you trying to tell me I was drunk all this time? Quite impossible! There's not a person who knows me who'll be taken in by that Banbury tale.' He laughed scornfully.

'I do not consider a capacity for drinking vast quantities of alcohol to be something to boast about. But you are right. Even you, in your excesses, could not stay inebriated that long. It only needed the merest drop of a suitable potion. . .' For the first time uncertainty crept into her voice.

'Are you saying you drugged me?' He stared at her incredulously, then he gave a triumphant laugh. 'Well, there's your weakness. No marriage would stand under those circumstances. Your efforts were wasted.'

'Were they, Kirkham? Perhaps not. There was quite a vogue a few years back for heiresses to be drugged and married off against their will, but I never heard of it happening to a man. Certainly not to a peer of the realm. How the gossips of town will enjoy the twist in the story. I shouldn't wonder if the ballad-mongers don't find it a source of inspiration. What would be a good title, I wonder? "The Reluctant Bridegroom, or The Tale of the Abduction and Seduction of a Noble Lord." It should sell well. Comical ballads always do.'

She had struck home! She could see she had by the look on his face. Kirkham had an Achilles' heel; his pride! It was what she had been banking on.

A flush of anger suffused Kirkham's face. 'Very well, mock away,' he snarled. 'But I refuse to admit that we are married. There was no legal wedding and I do not accept you as my wife.' He was not going to give in easily.

Melissa rounded on him again. 'You were happy enough to accept me as your doxy, though, weren't you? And now you are angry because I refuse to be sacrificed to your whims and pleasures!'

'My whims and pleasures have nothing to do with it! My greatest pleasure at this moment would be if you disappeared and I never clapped eyes on you again!'

Somehow they had both got to their feet now, and were facing one another.

'Then you should have thought of that earlier! Before you accepted another human being as a stake in a stupid card-game!'

'Do you think I would do such a thing deliberately?' bellowed Kirkham. 'I was drunk at the time, that was why.'

'I know you were drunk. Do you think it is any excuse? Or do you really think I want to be the wife of such a creature as you? I was forced to do it. I had no other choice, but let me assure you that now I am Lady Kirkham I intend to remain Lady Kirkham.'

'No!' His voice was low with fury. 'I will never tolerate it, do you hear?'

There was a long tense silence between them as they glared into each other's eyes.

'Then what do you propose we do?' asked Melissa, her voice unexpectedly quiet.

'We?' The sudden reasonableness of her tone caught him by surprise.

'Yes. We must come to some sort of agreement. On the one hand I say I am your legal wife. I have the papers to prove it. On the other hand you say it is all nonsense, that I lie. Yet you have done nothing to oust me from this house because you are not sure, are you? You fear I might just be speaking the truth——'

'What do you want?' demanded Kirkham. 'What are your terms? I presume you do have terms?'

Before she could reply the butler entered and announced, 'Mr O'Gallagher, my lord.'

The young man who was ushered in was stocky and with a shock of black hair. His face had an impish quality, as if designed for laughter and mischief. Now, though, he looked tired and drawn.

'O'Gallagher! The one man in all London I wish to see!' cried Kirkham. 'I have spent the entire morning looking for you.'

'And I you, Kirkham, my dear fellow. Seemingly we have been chasing after one another.' The new arrival moved forward to greet his friend, then his eyes lit upon Melissa and he came to an abrupt halt. 'Oh, no! Not you!' he moaned in a stricken voice. 'Say it is not so!'

'Good morning, Mr O'Gallagher,' Melissa said evenly. 'I am pleased to renew your acquaintance though your greeting is markedly unusual. It is an Irish form of address, perhaps?'

'Your pardon—er—my lady...madam... Miss—er...' stammered O'Gallagher, sweeping her a hasty and confused bow.

'"My lady" will do,' said Melissa.

'No it won't!' retorted Kirkham. 'If she is anything she is Miss Daubenay.'

Shaun O'Gallagher shook his head regretfully. 'I am afraid Lady Kirkham is right, I should have addressed her as my lady.'

'Lady Kirkham? My lady?' Kirkham repeated, appalled. 'What is this? You are my closest friend! Surely you aren't a part of this female's plotting?'

'I fear I must be, though I wish with all my heart I could deny it.' O'Gallagher sank onto a chair and buried his head in his hands.

'Explain!' demanded Kirkham. 'This creature insists she is married to me, but that cannot be!'

'Sadly, I fancy she is right. My friend, as far as I can tell you are legally and irrevocably a married man.'

'Explain,' repeated Kirkham, though in a more subdued voice. 'Explain, I beg of you.'

'It began when we were playing cards at Wall-eyed Kate's,' began O'Gallagher. 'You were having a streak of luck the like of which I had never seen——'

'I know that bit,' snapped Kirkham. 'Get on to the first mention of marriage.'

'This young fellow, Daubenay, had lost all night to you. It was obvious he was way over his head, but he would not give in, and you, generous fellow that you are, kept giving him chances to recoup his losses.'

'Ha!' snorted Melissa derisively. Both men ignored her.

'Then Daubenay offered his sister in lieu of the money he could not repay — great beauty, unimpeachable virtue and all that. You were interested but insisted upon seeing the goods —— Your pardon, your ladyship!' He amended at Melissa's angry cough. 'I mean you insisted upon making the acquaintance of Miss Daubenay first.'

'My brother sent a message that I was to come at once because he was in dire trouble.' Melissa's voice was shaking with fury. 'How could he have humiliated me so? When I meet up with him I will wring his neck!'

'No, you will not!' retorted Kirkham, 'for I intend to get to him first, after which encounter he will not have a neck left to wring. Now, O'Gallagher, what happened next?'

'One look at her ladyship and you were at her feet in adoration,' said the Irishman gallantly. Ignoring Kirkham's stifled groan, he continued, 'The then Miss Daubenay consented to participate only if marriage was involved.'

'And I agreed? I deserve to be sent to Bedlam!'

'By then you were in such a state and so enamoured of this lady I fancy that if she had asked you to put flowers in your hair and dance round Hyde Park naked you would have done so.'

'I wish I had,' said Kirkham sourly. 'It would have been the lesser of two evils by far. And what was your contribution to this?'

'I made the arrangements for the wedding.'

'You did! How could you do such a thing and still call yourself my friend?'

'Be reasonable, Kirkham!' protested O'Gallagher. 'I was somewhat the worse for wear myself by this time and, besides, I did not really take it seriously. Mock weddings are nothing new.'

'But you went as far as getting the special licence.'

'Indeed I did, with that Polly standing at my back all the time.'

'Polly? Who is she?'

'My maid,' said Melissa. 'You have not met her yet.'

'Are you telling me there are two of you in my household?' Kirkham was horrified.

'Yes,' said Melissa. 'Mr O'Gallagher may have thought he was making the arrangements, but in truth it was Polly guiding him all the time. She was at his back, as he says. And though he may have thought he was arranging a charade — I understand a certain type of gentleman finds such things amusing — Polly made sure that everything was legal and proper.'

'Are you telling me that a mere servant bamboozled

my friend over such an important matter?' Kirkham demanded, ignoring the fact that the Irishman had wilted somewhat beneath the scorn in Melissa's words.

'Polly is more than a servant. She is my friend and totally loyal. Her knowledge of the less fashionable areas of London is incomparable—it was she who suggested St Willibrod's as a suitable church for the ceremony, for instance. Above all, she was stone-cold sober all the time, a very definite advantage over both you and Mr O'Gallagher.'

Now both men wilted. Kirkham was the first to rally.

'I was not completely drunk. I was drugged,' he protested.

'A mild sedative, nothing more. Another of Polly's skills,' Melissa assured him. 'Even though your memories of the wedding may be hazy now, you were perfectly *compos mentis* throughout the ceremony. Ask Mr O'Gallagher.'

If Kirkham hoped for support from his friend he was disappointed, for the Irishman nodded his head. 'I fear it is so,' he said. 'You have no let-out by that means.'

'But there must be some way,' protested Kirkham. 'This marriage cannot be legal.'

This time the Irishman shook his head. 'I could find nothing,' he said. 'Not being able to catch up with you this morning, and having the most dreadful misgivings about what had happened, I decided to retrace our steps. I found St Willibrod's—I fear it does exist, but in such an appalling neighbourhood! I had my pockets picked twice between leaving the church and meeting the parson.'

'Parson?' asked Kirkham weakly.

'Yes, he was genuine too, I fear. He even showed me the record of the marriage in the parish register. He was very proud of it. I imagine they get very few society weddings at St Willibrod's.'

'I wish to heaven they had not had this one!' cried Kirkham. 'Did you find no cause for doubt? Something about this business must be illegal!'

'I regret to say that there was nothing.'

'A fine friend you turned out to be, letting me get myself into such a pickle and doing nothing to prevent it.' Kirkham was in a rage now.

'I know, I know!' The unfortunate Irishman was quite abject in his misery.

'If that is not typical!' exclaimed Melissa. 'You admit getting yourself into a pickle, then put the blame on poor Mr O'Gallagher. It was you who drank too much and gambled too much. It was you who agreed to the wedding and you who stood before the parson and took me as your wife. Mr O'Gallagher had little to do with it. I fancy that if he had tried until he was blue in the face to prevent you from getting in such a tangle it would have made no difference. You would have continued on your selfish way. You do not deserve such a friend as him, you really do not!'

'Thank you, my lady.' O'Gallagher seemed quite overwhelmed by her defence of him.

Kirkham glared at the pair of them, then grunted.

'For once I agree with you, but let this be the only time,' he said unexpectedly. 'O'Gallagher, I apologise. I had no business berating you. You are as good a fellow as ever lived, and if you could have got me out of this mess I know you would have done.'

'That is deuced handsome of you!' said the Irishman, springing to his feet. 'And I know your harsh words were born of your distress. But do not despair. I will go out again and see what else I can discover. As you say, there must be a flaw in this business somewhere.'

'You will not succeed,' said Melissa.

'Pay no heed,' put in Kirkham. 'Try anyway, and you will earn my undying gratitude.'

The room seemed very quiet after the Irishman had gone.

'We have not decided upon a plan of action,' Melissa said. 'We were about to discuss it before Mr O'Gallagher arrived.'

'What is there to discuss?'

'Quite a lot. You do not want to be married to me. I do not want to be married to you, yet here we are together. If we are not to provoke a most monumental scandal, which will do neither of us any good, we must reach some agreement.'

'I presume you have some sort of a scheme worked out?' Kirkham growled sourly.

'Yes, a simple one, but which seems to me to be the most effective. The world now considers us to be newly-weds, so to the world that is how we must appear. Privately we will lead separate lives and need have nothing to do with one another.'

Kirkham considered for a while.

'Why should I not simply throw you out of the house and have done with it?' he protested with sudden vehemence.

'Because you have no wish for scandal any more than I have. Also, you are beginning to remember more and more of the wedding and you are growing more convinced of its legality.'

'Poppycock!' snapped Kirkham, but without much conviction. It was bad enough having this appalling woman under his roof and claiming his name without her turning out to be clairvoyant into the bargain.

'How much is this going to cost me?' he demanded.

'Nothing!' Now it was Melissa's turn to be vehement.

'I have not entered into this marriage for money. All I want is to maintain my respectability.'

Kirkham did not look as though he believed her.

'In return for living here I will run your household and act as hostess to your friends, just as though this were a normal marriage. You will have no cause for complaint, I promise you.'

Again Kirkham looked doubtful, then he said, 'I suppose there is no alternative except to do as you suggest. But only until O'Gallagher uncovers proof that this marriage is a sham. Then you will be out of this house so fast you will be scarcely visible. Oh, and this Polly creature too.'

'That seems reasonable to me,' said Melissa. 'Let us shake hands on it.'

Kirkham was not in the habit of shaking hands with females, but he was willing to make an exception. At that moment one unanswered question was bothering him. It had been chewing at him all morning.

'Tell me,' he said at last. 'This so-called marriage took place yesterday evening, did it not?'

'It did.'

'Then we were together for the whole night?'

'For the best part of it, certainly.'

'Alone?'

'Of course we were alone.'

'During that time was the so-called marriage—er. . . did we. . .did I. . .?' His voice tailed away in unaccustomed embarrassment.

'Oh, Kirkham!' Melissa's eyelids were demurely lowered, and her long lashes fanned her cheeks. 'Oh, Kirkham, surely you remember?'

He regarded her anxiously for a moment, then he snorted.

'Pah!' he exclaimed. 'Pah!' and stalked from the room.

CHAPTER THREE

MELISSA decided that this must be the longest, most trying day of her existence. It seemed to consist of angry clashes, principally with her new husband, then long periods of waiting for something to happen.

'I wonder if any other bride ever found her first day of wedded bliss quite so tedious,' she complained.

'Likely not,' chuckled Polly. 'But then I doubt if any other marriage was quite like yours.'

'Very true,' agreed Melissa.

'And you have to admit that the surroundings are fine enough.'

Again Melissa was forced to agree. The library where she now sat was a splendid room. No, it was more than that, it was positively inviting with its rich russet-coloured curtains and finely carpeted floor. Shelf upon shelf of leather-bound books reached almost to the ceiling. Elegant writing-tables were ranged about the walls, cabinets of polished walnut held maps and prints, and comfortable chairs were everywhere. It had the appearance of being a room belonging to someone of refinement and culture.

Melissa wondered how Kirkham had managed to acquire it. No doubt it was part of his inheritance from some more cultivated ancestor. In normal circumstances she would have been in her element surrounded by so many books, but for the moment she felt fidgety and ill at ease, unable to settle to anything. If she could have gone out to walk off some of her restlessness it would have helped, but this she still did not dare to do.

'I anticipated many problems when I married Lord Kirkham, but one thing I did not expect was boredom,' she said.

'You're just not used to things yet. Wait until folks come on their bride-visits. You won't have a minute to call your own.'

'Such a state of affairs may never come about. Will London Society ever accept me as Lady Kirkham, I wonder?'

'If you are having any doubts I would be only too pleased to release you from all obligations.'

Kirkham's voice from behind her made her jump. She had not heard him enter. He seemed to bring with him a breath of the outdoors, for his hair was somewhat ruffled and the cold wind had brought more colour to his face. Someone more susceptible to male charms than Melissa might have considered him to be positively dashing. She, however, merely found him irritating.

'You know better than that,' she replied. 'You also know that any release must come from me, which is something I will never do.'

Kirkham did not reply. His attention was suddenly drawn to Polly, and his gaze took in her tall statuesque figure, which nearly matched his own for height. She looked spectacular and awe-inspiring. As his eyes travelled from her feet to the brilliant scarf she had twisted about her head in lieu of a cap his expression grew more gloomy.

'And you, I suppose, are Polly,' he said.

'Yes, my lord.'

'I can quite see why poor O'Gallagher did not protest at this so-called wedding, not with you at his back.' Kirkham turned to Melissa. 'I have just been to tell my granddam about this marriage nonsense. I could not let her learn of it from some other source. To say that she is not pleased at the turn of events is an understatement. Prepare yourself for a very uncomfortable interview with her soon.'

'You are hoping your grandmother will succeed where you have failed and oust me from your house? Really, Kirkham, you are despicable, using an old lady to get you out of scrapes!'

'Well, they say set a thief to catch a thief, don't they?' he said, heading for the door. 'Maybe it will work to set a termagant to catch a termagant.'

Less than an hour later Polly announced, 'The other termagant—whatever that might be—is downstairs demanding to see you.'

'A termagant is a brawling, bad-tempered woman, and it is no way for you to refer to Lady Kirkham—nor me!' Melissa said reprovingly.

'At least you knows who I mean quick enough,' said Polly cheerfully. ''Sides, it ain't my description of the pair of you, it's Lord Kirkham's!'

'I suppose I had better go and face her,' said Melissa. 'Will I do? Should I not wear my stuff gown? Would it not be more appropriate?'

'No, it would not,' said Polly decidedly. 'You look as pretty as a picture in that lilac merino. Just let me re-tie your sash. . .and tidy up your hair a little. . . There, you'll do. Now you're fit to meet the King, never mind Lady Kirkham.'

'Thank you, Polly.' Melissa gave her a quick hug. 'What would I do without you?'

'That's something you ain't never going to find out, not if I have any say in the matter,' said the maid.

That old Lady Kirkham's presence had already had an effect upon the staff was immediately evident, for the footmen on duty fairly snapped to attention as Melissa passed.

Outside the withdrawing-room she paused for a second, steeling herself for the coming ordeal. There was only one way she could tackle this interview, she knew, and that was with attack as the best means of defence. She entered the beautiful gold and ivory room and at once came under the scrutiny of a tall fashionably-dressed woman. Despite her age Lady Kirkham was very upright and decisive and she handled her quizzing-glass with a daunting authority. That this close examination was intended to intimidate her Melissa did not doubt. But she had not the slightest intention of being intimidated.

'Good afternoon, Lady Kirkham,' she said. 'You are very prompt. I was expecting you.'

'Expecting me, you say?' This was not the greeting that Lady Kirkham had anticipated. The quizzing-glass positively exuded disapproval. 'How so?'

'In your shoes, my lady, I would waste no time in inspecting any young woman who suddenly made a claim to be my grandson's wife.'

'Oh, you would not, eh?' The quizzing-glass descended a fraction.

'Certainly not, my lady. Nor would I delay in commencing an instant enquiry into her background. I am sure you have done this already. I dare say you called upon your lawyer on the way here.'

'You dare say so, do you?' The quizzing-glass was lowered a little more, and for the first time Lady Kirkham looked Melissa straight in the eye. It was an unwavering, antagonistic look, but Melissa did not flinch.

'I do, my lady. Though I must tell you that you could have saved yourself the detour, I am quite prepared to answer any questions you care to ask as frankly and honestly as I am able. First, however, would we not be more comfortable sitting down? I dare say this will be a prolonged interview, therefore will you take some tea?'

'Fraser can bring me cognac.' Lady Kirkham had a way of barking out her words in an alarming manner. However, she did sit down on one of the ivory brocade chairs, her back ramrod straight. 'Decent stuff, mind. Not the feeble rubbish he served me last time.' The quizzing-glass was raised again and pointed in Melissa's direction. 'You are a saucy young woman,' she barked. 'You are trying to get the upper hand. I am not used to saucy young women attempting to get the better of me. I do not like it.'

'I am sorry if I have offended you, my lady. It was unintentional,' said Melissa, meeting her glare squarely. 'However, if our positions were reversed, I feel confident you would adopt exactly the same strategy I am using now.'

That Lady Kirkham was taken aback by the frankness of this comment was evident. She dropped her quizzing-glass, letting it swing unhindered from the silken cord about her neck. She continued to regard Melissa, but now her light brown eyes, so unexpectedly like her grandson's, held a hint of puzzlement and curiosity. But Margaret, the Dowager Lady Kirkham, was not one to let surprise overcome her. She returned to the attack.

'Hoity-toity!' she declared. 'Since you threaten to be so honest you can tell me about your people. Who are they, eh? Answer me that!'

'My mother was a Chilcote, a granddaughter of Lord Hammington. I have a lineage equal to the Kirkhams.'

'You are doing it again! Being saucy! I know who Lord Hammington was without you telling me. And what of your father?'

'He was Major George Daubenay, of the Tenth Hussars.'

'That name is familiar. A gambler, was he not? Gambled away his own fortune and that of his wife, I believe. Well, you have nothing to be hoity-toity about there.'

'Sadly you are right, my lady. My father's weakness caused us much distress. It dragged us lower and lower. Can you wonder that I hate gambling above all things?'

'Did your mother's family do nothing for you?'

'My grandfather did not approve of my parents' marriage. At first it did not matter, for my mother had a good allowance during her lifetime, and a fortune of her own. . .'

'All of which your father lost for her?'

'Yes. It would be truthful to say that gambling alone has ruined us. First my late father, and now my brother. I tell you this so that you will understand how little I wanted to marry your grandson. If I had deliberately intended to trap a man into marriage, the last person I would choose would be another gambler. I have not the slightest wish to be your grandson's wife, but I was forced into it by circumstances. He is exactly the sort of man I despise.'

'Despise! You, a penniless chit, despise a Kirkham?' A faint flush of anger tinged Lady Kirkham's cheeks.

'I do. The fact that I am penniless has nothing to do with it. He is a gambler, a rake, a libertine. A man with wealth, rank and privilege but no sense of responsibility. As I say, the type of man I despise.'

'A rake? A libertine? No sense of responsibility, eh?' Lady Kirkham's bark had become positively threatening. 'Let me tell you a thing or two about my grandson, young woman. He might be wild and foolish, but he is kind, and he is never vicious. Some of these young blades about town care not who they hurt, but not Kirkham. As for his wildness, who can blame him? His father, our only child, died before he was born. After that the boy's mother, who was a fond and foolish creature, and my late husband both doted on the boy. He is the last Kirkham, the hope of us all. He was denied nothing, indulged at every turn, with only me ever to say nay to him or to curb his behaviour. After the way he was spoiled and pampered it is a miracle he turned out as well as he has. Yet you call him a rake and a libertine, indeed!'

Melissa was contrite. 'I beg your pardon, Lady Kirkham,' she said. 'I should not have spoken out so against Lord Kirkham. There must be much good in him, else you would not love him.'

The quizzing-glass was raised sharply and pointed at Melissa once more. This time there was more interest and less hostility in the gaze.

'I must be on my guard against you, young woman,' said Lady Kirkham, quite quietly for her. 'You are a deal more clever than I anticipated. To have detected my weakness upon so short an acquaintance was sharp of you. I take care to hide how fond I am of the rogue. It ain't good for him. You are not what I expected.' Lady Kirkham's voice suddenly resumed its bark. 'I expected you to be a painted doxy.'

'It is exactly my refusal to become a doxy, painted or otherwise, which lies at the root of this whole marriage. I presume Kirkham has told you the details?'

'He has. You had no call to inflict this marriage business on him, though.'

'You think not, my lady? May I ask how you would have tackled matters in the same circumstances?'

'It would never have occurred. You were stupid,

allowing your reprobate of a brother to get you in such a fix.'

'Perhaps I was, my lady, but I love my reprobate brother as much as you love your reprobate grandson. We are both fools but we cannot help ourselves.'

Lady Kirkham's expression registered shock and incredulity. Clearly it had been a long, long time since anyone had called her a fool. Then surprisingly she emitted a strange snort which might, to one of strong imagination, have been a laugh.

'In that case, given the same circumstances, I hope I would have had the courage and intelligence to devise such an ingenious solution,' she said.

'I am certain you would, my lady,' answered Melissa, intensely relieved by this unexpected easing of tension. 'And of one thing I must assure you. I am sure you do not wish to recognise me as your grandson's wife, but whether you do or not, I promise you I will always behave in a manner as befits one who is your granddaughter-in-law. It is not my intention to cause any scandal. You will never have cause to be ashamed of me.'

'You say so?'

'I do, my lady. I swear it. And one thing more — Kirkham thinks I mean to hang on to his coat-tails to the end of his days. In truth, as soon as the time is appropriate, I would like nothing better than to slip out of his life completely. I only threatened to plague him because he annoyed me and I wished to punish him.'

This time there was no mistaking Lady Kirkham's laugh.

'Serves the young rascal right!' she declared. 'Well, whether you are legally wed or not I cannot tell, not until my lawyer has gone into the matter. But let us get one thing straight. That there will be talk is unavoidable, but we can pass the bizarre nature of the wedding off as another of Kirkham's pranks. However, I will not have any other hint of scandal breathed abroad in connection with this so-called marriage. Our family honour must remain unscarred. Lady Kirkham you claim to be, so Lady Kirkham you will be, in the eyes of Society at least. To accomplish this effectively the world must see that you have my approval.'

'Does this mean that you accept me as your grandson's wife?' Melissa was astounded by the idea.

'Certainly not! At least, not in private. If the marriage proves a sham, as I suspect it will, then I will take whatever steps are necessary to rectify matters.'

Melissa thought it prudent not to enquire what these steps might be.

Lady Kirkham's quizzing-glass was evidently a barometer of her mood, for now she nonchalantly let it fall. Then she unclasped the splendid pearl necklace she had about her neck and handed them to Melissa.

'The Kirkham pearls,' she said. 'Put them on.'

'But I cannot take them. They are far too valuable,' protested Melissa. 'And beautiful,' she added softly, her fingers caressing the silken smooth surface of the pearls.

'Put them on,' insisted Lady Kirkham. 'Do not worry, I do not make such gestures rashly. I pride myself that I am a good judge of character. I have reservations about you being my grandson's wife, but I do not take you to be a jewel thief. Besides, if you ran off with them it would do you little good, you would never be able to sell them. Everyone knows them, they are a family heirloom. To Society at large they will be a sign of my acceptance of you. Anyone who dares to look askance at you will answer to me.'

Melissa could quite see that this would be a powerful

deterrent against snubs and set-downs. 'Thank you,' she said. 'I accept them gratefully, though I regard them as being on loan. They will be returned to you when I leave Lord Kirkham.'

'Indeed they will,' said Lady Kirkham in a voice which brooked no argument. Now she looked the younger woman up and down. She could find no fault in the simple yet elegant way Melissa's fair curls were dressed, nor yet in the delicacy of her features or her graceful figure. It was a different matter when she regarded the lilac merino gown. Taking in every worn thread and every faded patch, Lady Kirkham frowned. 'That will not do, not for someone claiming to be my grandson's wife. I suppose you have nothing better? Then I will send Madame Elise to you. She is my mantua-maker, she will fit you out appropriately.'

'No, thank you,' said Melissa firmly. 'It was never my intention to take money from Lord Kirkham——'

'In that case what do you intend to do? Wear that rag when you go out to dine? When you entertain guests? When you go driving in the park? You will scarce be an asset to him dressed like that. Worse still, it would set tongues wagging. If I were to give such a garment to my maid she would leave me instanter. No, you will have Madame Elise devise a fitting wardrobe for you. I am assured of her discretion—she values my custom too much to be otherwise.'

'Such a scheme would cost a fortune. My lady, I would prefer not!'

'And I insist that you do. Do not worry about being under obligation to Kirkham, for the cost will come from my purse. Two things I want above all else—to avoid a scandal and for my grandson to abandon his wild ways. This escapade just might shock some sense into him, and if you can play your part then it will be worth the cost of a few gowns and a bonnet or two.' Lady Kirkham rose to leave. 'I might even make you a small allowance. The more I consider it, the more I begin to think matters may not turn out as grim as I first anticipated. Kirkham has been in some scrapes in his time. Maybe, for once, this one will be of benefit to him.'

Lady Kirkham looked at the lilac merino again. 'You are not intending to go abroad in that, I trust? I suggest you are indisposed for a day or two, until Madam Elise has had time to get things in hand. A diplomatic touch of *la grippe* would do.'

So saying, she swept out of the house between twin lines of footmen whose smartness would have been a credit to the Grenadier Guards, pausing only to glare at one unfortunate flunkey and rasp out, 'Do you call that wig powdered? You have scarce enough powder on to cover a mouse! See to it at once!' she permitted herself to be handed into her carriage. As she drove away, the servants sagged visibly with relief and returned indoors.

For Melissa, however, relief was tinged with astonishment. Never for one moment had she anticipated gaining such an ally as Lady Kirkham.

Her incredulity was shared by Kirkham himself when he returned. He took one look at the pearls about her neck and his jaw dropped.

'What are you doing with those?' he demanded.

'Lady Kirkham insisted that I wear them.'

'She did? She gave them to you? I was certain she would have driven you from the house, neck and crop, by now, yet she presents you with one of our most treasured possessions. How did you manage it? Did you drug her too?'

'Now you are being foolish,' said Melissa reprovingly.

'I think Lady Kirkham intends the pearls to be my badge of respectability.' She decided not to mention that she personally regarded the necklace as merely being on loan.

'Do you mean my grandmother believes your story?' he asked incredulously.

'Not entirely,' she was forced to admit. 'She is having the validity of our marriage investigated, which I suppose is only natural.'

'I do not recall your showing the same understanding when I questioned that same validity,' Kirkham protested.

'You were at the ceremony, Lady Kirkham was not!' Melissa pointed out sharply. 'In the meantime she is determined there shall be no scandal.'

'Does that mean she wants you to remain here, in my house?'

'She does! It is the only way to still wagging tongues. Lady Kirkham and I have reached an understanding.'

'And what form does this understanding take?'

'Only what you and I have already agreed upon — to behave in public as much like a newly-wed couple as possible. But do not worry, you have a short reprieve before you need be seen about town with me. Your grandmother has decreed that I have *la grippe* until my wardrobe is fit for the world's scrutiny.'

'And how long might this indisposition last?'

'A mere day or two, so Lady Kirkham's mantua-maker assures me. She has been here already, with her tape-measure and her pattern-books. She has promised to complete the basic essentials of my trousseau by the day after tomorrow.'

'Trousseau! The day after tomorrow! Is a man to have no respite from his troubles?'

'Not when his troubles were self-inflicted,' stated

Melissa. The dressing-bell for dinner came as a welcome interruption.

'My sign for leaving the house,' said Kirkham, springing to his feet. 'I have no heart for dining at home tonight. I need some cheery company.'

'What, you would abandon your bride of one day to dine with friends? And when she is ill, too? What will the world say to that?' Melissa spoke reprovingly.

Kirkham halted in his tracks. 'I suppose you are right,' he said glumly. 'It seems my reprieve was shorter than I had anticipated.'

It would be an exaggeration to describe the conversation at dinner as sparkling. For the sake of the servants Melissa and Kirkham kept up an exchange of polite comments, but it was stilted in the extreme. The soft gleam of candlelight upon polished wood and fine china evoked an almost intimate atmosphere which should have helped ease the tension, instead it only made things worse. Afterwards, in the withdrawing-room, matters were even more awkward. Long difficult silences lay heavy on the air. Even the crackle of logs in the ornate marble fireplace—one of Mr Robert Adam's most inspired creations—failed to animate the situation.

'We appear to be able to quarrel with great fluency; it is at normal conversation that we flounder,' observed Kirkham. He nodded towards the piano. 'Do you play?'

'I did once,' Melissa admitted. 'Doubtless my fingers have got out of the way of it now.' Her own piano had been a very early victim of her father's gambling debts.

'Try, anyway, if you please, just to alleviate the boredom.'

Melissa went to the piano, selected the most simple piece of music she could find and sat down. The results were not encouraging. If the conversation had been halting, her attempts at playing the piano were even worse. Long before she had reached the end of 'Bushes and Briars' all semblance of tune had been well and truly eradicated.

'I am glad you played,' said Kirkham, as she faltered to a stop. 'It makes the silence seem infinitely preferable.'

'That is scarcely gallant.'

'I do not feel gallant, I feel bored. What I need to liven things up is a bottle of decent claret, a pack of cards and some cheerful companions. The cards and the claret I can procure at the pull of a bell-rope. In the absence of the companions I don't suppose you. . .?' Melissa's look of scorn brought him to an abrupt halt. 'No, I don't suppose you would,' he finished.

'Since your ability to amuse yourself is strictly limited, I suggest we play backgammon,' said Melissa.

Kirkham opened his mouth to pour derision on this idea, then he realised it was the only hope of entertainment available to him.

'Very well,' he said resignedly. . .

'That was a very long and trying evening,' said Melissa to Polly later, in the bedroom. 'A most fitting end to a long and trying day. I fear Lord Kirkham and I did very little to promote the cause of happy marriage; we scarce managed two words together that were agreeable. Goodness knows what the servants made of it!'

'The general opinion below stairs is that you were both bashful when anyone else's eyes were on you,' Polly informed her. 'It was only when you were alone that you behaved like a pair of turtle-doves — at least, that is the talk in the servants' hall.'

'Then the servants must have a keener imagination than I have, for I admit that the idea of a bashful Lord Kirkham defeats me entirely.' Melissa's words ended in an enormous yawn. 'I will be thankful to get my head on the pillow; I am exhausted,' she confessed, climbing into bed. 'Are your quarters comfortable?' she asked belatedly.

'A deal better than at Newgate Street,' Polly informed her cheerfully. 'Goodnight.'

'Goodnight.' Melissa was so befuddled with sleep she was scarcely aware of Polly leaving the room.

She was wide awake within minutes, however, when the door opened again and in walked Kirkham, dressed in nightshirt and dressing-gown.

'What is the meaning of this?' she demanded, sitting bolt upright and clutching the bedclothes to her.

'I would have thought it obvious. It is late and I am tired. I am coming to bed.'

'Not in this bed you are not!'

Kirkham placed his candle on the night-table with great deliberation.

'Madam, this is my bed and I intend to sleep here,' he said.

'But I am in it!'

'So I have noticed. Nevertheless, it is a large bed, there is plenty of room for two—and you do keep insisting that we are man and wife, do you not?'

'Only to the world, not in bed,' said Melissa in alarm. She had always been aware that Kirkham might attempt to take advantage of the situation in this way, but somehow she had thought him too much of a gentleman—correction, she had *hoped* he would be too much of a gentleman. Evidently she was wrong. Confident as she was that their marriage was legal, she had no intention of losing her virginity to Kirkham.

'The honourable thing would be for you to sleep elsewhere,' she said, hoping she sounded less nervous than she felt.

'I am too tired to be honourable, and this is my bed, as I have already pointed out. If you object to my presence you can always find another room for yourself; there are plenty available.' Kirkham divested himself of his dressing-gown and climbed in. 'Of course,' he said, as with a squeak of protest Melissa began to scramble out of the other side, 'the fact that we spent our second night apart so soon after our wedding is bound to be commented upon by the servants. I should not wonder if the news reached my grandmother and she would not be at all pleased. It would hardly add credence to the idea that all is well with our marriage.'

This was true. Melissa paused in her flight.

'I promise you I have no designs on your virtue. But if you are still worried. . .' He took a long feather bolster and thumped it firmly down between them. 'There, the Great Wall of China could not prove a better barrier.'

Reluctantly Melissa settled back in bed, perching herself on the very edge to be as far away from him as possible.

Kirkham snuffed out the candle. 'You can come further in than that, there is enough room,' he said, a disembodied voice in the darkness.

Melissa did not move.

'Oh, please yourself, I am too tired to argue.' He spoke irritably. 'Only, if you fall out of bed in the middle of the night do not expect me to come and help you back in. The servants can find you still on the floor for all I care.'

Melissa did not reply. She had not heard him. She was fast asleep.

CHAPTER FOUR

A PROCESSION of footmen tramped upstairs, their arms piled high with parcels and boxes. At their rear Madame Elise fussed and worried like an over-anxious sheepdog.

'*Allez*! *Allez*!' she puffed. 'We 'ave not got all ze day. We must make ze 'urry.'

'Madame Elise, what does this mean?' protested Melissa, as the servants set down their loads.

'My lady, 'ere we 'ave ze little bit of *votre* trousseau. *Vous* were expecting it today, *non*?'

Melissa bit back a smile. Madame Elise's French accent was as inconsistent as it was false. There was no disguising the fact that the mantua-maker's dropped 'h's owed more to Putney than to Paris.

'I was expecting it today, yes,' she said, waving a hand at the packages which spilled over from the dressing-room into the bedroom. 'I was expecting a few garments, not this vast array.'

'But *vous* 'ave 'ere only ze bare essentials, I assure *vous*, my lady.'

'I fear there must be some mistake. Lady Kirkham mentioned a few dresses and a bonnet or two.'

'A few dresses and a bonnet or two?' Madame Elise looked astounded at the idea. Then her round, painted face broke into a wide smile. '*Vous* will 'ave *votre* little joke, my lady,' she beamed. 'I promise *vous* there is no mistake. Lady Kirkham instructed me 'erself to fit *vous* out for the whole season. These are but a few things to tide *vous* over, so to speak.'

Melissa did not know what to say. She had never expected Lady Kirkham to show such generosity, and she felt uneasy at accepting so much.

'Start trying on a few things,' said Polly, who was already beginning to investigate among the tissue-paper and packing muslin. 'Lady Kirkham wouldn't have ordered all this if she hadn't thought it worth her while.'

'Hindeed not,' said Madame Elise, firmly removing a cream satin creation from Polly's grasp. 'Lady Kirkham isn't a lady to say one thing one day and somezing else ze next. Per'aps *votre* ladyship will condescend to try this first. It 'as ze overdress of blond lace to go with it. If *vous* please, my lady,' she implored as Melissa still hung back. 'I 'ave my instructions from Lady Kirkham. She was very particular about what she wanted *pour vous*.'

Starved of pretty things for most of her adult life, Melissa regarded the tantalising finery which was now strewn over the room. It would have taken an iron will indeed to have resisted such delights.

'Very well, I will try on one or two garments,' she said. 'You must accept, though, that it does not mean I agree to keep them.'

'*Naturellement, votre* ladyship.' Madame Elise had been serving the gentry for far too long to regard any purchase as definite until she actually held the payment in her hand. 'Timms, don't stand there like a block of wood! Make *votreself* useful!'

The unfortunate Timms, Madame Elise's assistant, scurried forward and sank to her knees, ready to give her undivided attention to recalcitrant hemlines. A moth-like creature clad in black, she never spoke. Melissa wondered if the poor woman had spent so much of her life with her mouth full of pins that she had lost the art of conversation. It was Madame Elise herself who attended to the main fitting of each garment. Slightly ridiculous she might be, with her fake French accent, but there was no denying her skill as a dressmaker. Melissa tried on a bewildering succession of exquisite day dresses, evening gowns, pelisses and cloaks. To her bedazzled eyes each looked to be the ultimate in elegance and fit. Madame Elise proved less tolerant, and tweaked, pulled and pinned at each garment until it met with her exacting standards.

'Timms will 'ave that ready for *vous* in an hour, my lady,' or, 'Timms will make ze alterations by dinnertime, *votre* ladyship,' was her constant comment.

Even allowing for the mantua-maker's censorious eye, which picked out the slightest imperfection, there was still a satisfactory number of garments which met with her full approval. With each one she selected an appropriate number of bonnets, shawls, and other accompanying delights for Melissa's consideration.

As well as her undoubted skill as a dressmaker, Madame Elise betrayed another valuable asset, her discretion. It was most unusual for a mantua-maker, especially one at the top of her profession, to be asked to provide every single item for a lady's wardrobe. Elsewhere such a commission would have excited comment and interest. Madame Elise did not even register curiosity. She produced underwear, shoes and all manner of other things as if being asked to do so was the most ordinary thing in the world.

'Superb! *Votre* ladyship will be all the rage.' The dressmaker stood back and admired her handiwork, a beam of happy satisfaction on her face. 'It 'as been a long time since we 'ave 'ad the honour and pleasure of dressing anyone 'alf as beautiful as *votre* ladyship. Hisn't that so, Timms?'

Timm's mouth twitched in agreement at either side of its load of pins.

Melissa regarded herself in the mirror, quite unable to quell a thrill of excitement. She did look good. The fine woollen gown she had on was of the same deep violet-blue as her eyes. Worn under a velvet pelisse of exactly the same shade, and with a matching bonnet, the outfit complemented her delicate colouring and slender figure to perfection.

'That will serve very well,' barked a familiar voice. 'At least you will not disgrace us. I dare say you will turn a few heads into the bargain.'

Lady Kirkham stood in the doorway, her quizzing-glass actively taking in every detail of Melissa's ensemble. If she felt ill at ease at entering someone else's dressing-room unannounced and uninvited she did not show it. She cleared the nearest chair with one sweep of her ebony cane, and sat down, not caring that half a dozen delicate creations fell to the floor.

'What else is there?' she demanded.

Obediently Madame Elise held up garment after garment for her scrutiny. Not certain whether to be annoyed at such a cavalier manner or not, Melissa decided it was foolish to take umbrage. From what little she had seen of her grandmother-in-law, that lady had a code of behaviour all her own. Besides, she was paying for everything.

'I am glad you have come, Lady Kirkham,' she said.

'You are?' The old lady looked surprised and rather disbelieving.

'Certainly. I wish to know how many of these garments I am to keep.'

'How many? Why, all of them! Not that bronzy-green thing on the sofa, though!' Stretching out her cane, her ladyship knocked the offending gown to the floor.

'Can't abide the colour. When I was a girl we used to call that goose-turd green!'

In fact it was a subtle shade, the latest thing and very elegant, but no one argued. Without a word, Madame Elise gathered it up and whisked it out of sight.

'I cannot accept such generosity,' protested Melissa.

'Yes you can. I thought we had settled that argument. The news is out that you are married to my grandson, and the moment you go into society the old tabbies will scrutinise every stitch of your bride-clothes. No Kirkham has ever been accused of being shabby, and I refuse to start now. And you may as well keep that on,' she added, as Melissa began removing her bonnet.

'May I ask why?' asked Melissa.

'You have been indisposed for quite long enough; it is time Kirkham and you were seen in public. We will go for a drive in the park.'

Melissa's heart sank at the prospect of facing London Society, even from a carriage. She opened her mouth to object, to beg for another day or two's grace, then closed it again. In another day to two things would be no easier. Far better to face it now. A footman appeared at Lady Kirkham's energetic tugging of the bell-rope.

'My compliments to Lord Kirkham. Tell him I want to see him here,' she barked.

'I beg your pardon, my lady. I am afraid his lordship is not at home.' The footman spoke the words too mechanically for conviction. Certainly Lady Kirkham was not persuaded.

'Yes he is!' She prodded the unfortunate man in the stomach with her cane. 'He will be in the library, by the fire. He imagines he is invisible, slumped down in that big chair of his, but he is wrong. I know he is there and I would see him here immediately.'

The footman did not need to be urged to hurry; he fairly flew from the room. His feet could be heard clattering down the stairs. A few minutes later there was a knock at the door and Kirkham entered. His face did indeed have the flush of one who had been contentedly sitting by the fire, and his expression was that of one who was not at all pleased at being disturbed.

'Madam, I did not know you were here,' he said giving his grandmother a dutiful kiss on the cheek.

'Liar!' she retorted.

Clearly there was nothing unusual in this grandmotherly comment, for he neither flinched nor frowned. He looked at Melissa. A brief flicker of appreciation crossed his face as he regarded her, but he suppressed it smartly.

'You appear to be ready to go on an excursion,' he said.

'We are all going on an excursion,' barked out Lady Kirkham, before Melissa could say a word. 'We are going for a drive in the park.'

'Surely not, Grandmother.' He spoke persuasively. 'The afternoons are still short. By the time I send to have my coachman harness up the team and I have changed my clothes it will be dark.'

'I have already sent word to Pentecost to lay out your things. You can be ready in ten minutes. My barouche is at the door and the horses have been waiting quite long enough already.'

'Madam, it takes a man of fashion a good hour to prepare to face the world. My neckcloth alone. . .'

'Ten minutes!' snapped Lady Kirkham.

'In that case I will be ready in ten minutes,' he said with resignation. Then, unexpectedly he looked at Melissa and said, 'Is there a muff or something to go with that rig you are wearing? It's deuced cold out of doors.'

'Yes, my lord. I 'ave 'ere just the thing for *votre* bride.' Madame Elise dashed forward with a muff and tippet of soft grey fur.

Kirkham gave a curt nod of approval and left the room.

Melissa was quite taken aback by his consideration. For all he disliked her, he had been concerned in case she might be cold. Perhaps Lady Kirkham was right, and he did have a kindly streak. The old lady must have been thinking along similar lines, for she said, 'You would think a fellow who was so thoughtful would have more consideration than to wear such a gaudy weskit, would you not? It has quite given me a megrim.'

'Then maybe we should abandon our drive if your ladyship is not feeling well,' Melissa said hurriedly.

Lady Kirkham gave her a glare. 'Do me good, a bit of fresh air. Clear my head!' she barked.

With an ill-concealed sigh Melissa took up the muff and allowed Polly to arrange the tippet about her neck. Lady Kirkham had decided they were going for a drive. There was no point in arguing.

Upon being handed into the carriage Melissa made to sit beside Lady Kirkham, only to be jabbed sharply in the ribs by that lady's very pointed elbow.

'Other side!' barked the old lady. 'Sit by my grandson. It is what the world expects of newly-weds. And take that scowl off your face, Kirkham. You have your bride with you! You are happy, do you hear?'

The glowering look about his brows did not lift.

Melissa could not blame him. It was an awkward enough situation, sitting there thigh to thigh, muffled by the same rugs, their feet sharing the same foot-warmer, without having to look happy as well. She tried moving away from Kirkham, to avoid any contact with him but the grooms had done their work efficiently. She was firmly wedged against him by rugs and blankets.

In spite of these precautions it was cold in the open barouche. She feared her first appearance in Society was likely to be with a red nose, especially as they bowled along through the London streets at a cracking rate. Before long, however, she began to find the drive exhilarating. Any outing would have been agreeable after being confined to the house for several days, and she had the added novelty of riding in a carriage. True, Kirkham's presence was something of a drawback, but her new husband's company in the open air was infinitely preferable to being with him indoors.

The carriages were growing more numerous, forcing them to slow down so that by the time they entered Hyde Park they were barely going at a walking pace. They found themselves well and truly under the public gaze, and London Society had no reservations about staring at them to its heart's content. If there had ever been any doubts that news of their wedding had spread all over town those doubts were dispelled now.

'Do not sit there like a pair of Aunt Sallies,' barked Lady Kirkham, as Melissa and Kirkham stared woodenly ahead trying to ignore the curious stares. 'Be animated!'

Not an easy order to obey, not when under such unwavering scrutiny.

'Well, you wanted to enter the *beau monde*; I hope you are satisfied,' said Kirkham out of the side of his mouth, at the same time doffing his hat to a lady and gentleman in a curricle.

'I did not want it, I had no alternative,' replied

Melissa in a similar manner, acknowledging the bows of two middle-aged gentlemen.

'What are you two talking about?' demanded Lady Kirkham. 'Sit closer together! Look more amicable! Everyone's eyes are upon you, you are the sensation of the day, the pair of you, and yet you waste your opportunities.'

It was true that the arrival of their barouche was causing great excitement. People were running alongside to get a better view of them, and even standing up in their own carriages to take in every detail of Lord Kirkham and his mysterious new bride. Melissa felt intensely uncomfortable.

'It is a pity these people have nothing better to do with their time,' she muttered.

'If they had, then the whole framework of Society would collapse,' said Kirkham. 'It only survives through idleness and an overwhelming desire to know other people's business.' As he spoke he caught her hand and tucked it under his arm.

Taken unawares, Melissa tried to pull away, but he held her too firmly.

'That is not much better,' rapped out Lady Kirkham. 'You are doing no good in the barouche. You must get out and walk! Mingle more!' Before either of them could protest she had called the carriage to a halt and ousted the pair of them with a few well-aimed, subversive prods from her cane.

Melissa and Kirkham were forced to stroll arm in arm through the fashionable throng, smiles so fixed on their faces that Melissa was convinced they must both look slightly demented. Their stroll was not prolonged. After a few minutes they were accosted by a sprightly elderly gentleman.

'Kirkham! Kirkham! What is this I hear?' he demanded. 'Have you truly got yourself a wife?'

Melissa felt Kirkham's arm tense beneath her hand.

'Indeed I have, sir. My love, I beg leave to introduce you to my godfather, Lord Layfield. Sir, it is my pleasure to present to you my wife, Lady Kirkham.'

Melissa was conscious of the shudder he gave when he referred to her as Lady Kirkham. It almost matched hers at being addressed by him as 'my love'. Nevertheless, her smile did not falter as she sank into a curtsy. Lord Layfield gallantly kissed her hand, his pale blue eyes peering at her, as if assessing every jot of her character.

'Knew your grandmother, you know!' he exclaimed suddenly. 'What a pair of eyes she had too, the lovely creature.' Then a huge grin spread across his lined face and he thumped Kirkham amiably in the chest. 'You young dog!' he roared approvingly. 'There's no knowing what prank you will be up to next, is there? Fancy running off and getting married without telling a soul! Might have known you would choose the pick of the crop. Nothing wrong with your taste! You are your grandsire all over again.'

Somewhat startled, Melissa realised she being compared to old Lady Kirkham. While she was working out whether or not this was a compliment Kirkham looked down at her with a false smirk on his face and replied, 'Let us just say that I have had extraordinary luck.'

The ambiguity of this remark was not lost on Melissa, and she was obliged to readjust her smile.

Fortunately Lord Layfield noticed nothing amiss. 'I am glad you appreciate it,' he said. '"Too good for you"! That is how your grandmother describes this pretty bride of yours, and there is no better judge of character than dear Meg.'

Now Melissa really was taken aback, both at learning that Lady Kirkham was supporting her so strongly and at hearing the august lady referred to familiarly as 'Meg'. Kirkham, too, was lost for words, so she stepped into the conversation.

'I am sure I am not too good for my dear Kirkham, my lord,' she said sweetly. 'Though I hope I will simply be good for him.'

'Well said, my dear! Well said!' chortled the old gentleman, evidently unable to hear Kirkham grinding his teeth. 'Now, my boy, I do not suppose we will be seeing you at White's for a while, not with such a charming distraction. When you do come, though, you will be obliged to stand us all a bottle or two in celebration. You will not get out of it, do not think you will.'

'I promise to do my duty by my fellow members,' said Kirkham with unexpected fervour. 'I will stand you all the finest the cellars can afford.'

They bade farewell to Lord Layfield and continued on their promenade. Melissa could not help noticing that Kirkham seemed more relaxed after the meeting with his godfather. She did not understand that Kirkham's tension lay in the old gentleman's standing rather than his character, for Lord Layfield was a very influential member of White's, the exclusive gentlemen's club to which Kirkham also belonged.

During these last few days a fear had been growing within Kirkham. What if the unconventional nature of this marriage fiasco were to cause him to be expelled? In the past his japes and pranks had earned him disapproval among the older, more staid members of White's. Once or twice he had received stern warnings to mend his ways. But a sudden and secret marriage was far more serious than introducing a pair of polecats into a boring reception, or riding his horse through the card-room at the club. Might the aura of scandal surrounding his wedding be enough to have him blackballed? With the prospect of social ruin staring him in the face, Lord Layfield's approval of his so-called marriage had come as a great relief. He still had an unwanted wife hanging about his neck, but at least he was still able to go and drink and game with his friends! Eventually! This playing the happy bridegroom was the very devil!

The progress of Melissa and Kirkham was slow, for they were forced to halt every few yards to receive congratulations and to exchange introductions. Much to their mutual surprise not one person regarded them with suspicion or suggested that there might be something havey-cavey about their union. The general consensus among the men they encountered seemed to be that Kirkham was the luckiest of fellows to have captured such a beauty. As for the women, they smiled sentimentally and spoke of love-matches and how romantic they were. Whether this general approval was attributed to the combined acting skills of Melissa and Kirkham or to Lady Kirkham's austere figure waiting in the barouche for them, there was no knowing.

'If I hear that phrase once more I will throttle the speaker, I care not whether it be man, woman or child!' snarled Kirkham through clenched teeth when eventually they were permitted to climb back into the carriage.

'And what phrase might that be?' demanded his grandmother.

'Why, "What a charming pair you make, to be sure",' he mimicked in a falsetto voice.

'And, "How delightful to see a young couple so well suited!"' Melissa's tone matched his.

'Stop it, the pair of you!' ordered Lady Kirkham. 'I will not have you mocking other folk. Simply be glad that no one asked any awkward questions.'

She was right, of course. Melissa had to admit that the outing had gone far better than she could have anticipated, without any of the difficulties she had feared might arise. Thankfully she allowed the rugs to be tucked about her. Now that the tension of her first foray into Society was easing she realised that she was very cold. The footwarmer had long since cooled, and it was disconcerting to discover that her only source of warmth was Kirkham, squeezed in beside her.

'I suppose we are well matched in a way,' he remarked bitterly. 'I do not want you, and you do not want me. You cannot get a better pairing than that.'

Then, unexpectedly, he reached across and tucked the rug more firmly about her, making sure she had every protection possible against the chill wind. Melissa felt she should have made some retort to his comment but his kindly gesture was so at odds with his acid words that she was surprised into silence.

Lady Kirkham, however, suffered no such constraint. 'Stop being peevish,' she ordered. 'You have no one to blame but yourself.'

Now Kirkham was at a loss for a reply, and so they completed the journey back to Hanover Square in silence.

Lady Kirkham would not come in to the house. 'I am engaged to dine with Lettie Chippenham,' she said. 'An awful dinner, no doubt, but good conversation. I shall be back tomorrow afternoon, I shall expect you to be ready.'

'For what?' asked Melissa.

'To receive your bride-visits, of course. From two of the clock I have said you will be At Home to all polite society who wish to pay their respects to the new Lady Kirkham.'

'Then my presence is not necessary,' declared Kirkham.

'Some men are happy to desert their brides on these occasions,' said his grandmother, 'even though they have been wed a scant three days. Other men are happy to remain.'

'Perhaps I will remain,' Kirkham said prudently.

Together they stood in the doorway until Lady Kirkham's barouche had driven away, its carriage-lamps flaring in the dusk.

'Thank goodness that is over!' exclaimed Kirkham as they went indoors.

Exactly what he referred to was not clear. It might have been getting away from public scrutiny, being out of the cold, or escaping from Lady Kirkham's undeniably restricting presence. Melissa fancied the latter, especially when he gave a chuckle.

'Poor Grandmother. I do not envy her dining at Lettie Chippenham's. Her cook has only three types of dish, the inedible, the indigestible, and the unrecognisable. I must say I am starving. I hope Bertrand has something decent for us tonight. If it is half as good as last night's dinner I shall not complain.'

Bertrand certainly gave his employer no grounds for complaint. It might have been the excellence of the food, it might have been their shared dislike of the excursion they had endured—whatever the reason, that evening was the most agreeable Melissa and Kirkham had spent together. Backgammon had been discarded in favour of chess, a game at which Melissa was adept, and at which, to her surprise, Kirkham excelled. Their customary battle of words now became a battle on the chessboard. Cosily set out by the fire, it proved to be unexpectedly pleasant and absorbing. For once they passed an entire evening without either of them being bored.

Next morning it rained. Melissa regarded the grey sky above and the damply gleaming cobbles below with hopeful anticipation. Perhaps the weather would dissuade any callers. Where Kirkham had gone she did not know, nor was she particularly bothered. For herself she had planned a quiet, comfortable hour or so reading.

The library was rapidly becoming her favourite room. To have innumerable books to choose from after years of deprivation was a heady experience, and to do so in such pleasant surroundings doubled her enjoyment. She was somewhat puzzled, however. The library shelves were stacked with splendid leather-bound volumes which at first she had considered to be a legacy from earlier Kirkhams. Many did prove to be old, of course, but a surprising number turned out to be modern publications covering a multitude of subjects, not to mention a quantity of novels and poetry. It was not unknown, she knew, for wealthy householders to order books in bulk simply for the decorative qualitites of their bindings, but in such cases then surely the pages would remain uncut? Here, in Kirkham's library, every page was cut and many had marginal notes written in a bold flowing hand, showing that they had been read with care and attention.

Opening a large, beautifully illustrated book on the flowers and plants of the East Indies she happened to glance at the flyleaf. There, among the list of people who had paid towards the publication of the work was a familiar name:

'Kirkham, Lord.'

Kirkham's father, perhaps? But no, judging by the date on the title page the book was a mere two years old.

She replaced it and, moving along the shelves, took out another volume, some sort of treatise on the possible applications of steam-power. There it was again! Kirkham's name among the list of subscribers. One after another she scrutinised books at random and most claimed Kirkham as a subscriber and patron. It was very puzzling. If they had been books on horse-management, or racing manuals, or studies on how to win at casino, she could have understood it, but these were on much more learned subjects.

As she was replacing the last book the door opened and in came two footmen, carrying a weighty box between them.

'Your pardon, your ladyship, we didn't realise you were here,' said the first, and they made to withdraw.

'No, come in and finish your task, whatever it is. You are not disturbing me,' she said.

'Thank you, your ladyship.'

With evident relief they carried in their burden and set it on the floor. Hard on their heels came Kirkham himself, his face alight with anticipation.

'Ah, they have arrived!' he exclaimed. 'Splendid. . .' His voice tailed away as he saw Melissa and the happy expectation faded from his face. 'Oh,' he said dully. 'You are here.'

It was as if her presence had taken away all his pleasure and Melissa felt unaccountably stung.

'I was just going,' she said, preparing to follow the retreating footmen. 'I have no wish to intrude.'

She had almost reached the door when he called her back.

'There is no need,' he said swiftly. Then as she turned he added, 'Do not leave because of me. You were choosing a book for yourself?'

'I was,' said Melissa, somewhat taken aback by his apology. 'I have just finished *The Lady of the Lake*.'

'You have a taste for the poems of Sir Walter Scott, have you? You will find his *Lay of the Last Minstrel* on that third shelf there. Or there are novels on the shelves beyond the fireplace. I think I may even have a copy of *The Mysteries of Udolpho* somewhere or another.'

For a moment Melissa suspected that in this last remark he was sneering at her taste, and her head went up smartly. Then she saw mischief in his brown eyes and realised he was joking.

'I fear *Udolpho* is a little lurid to be my usual choice,' she said. 'However, I would be glad to read it aloud to you, if you would not deem it too frightening.'

'I would not put you to such trouble. Maybe the works of Mrs Edgeworth would be less of a strain on the nerves? You will find a selection of them on the second shelf. They are bound in blue calf.'

'You certainly know the layout of your library,' said Melissa, going to the shelf as directed and finding the neat row of blue leather volumes.

'So I should. I spend more time here than in any other room in the house. I find such good companionship in books, and solace too.'

Melissa looked at him curiously, her attention caught by a wistful, almost sad note in his voice.

'Would you object if I attend to my box while you browse?' he asked, suddenly lively again. 'It is Mr Lackington's regular offering to me. Hopefully it will be the pick of his bookshop.'

'Please, go ahead. . .' Melissa replied. 'You do not go to choose your own books?'

'Indeed I do,' Kirkham was rummaging in his pockets. 'Most of the contents of the box are the result of an agreeable afternoon spent combing Lackington's shelves. However, if he comes across anything else he thinks might interest me he includes it in the parcel. He is a good fellow, he is not often wrong in his judgement.'

Melissa was becoming more and more confused. A Kirkham who loved books, who spent hours in the bookseller's, did not equate at all with her impression of a dissolute rake. She could have half imagined he was joking when he expressed a love of reading, if he had not been so precise in his knowledge of his own library. Maybe she had not been quite fair to him. It was just possible his character was less frivolous than she had imagined.

In the meantime he was still going through his pockets with the agitated air of a man who had lost something.

'You have not seen my pen-knife about the place, have you?' he asked at last, looking about him on desk and table-tops.

'I do not recall seeing a knife,' said Melissa, helping him to search. 'What does it look like?'

'Nothing out of the ordinary. It is quite a frippery thing, made of gold, and engraved with our family crest.'

By its description the knife did not sound insignificant to Melissa, nevertheless, she continued to help look for it.

'It is no good,' she said, after a while. 'It is not here. I have even searched down the sides of the chairs to no avail. Shall I ring for the servants to look?'

'No, thank you, that is not necessary. Yet it is strange.' Kirkham shook his head in puzzlement. 'I have always kept it in my waistcoat pocket without mishap, and now it is gone.' He gave a rueful shrug. 'I fear I have acquired an aptitude for losing things. If you knew the number of seals and shirt-studs, cravat-pins, and toothpicks that I have missed over the last few years you would be amazed. Pray do not exert yourself any further. Carry on looking for something to read. I will just have to use another knife.'

Taking one from the desk drawer he proceeded to slit open the cords which bound the box.

'Ah, wonderful! Lord Byron's *Childe Harold*! I have had to wait an age for that. And another Mrs Edgeworth. . . Let me see, what it is called. . .? *The Absentee Landlord*! That sounds promising indeed.'

As he examined the contents of the box he kept up a running commentary, exclaiming at some books, expressing interest at others, until at last he declared, 'Come and see these! Did you ever see such illustrations? They are not to be missed, believe me!'

Unable to contain her curiosity, Melissa did as she was bid, and at his elbow she regarded the beautifully coloured pictures of exotic birds. There was no going back to the bookshelves: she helped him unpack the box, sharing with him the delights it held.

'Well, Lackington has lived up to his reputation,' Kirkham announced, holding a book in each hand. 'There is not one I want to return to him. I had no idea you shared my passion, though.' There was approval in his voice.

'Oh, yes! Though I have had little enough opportunity lately.'

'No, I do not suppose you have.' He looked at her thoughtfully. 'Which of these would you most like to read?'

'That is a hard decision. The *Childe Harold*, I think.'

'That would be my choice too. Excellent. Here!' He handed her the book. 'You shall read it first.'

'But I could not take it. You have waited a long time for it, you said so yourself.'

'In that case another day or two will be no hardship.'

'Since we are both so eager for Lord Byron's poetry, why do we not read it aloud tonight, turn and turn about. That way we will read it together.'

'Now that is a splendid notion! One of Bertrand's rapidly improving dinners, a game of chess and a good book. That sounds to be a very pleasing evening.'

'We have the bride-visits to endure first,' Melissa reminded him.

For a moment he looked downcast; then he cheered up. 'At least we have something to look forward to once they have gone.'

'So we have.' She nodded in agreement.

Only afterwards, when she was dressing for the afternoon, did she realise what had happened. Relations between her and Kirkham had become almost amicable. She was actually happy at the thought of spending the evening with him. It was incredible! And all because he liked reading! Maybe he did love books. That did not alter the fact that he was still a gambler and a rake. At the moment he was obliged to stay at home to guard the precious Kirkham reputation. But soon, when he was no longer obliged to play the devoted bridegroom, he would undoubtedly show his true colours once more. Kirkham was a dissolute gambler through and through, and she would be a fool to forget it.

CHAPTER FIVE

ONE morning Melissa had barely settled herself in the withdrawing-room with a piece of particularly uninspired embroidery when a maid entered.

'If you please, your ladyship, Madame Elise has arrived,' she announced.

'Madame Elise? What does she want?'

'She said something about a fitting, your ladyship.'

'Fitting. . .? Oh, I suppose I had better come.' Melissa had not been expecting the dressmaker to call, nor had she any idea what garment was to be fitted.

When she reached her dressing-room she found Madame Elise surrounded by bandboxes and tissue-paper, with the silent presence of Timms hovering in the background, pins already clamped between her lips.

'Ah, *votre* ladyship,' beamed the dressmaker. 'Hit 'as been a bit of a rush, but we 'ave managed to complete *votre* gown. Just one *dernier* fitting, avec *votre* permission. . .'

'I don't understand,' said Melissa. 'Which gown are you talking about?'

'Why, *votre* ballgown, your ladyship, the blue satin.'

'What ball gown? What blue satin?'

'But you ordered it specially *pour* the ball *ce soir*, at Lady Pearmain's.'

'I have no recollection of it.'

'Well, per'aps *votre* ladyship did not, but Lady Kirkham was *très* clear on the matter.'

'Ah!' Recollection came flooding back. There had been a bolt of blue satin and some talk of its suitability for a ballgown. That had been when Melissa had put her foot down with great firmness. She had accepted Lady Kirkham's point of view that she needed an adequate wardrobe, and she had had no option but submit to the old lady's generosity; however, she had her limits. One ballgown she had agreed to. Of ivory silk trimmed with lace, it already hung in her clothes-closet having been worn only once. She did not need another ballgown, and she said so.

'Put the blue satin and all the fal-lals that go with it back in their boxes and take them away,' she instructed.

'But *votre* ladyship!' Madame Elise came as close as she dared to protesting as she repacked the boxes. '*Vous* 'ave only the one gown. To wear it again so soon . . . and at Lady Pearmain's. . . What Lady Kirkham will say I dare not think.'

She was still protesting as Melissa steered her, her boxes, and the inevitable Timms firmly from the room—only to collide with Kirkham outside the door.

'What the devil's going on?' he demanded testily. 'Can't a man walk from one room to another without falling over bandboxes?'

'*Mille pardons, votre* lordship.' A flustered Madame Elise attempted to regain her grasp on the boxes, failed completely and finery cascaded all over the floor.

Kirkham's eyes rolled heavenwards in exasperation. 'In future, madam, if your dressmaker proves unsatisfactory, is it too much to hope that you can eject her more quietly?' he demanded.

Madame Elise's lower lip quivered at this slur on her integrity, while Melissa's mouth tightened at his tone.

'Madame Elise is not unsatisfactory,' she said coldly. 'I am merely returning a gown because I did not order it and I have no need for it.'

This was too much for Madame Elise. 'The Dowager

Lady Kirkham was most definite...*Votre* ladyship's ivory silk is very well but for Lady Pearmain's...'

'This is something for tonight's ball, eh?' Kirkham regarded the sea of blue satin on the floor. 'Does it not please you?'

'I do not know. I have not looked at it.'

He glared at her for a moment, then he turned to Madame Elise. 'You, Madame Whatever-your-name-is, take these things back into her ladyship's dressing-room, then go. Wait below stairs until you are sent for.'

'*Oui*, my lord.'

Madame Elise's expression of relief and triumph was not lost on Melissa, but she waited until the dressmaker had gone before she rounded on Kirkham.

'And what do you think you are doing, countermanding my orders in that high-handed manner?' she demanded.

'I might equally ask what you are about,' he retorted. 'Though I do not need to ask. I can guess exactly what your game is. You are returning that ballgown for one reason only. To belittle me tonight and make me look a penny-pincher.'

'I do not believe my own ears!' She stared at him incredulously. 'Why should what I wear make any difference to you?'

'Your memory is proving appallingly short, madam. Until recently you were claiming me for your husband. Indeed, to my intense regret, that is how Society now sees me. What you wear does affect me, for it reflects upon my qualities as a spouse and provider.'

'Nonsense!' snorted Melissa.

'It is not nonsense. It is a regrettable fact of modern life. I will not have you going abroad dressed in a manner likely to disgrace me.'

'Your honour must be a fragile thing if my wearing the same ballgown twice will damage it so easily.'

'It is not what you wear, madam, but where you wear it.' Kirkham spoke in the tones of a man curbing his anger with great difficulty. 'Tonight we are engaged to dance and sup at Lady Pearmain's. Lady Pearmain, may I inform you, is one of the foremost hostesses in town. She has the keenest eye and the sharpest tongue from here to Kent, and gathers about her a horde of like-minded harpies who do their best to emulate her. Within five minutes of you entering the house they will have priced everything you are wearing from the comb in your hair to the bows on your shoes. Moreover, they will be familiar with everything you have ever worn since you entered Society so precipitately. Not a handkerchief, not a ribbon, will have escaped their notice. That, madam, is why you will wear the new ballgown tonight. I will not have those vinegar-tongued crones passing it about town that I am a shabby fellow whose wife only has one ballgown.'

'You keep saying I am not your wife.'

'I know!' roared Kirkham, his patience at an end. 'But in the eyes of the world. . . Oh, never mind the arguments. Just wear that new gown tonight!'

'No,' she declared. 'I wear the ivory silk or I do not go.'

'I hope you are not planning a second bout of *la grippe* so soon, madam. That would really stretch everyone's credulity; and, if you recall, we have an agreement to prevent tongues wagging at all costs. Therefore you will go and you will wear the new dress.'

'I will not,' she retorted.

'Is it too much to hope that you have a sound reason for your intractable attitude?'

'Of course I have a sound reason.' Melissa raised her

chin proudly. 'I entered this marriage as a matter of expediency. It was never my intention to profit financially from being your wife. Already I have been obliged to receive more of Lady Kirkham's benevolence than I would have wished. But enough is enough. I accept nothing more. My pride will not permit it.'

Kirkham gave a growl of fury. 'And my pride will not permit me being seen abroad with a shabby wife — or even a shabby so-called wife,' he snarled through gritted teeth. 'You, madam, will accompany me to Lady Pearmain's tonight wearing that new gown, even if I have to put it on you myself!'

'Do not threaten. . .' Melissa began, then she saw the look on his face. If ever she had considered Kirkham to lack resolution and determination then that consideration faded at the steely expression in his eyes. He took a step forward. Sharply she retreated into her dressing-room.

'You would not dare,' she declared, round the safety of the stout mahogany door.

'Madam, do not try me too far,' he snarled in reply.

He began to move forward. There was no denying that he meant every word. With a startled cry Melissa slammed the door on him and locked it. Only when she heard his angry footsteps recede along the corridor did she venture to turn the key and summon Madame Elise back to her dressing-room. She and Kirkham would go to Lady Pearmain's ball and she would wear the new blue satin gown. In the circumstances it seemed the most prudent thing to do.

All the *haut ton* appeared to be attending the ball. From end to end Brook Street was aglow with carriage lamps and flambeaux. Coachmen attempted to urge their horses further and further into the tightly packed jam, while impatient passengers thrust elaborately dressed heads from carriage windows to demand what the devil was causing such a delay.

Melissa and Kirkham had not exchanged a word since leaving Hanover Square. Now Kirkham gave a disgruntled sigh.

'Just what I feared,' he groaned. 'A sad crush. If it is like this outside, imagine what a press of people will be in the house. Still, we do not need to stay long. Once supper is done we can make our excuses and leave.'

'Perhaps I could suffer another onset of *la grippe*,' said Melissa waspishly.

Kirkham's eyes glittered with anger. 'It will suffice for you to claim fatigue,' he replied. 'Ah, we have reached the door at last. Now we must play the devoted newly-weds.'

'And a masterly task that will be,' muttered Melissa, half to herself. 'We'll be asked to appear at Drury Lane next.'

'Just so long as it is for a farce and not a romantic piece about lovers,' snapped Kirkham, getting out of the carriage. Then a transformation swept over him as he turned to help her out. A fond smile, which to Melissa's eyes looked false and idiotic, spread across his face as he grasped her hand.

'Go carefully, my love,' he said. 'There, you have nothing to fear, for I have you safely.'

The mock-tender tone of his voice made her grit her teeth. She half expected him to let go suddenly or cause her some other disaster. Fortunately he did not, and though she hated to admit it she was grateful for the security of his grip. It was no easy matter getting out of a carriage with dignity when hampered by a long train and a plumed headdress.

She had set out for this ball in an ill humour, one she maintained with difficulty as, on Kirkham's arm, she climbed the steps to Pearmain House. Kirkham's ultimatum on the subject of the ballgown, plus his extraordinary steadfastness in ensuring his demands were carried out, had both shaken and surprised her.

How dare he? she had fumed silently all the time Madame Elise and Timms had been busy making the last-minute alterations. How dare he tell me what to wear and when to wear it?

Her fury had received a serious setback when she had taken a first look at herself in the mirror. The gown was simpler in style than was the usual mode of the day, relying for effect upon the impact of its colour — a blue as soft and delicate as a speedwell petal — upon the lustrous sheen of the heavy satin, and upon the rich borders of embroidered lily of the valley which decorated the front and the hem. It was a superb creation, far and away the most beautiful dress she had ever owned, and it showed off to advantage her slender figure and fair colouring. She tried with all her might to wish she was wearing the ivory silk, but it was no use.

Her grumpy mood received a second blow when they finally entered Pearmain House and she removed her wrap. Kirkham, who had been lounging against the wall in the entrance hall waiting for her, straightened up as she approached. Then he seemed to take a second look at her, as if unable to believe his eyes. The silly pseudo-fond expression faded from his face, to be replaced by genuine admiration. Reaching out, he took her hand and pressed it to his lips.

'Madam, all other ladies present will fade into insignificance when you enter,' he said softly.

It was just the sort of extravagant compliment he frequently paid her in public, and Melissa tried to respond in her usual way — with a demure flutter of her long lashes and a low response. On this occasion, however, there was a hint of something perilously close to sincerity in Kirkham's voice. It brought warm colour flooding to her cheeks and made her unable to think of a suitable reply.

Then Kirkham spoiled the moment. While still bent over her hand he murmured so that only she could hear, 'There, was I not right to insist upon the new gown?'

Anger surged through Melissa, though she dared not let it register on her face. Instead she withdrew her hand from Kirkham's grasp so sharply that he almost overbalanced.

'What, staggering already?' said the familiar voice of Lady Kirkham. 'You have not arrived foxed, I hope.'

'No, Grandmother, I am merely drunk with love,' sighed Kirkham, in such a sickly sentimental voice that Melissa longed to hit him.

'Do not overdo it, for pity's sake!' Melissa hissed as the three of them climbed the marble staircase to the ballroom.

'There is no fear of that,' replied Kirkham. 'Look at the doting smiles all about us. These old dames thrive upon such tender-hearted utterances.'

'Maybe, but my stomach does not,' she retorted.

They reached the head of the staircase where they were announced and greeted by their hostess. Within ten seconds of being under the relentless scrutiny of Lady Pearmain Melissa was forced to admit Kirkham had been right. Those steel-grey eyes were assessing everything she had on, right down to her chemise and petticoat at a guess.

'Why, Meg, the chit is quite presentable,' drawled Lady Pearmain insolently.

Lady Kirkham made no appearance of being put out.

'Which chit would that be, Hetty?' she asked calmly.

'If you mean that piece of muslin your son is drooling over then I fear your taste, like his, is sadly adrift, for I have never seen thicker ankles nor a worse-dressed head in my life.'

Without waiting for a response she moved on, propelling Kirkham and Melissa before her.

Kirkham gave a snort of laughter. 'No one slights our family lightly when Grandmother is about,' he said into Melissa's ear. 'Putting such people down is her chief delight in life.'

'After whist,' declared Lady Kirkham decisively. 'I am glad Hetty has got a decent number of tables laid out away from the hurly-burly. Off you go, you two, and leave me to my cards in peace.'

Melissa and Kirkham had no alternative but to obey, for as Lady Kirkham turned off into the card-room they were carried along by the crush towards the dancing. At least, most of the other guests were heading in the direction of the ballroom floor. One stout lady was forcing her way against the tide. Clad in a virulent green brocade and with a collar of huge emeralds about her neck that would have brought a lesser woman to her knees, she breasted her way through the oncoming bodies, not caring who fell in her path. Melissa realised they were on a collision course with this fearsome creature.

Kirkham did not flinch. 'Why, Mrs Hurst, how delightful to see you again.' He made a low bow. 'And Miss Hurst too. Such a pleasure.'

Belatedly Melissa noticed that there was a smaller, slighter figure behind the green edifice, entirely shielded from view by Mrs Hurst's brocaded bulk.

'My dear, may I present to you Mrs Hurst and her delightful daughter?'

Melissa had to give Kirkham full marks, he did not

let the glare of terrifying hostility in Mrs Hurst's eyes deter him. Mrs Hurst, however, was in no mood to be presented. Turning her glare on Melissa, she uttered a stentorian 'Hrumph!' and ploughed a way between them. Scurrying behind her mother, her small face scarlet with mortification, Miss Hurst paused long enough to bob them each a hurried curtsy then rushed away.

Among the willing hands that steadied Melissa and Kirkham were those belonging to old Lord Layfield.

'As severe a snub as ever I've seen,' he chuckled. 'That's what you get for spurning the girl, my boy. But it's nothing to what you'd have suffered if you'd married her! Your grandmother's in the card-room, is she? Then I'll join her.'

'You were thinking of marrying Miss Hurst?' asked Melissa incredulously.

'It did cross my mind. Her mother was pushing me towards it, certainly,' said Kirkham.

'Ah, the mouse and the dragon.'

'I beg your pardon?'

'That was how you once described them to me, though you mentioned no names.'

'I did? I have no recollection of it, but now I think on it, it is a very apt description. Did you see how that woman was breathing fire? Every footman's wig for twenty yards is frizzled.'

'You exaggerate, my lord, though not by much,' replied Melissa suppressing a chuckle. 'And, unconventional though our union may be, you owe me one debt of gratitude for having saved you from such a mother-in-law.'

'Indeed I do!' His look of utter astonishment was so comical that Melissa could not hold back her laughter. Her mirth was infectious, and Kirkham joined in heartily, causing people round about to smile also and remark how delightful it was to see such a happy young couple.

It was as well that Melissa did not hear their comments, for it still made her uncomfortable to be regarded as a blissful newly-wed. Unexpectedly she felt quite grateful to Mrs Hurst. That lady's appalling behaviour had broken the ice which always seemed to exist between her and Kirkham when they were on public show. Their laughter had swept away all awkwardness, causing her to look forward to the evening. For once she felt there was a chance she might actually enjoy herself.

'With your permission, madam.' Kirkham held out his hand for her dance card, scribbled furiously for a minute or two, then returned it.

'You have written yourself in rather a lot,' said Melissa.

'It was done on purpose. That way everyone will see us as devoted and united.'

Melissa added up the number of dances with Kirkham's name beside them.

'Siamese twins would be hard put to it to be more united,' she remarked. 'I wonder you propose to neglect me during the schottische and the polka. You are not afraid tongues will wag?'

'They are duty dances. I have my social obligations, you know,' he retorted a might testily. 'If you object to dancing with me frequently you are at liberty to withdraw any time you choose.'

At once Melissa regretted her acid comments. To tell the truth she was relieved to see his name so often on her programme. The more they danced, the less need they would have to fend off other people's pertinent — and sometime impertinent — enquiries. Besides, on the one other occasion when she had danced with Kirkham, at a much smaller, less fashionable ball than this, she had found the experience surprisingly pleasurable.

'I do not object to dancing with you,' she said hurriedly. 'I am sorry if I sounded as if I did. I accept that, for all your faults, you are an exceedingly good dancer——' She stopped abruptly, conscious that again her reply had sounded sour. It had been her intention to say something nice for once. Since she had become Lady Kirkham her tongue had somehow taken control of her brain, uttering churlish comments of its own volition. To her surprise Kirkham laughed.

'That's the nearest thing to a compliment you have offered me yet, madam,' he grinned. 'My character must be improving. Come, let us take our places in the dance while we are still on amicable terms.'

Unexpectedly they remained on amicable terms for most of the evening. Once or twice Melissa noticed Kirkham's eyes stray longingly towards the card-room. Not the one where his grandmother was playing whist, but the one more discreetly placed, where, by the excited yells that emerged from time to time, the play was lively and the stakes high. But, to give him his due, he made no attempt to abandon her and go to join the game.

Kirkham could be excellent company when he put himself out, and he was on fine form that night. Laughter and smiles seemed to follow them about the room. Melissa's previous life had been sorely lacking in merriment, and she would have been less than human if she had not found herself thoroughly enjoying the evening. The elegant company, the excellent music, the infectious rhythms of the dance, all combined to give her pleasure. It was halfway through the ball before she allowed herself to admit to one more pleasure. That of being partnered by the handsomest man in the room.

It had grown excessively warm and Kirkham had gone to fetch her some lemonade. While she waited for him Melissa amused herself with watching the passing throng; the ladies in their elegant gowns, plumes nodding, jewels sparkling; the young blades in the exaggerated neckcloths and skin-tight jackets; the military men in scarlet coats, gold braid and immaculate white breeches; men of fashion clad in the more sombre mode made popular by Mr Brummel. Then she saw him coming back to her. His dark head topped every other man's in the room, his movements seemed more athletic, his shoulders, beneath the superb fit of his coat, wider and more muscular. Above all, as he approached her his face lit in a vivid smile displaying strong white teeth, showing no hint of the sickly false grin he often wore when accompanying her in public. He looked devastatingly handsome.

'Your wish is my command, madam,' he said, setting the lemonade in front of her. 'And not above half of it spilled down my weskit. Pray congratulate me on my dexterity.'

There was not a single drop marring the front of his gold brocade waistcoat, but Melissa did not notice; she was conscious only of a sudden feeling of elation because no other woman had such a good-looking partner.

Her feeling of euphoria was excessively brief. It was followed swiftly by astonishment and chagrin. How could she think such a thing! About Kirkham, of all people! She was obliged to take a swift drink of lemonade to restore her composure. The result was disastrous.

'I only wanted you to praise my abilities as a waiter,

not choke yourself to death,' said Kirkham, patting her on the back.

'The lemonade — went down — the wrong way,' spluttered Melissa. She took a deep breath. 'There, I am better,' she said at last, mopping her eyes.

'You are sure?' He looked at her with concern. 'This next dance is mine, I believe. We will sit it out until you have completely recovered.'

'There is no need, truly,' she assured him. 'I have stopped coughing. See, they are making up the sets for the cotillion. Please let us join in.'

Her eagerness to dance owed more to a sudden need for activity than a wish to join in the cotillion. She did not want to admit that such favourable thoughts about Kirkham had ever occurred to her. Better by far to concentrate upon the complex figures of the dance; anything was preferable to being forced to dwell upon her terrible lapse.

In theory the idea was excellent, but she had forgotten that during the dance she would feel the firm grasp of his fingers on hers, have his arm encircling her waist, feel his body close to hers as they moved to the music. Far from restoring her composure Melissa felt increasingly agitated.

When the cotillion was at an end she was relieved to notice that the ribbon had been torn off one of her satin slippers and she had an honest excuse for begging to withdraw.

The ladies' retiring-room was some distance from the dancing. Melissa was grateful to hand her damaged slipper over to a maid and then sink into a chair.

It took some time before the cool tranquillity of the retiring-room began to have its effect and her normal common sense reasserted itself. It had been a touch of the vapours, nothing more. She had never considered herself to be prone to such things, but clearly she was not totally immune. The excitement of being at such a fashionable assembly, plus the heat of the room, had inflamed her sensibilities — that was it! Normally she despised females who were susceptible to any man in their line of vision simply because he was male. Evidently, in certain circumstances, she had to count herself among their number. It was not agreeable to learn such a disconcerting fact about oneself — but it was a great deal better than the idea that she found Kirkham attractive.

For the first time she became aware that she was not alone in the retiring-room. A small, slight figure was sitting squashed up tightly in a corner of the sofa, as if fearful of being accused of taking up too much room. To Melissa's consternation she recognised her.

'Your pardon, Miss Hurst, you must think me very rude. I did not see you sitting there,' she said.

'Your apology is not necessary, your ladyship, I assure you,' replied Beth Hurst. 'After the heat of the ballroom it is very refreshing to sit quietly with one's eyes closed, is it not?'

'It is indeed,' Melissa responded, though she had not been conscious of having closed her eyes.

An awkward silence followed.

'Are there not a great many elegant people here tonight?' said Miss Hurst.

'There are. This must be one of the most fashionable gatherings of the season.'

Once more silence fell.

'Oh, Lady Kirkham, I have been so remiss. What must you think of me? I have not offered you and Lord Kirkham my felicitations upon your wedding and my wishes for a long and happy life together.'

Melissa could bear it no longer. Here was this nice

quiet little creature struggling to make polite conversation when she, Melissa, had probably ruined her life by stealing her suitor. Hobbling over to the sofa she sat beside her.

'Miss Hurst,' she said. 'You must be the kindest, most forgiving creature in the world, which is why I feel I must speak frankly. When I married Lord Kirkham I had no idea that there was any sort of understanding between you. As for Lord Kirkham's actions. . .well, there were special circumstances which I cannot divulge, but I know I speak for him when I apologise on both our behalves for any distress we may have caused you. We never set out to harm you in any way, and if we have then we are dreadfully sorry.'

'How very nice of you, your ladyship.' Beth Hurst's small face grew pink with pleasure. 'But you have no cause for regrets. There was never any firm commitment between Lord Kirkham and myself, except in Mama's understanding. When I offered you both my felicitations I meant every word. I hope you will be very happy. Save that Mama is exceeding cross, you have done me no harm at all.'

'I am heartily glad to hear it.' Melissa regarded Miss Hurst keenly. 'You will pardon me if I seem impertinent upon so short an acquaintance, but you sound almost relieved that you are not marrying Lord Kirkham.'

'I am,' confessed Miss Hurst.

'Indeed?' It was ridiculous how such a note of indignation should have got into Melissa's voice, but it had.

'I mean no disrespect to Lord Kirkham,' Miss Hurst said hurriedly. 'He is a most handsome gentleman, and he has always been polite and courteous to me. No one could have been kinder, but. . .'

'But?'

'I find him rather alarming.'

'Alarming. . .? Kirkham. . .?' said Melissa in astonishment. 'But he would not hurt a fly!'

'I do not blame you for sounding surprised. You are very beautiful and at ease in Society. I dare say people do not alarm you. Unfortunately I frighten easily. I cannot help it. I tried extremely hard not to be afraid of Lord Kirkham, for Mama's sake. It was no use. He is such a lively gentleman, you see, and very energetic. I find conversing with people difficult at the best of times. In his presence I was completely overcome with nerves and could never utter a word. He must think me a most terrible mouse.'

This was too close to Kirkham's opinion for comfort.

'Yet you have no difficulty in talking to me,' Melissa observed swiftly.

'No, I do not, do I?' said Miss Hurst in surprise. 'How extraordinary!'

'Perhaps it is because I am not half so much at ease in Society as you imagine,' said Melissa. 'Please believe that you are not the only one who gets nervous.'

'Not you, Lady Kirkham!'

'Yes, me.' Melissa smiled at the girl's incredulity. 'The repairs to my slipper seem to be taking an age, but that is no reason for you to stay. I hear the orchestra tuning up for the next dance. Your partner will be looking for you.'

'I have no partner for this dance,' said Beth Hurst candidly. 'Nor had I one for the last. That was why Mama banished me to the retiring-room until both were over, in order not to shame her.'

'I am sure no shame is involved,' said Melissa, indignant on the girl's behalf. 'As soon as I get my slipper back we will find you partners enough.'

'Thank you, my lady, but I am sorry to say that I do

not think Mama would agree. It is not that I lack offers. It is that Mama is excessivly particular. Mr Woodley would have danced with me but she sent him away because he had already partnered me twice.'

'Ah,' said Melissa, noting the flushed cheeks and the bright eyes. 'This Mr Woodley, I gather he is not alarming.

'No, he is very kind and gentle. I am rarely nervous with him.'

'And you love him very much.' It was a statement, not a question. Beth Hurst's face betrayed her feelings. She looked positively pretty. 'I suppose he is poor and has no prospects, that your parents disapprove of him.'

'I do not think he can be poor,' said Beth thoughtfully. 'He already has a very pretty estate that borders ours in Sussex, plus a clear forty thousand a year, and I believe he will inherit as much again by and by. I do not think that that is poor, do you, Lady Kirkham?'

'No,' replied Melissa gravely. 'I do not.'

'And it is only Mama who does not approve. Papa is exceeding fond of him, and is always glad when he calls. I think Papa would give his consent for Mr Woodley to pay his addresses to me, but sadly Papa is an invalid.'

She did not need to say more. Clearly Mr Hurst's opinions were discounted by his overbearing wife.

'Then why does your mama disapprove of Mr Woodley? He is wealthy, has good prospects, and must be of good character or your father would not like him.'

'He has no title,' said Beth, and all the happiness went from her face. 'Mama has set her heart upon me having a title.'

For a few moments Melissa's thoughts were occupied by some very uncomplimentary opinions of Mrs Hurst.

Before she could say anything, however, the rather harassed maid returned bearing the repaired slipper.

'Your pardon for taking so long, your ladyship,' the girl said breathlessly. 'I had to go right up to the sewing-room to find the right shade of blue thread.'

'All that concerns me is that your stitches are stout,' Melissa replied, and was rewarded with a relieved smile. She put on her slipper and turned to Beth Hurst. 'Now that I am decently shod once more I would suggest that we return to the fray together. However, such a course might make things difficult for you, therefore I will go first. But I implore you to return to the ballroom soon. You have hidden away in here long enough. You have nothing to be ashamed of. Besides, though you may not dance with your Mr Woodley no one can prevent you from looking at one another. Hold your head high, Miss Hurst, and rejoin the assembly.'

'I will, Lady Kirkham, I will!' Beth Hurst's face positively beamed. 'And thank you. . . Oh, thank you!'

Melissa was not sure what she had done to deserve such gratitude, save persuade a timid young girl to disobey her mother. What if Mr Woodley was really a scoundrel and Mrs Hurst was perfectly justified in rejecting him?

As she returned to the ballroom she realised that her original problem, her extraordinary reaction to Kirkham, had not faded from her recollection. For a short while she had thought she had got the matter in its proper perspective, but she had been wrong. It had only taken Beth Hurst's obvious relief at having escaped marriage to Kirkham to arouse in her a protective indignation. Surely nothing could have been more bizarre? Being provoked because another woman had no wish to marry her husband! Yet, she had been. She had been resentful on Kirkham's behalf, seeing Miss Hurst's rejection of him as a slight.

Kirkham rose at her approach. She wished the welcoming smile on his face did not look so genuine. Oh, where was the idiotic fixed grin she could dislike with such ease?'

'There you are at last,' he declared. 'I thought the gypsies had run off with you.'

'No doubt you paid them handsomely to take me away. What a pity they gulled you.' Her retort was meant to be one of her acid-tongue comments, but even that failed her. Her words came out as a light-hearted response.

'Clearly I didn't pay them enough,' replied Kirkham in the same vein. 'I must see they have another half-crown next time. But I intend to take advantage of your unexpected return and ask you to accompany me for the next dance. It is a waltz, a favourite of mine, and I am sure my name is writ clearly beside it.'

'Indeed it is, my lord!' She feigned surprise to hide her dismay as he led her on to the floor. Why did it have to be a waltz? Why could it not have been a country dance with a minimum of physical contact and the maximum of partners. Heartily she cursed Lady Pearmain for not being one of those puritanical hostesses who still forbade such licentious activity at their assemblies.

'You do not like the waltz?' asked Kirkham after they had been dancing for a few minutes.

'Yes, I like it. Why do you ask?'

'Because you have gone all stiff and forbidding. Let me draw you closer, then you will be able to follow my lead much more easily. It is an exceedingly enjoyable dance, in my opinion.'

Melissa's head told her that it was very disagreeable

being held tightly by Kirkham, that to feel the warmth of him, to be aware of his every muscle, was unpleasant in the extreme. Unfortunately her head did not seem able to communicate with the rest of her. She found herself melting against him, being intoxicated by the feel of him against her, responding to his every movement. Never in her life had she felt such sensations. It was dreadful of her, and she was certain that every eye in the place must be on her, condemning her behaviour. Astonishingly, when the final chord died away, not a soul seemed to be looking in her direction.

'That was splendid,' said Kirkham, tucking her arm through his. 'I enjoyed that exceedingly.'

Melissa did not dare speak. She merely muttered incomprehensibly. Thankfully she allowed herself to be returned to her seat, conscious that the weak sensation in her knees had nothing to do with the energetic steps of the waltz. She did not know what was happening to her, and she was not sure she liked it.

In a determined effort to restore her equilibrium she concentrated hard upon the people in the room. It was some minutes before she spotted Miss Hurst sitting beside her mother. Silently Melissa applauded her for summoning up the courage to quit the tiring-room. The Hursts were not alone. A tall young man was standing in front of them. It was evident from across the room that Mrs Hurst was dismissing him in no uncertain terms, but the young man stood his ground, evidently using all his powers of persuasion. The look of adoring hopelessness on Beth Hurst's face told its own tale. This had to be Mr Woodley. But Melissa decided to make sure.

'My lord,' she said. 'The auburn-haired gentleman across the room, the one in the dark-green coat, do you know him? He closely resembles an acquaintance of my brother's.'

'What, Gerard Woodley? I shouldn't have thought he would have had much in common with your brother. A sound fellow, is Woodley. Everyone says so.'

Such was the shattered state of Melissa's nerves that she failed to notice Kirkham's uncomplimentary comments on her brother, much less respond to them.

'Then it cannot be the same gentleman,' she replied mildly.

Her immediate feeling was one of relief that she had not encouraged Beth Hurst's affections for an unsuitable young man.

The ball was over, and the guests made their exits from the ballroom even more slowly than they had entered. By pure chance Kirkham and Melissa found themselves not far behind the verdant bulk of Mrs Hurst. She was clinging to the arm of old Lord Layfield, ostensibly for support. A pretty vain hope in view of the great disparity in their sizes.

'I am surprised your godson, Kirkham, did not spend more time gaming tonight,' boomed Mrs Hurst. Obviously she did not know Kirkham himself was in earshot, nor did she care. She continued, 'Maybe he has learned his lesson, and not before time; being a rake and a gambler and a dissolute has always been his forte. How satisfying that it has caught up with him at last. I suppose you know the *on dit* is that he won that new wife of his in a game of cards. Goodness knows what her background is! That should quench the Kirkham pride well and truly.'

A stir of mixed embarrassment and speculation swept through the people round about. Melissa gazed at Kirkham with concern, felt him tense, saw his mouth tighten. A less courteous man would have given the objectionable woman a vicious set-down—but not Kirkham. He would never be impolite to a lady, no matter what the expense to himself. Therefore Melissa fumed with fury all the more on his behalf. How dared that woman speak so of him? How dared she refer to him without using his title! Who did she think she was?

'Is that what is being said?' replied Lord Layfield in icy tones. 'Then no wonder the fellow has given up gambling. He could not expect to be so lucky twice.'

'Indeed not,' added Melissa, unable to contain her anger. 'Another time, madam, the prize might be you. No man would risk that!'

So saying she stalked forward, thrusting her way through the crush, past a stunned Mrs Hurst. She did not notice that she had left her husband behind, staring after her with incredulity and amusement. Only one fact occupied her angry mind. It was that no one insulted Kirkham and remained unscathed, not while she was around!

CHAPTER SIX

MELISSA awoke next morning feeling decidedly ill at ease. Had she been right to admonish Mrs Hurst quite so sharply the previous evening? Would it not have been better to have maintained a dignified silence and pretended to ignore the wretched woman? Left to herself she had no regrets whatsoever, save that she had not thought of enough insults in time. It was Kirkham she was bothered about. Had she let him down? This in turn led to more uneasiness. Why on earth should she care what damage she had done to Kirkham's reputation?

Much troubled on both counts, she sat up in bed with a sigh. Beyond the great feather bolster that nightly divided their bed her husband slept as soundly as any babe. She was sorely tempted to wake him and get at least one matter sorted out, but she knew from experience that Kirkham deprived of his sleep would be in no mood for serious discussion. In the carriage, on the way home from the ball, she had tried to discover his true feelings about her treatment of Mrs Hurst.

His only response had been to say, 'Madam, Lady Kirkham—even a would-be Lady Kirkham—does not bother herself about what other people think of her behaviour. Such anxiety is for the lesser orders.'

She had not been sure whether or not he had been serious. At one point she thought she even detected a glint of amused approval in his eye, but in the uncertain, unsteady light of the carriage it had been hard to be sure.

Now she felt too restless to lie any longer. Moving quietly to avoid disturbing the sleeping Kirkham, she slid out of bed. Gently pulling the covers more comfortably up over his shoulders was an automatic gesture, one she regretted the moment it was done, but by then it was too late.

She breakfasted downstairs, and somewhat to her relief Kirkham did not put in an appearance.

'His lordship has decided to breakfast at his club, my lady,' she was informed. 'He spoke of an appointment with Mr O'Gallagher.'

She suspected that Kirkham's absence probably had more to do with his disapproval of her behaviour than a wish to see his friend. For the third time that morning she heaved a deep sigh, and decided to seek sanctuary in the library. When she entered she found Fraser presiding over a scene of chaos. A battalion of housemaids and footmen were dismantling the room, pulling out furniture, removing cushions, lifting down stacks of books.

'Goodness, no one told me the place was to be refurbished!' she exclaimed.

At the sound of her voice the butler swung round. 'Your pardon if you are being inconvenienced, my lady,' he said apologetically. 'I will do my best to have things set to rights as soon as possible.'

'Then you are not preparing for the decorators?'

'No, my lady. We are looking for his lordship's snuff-box.'

'His snuff-box?'

'Yes, my lady. His lordship is certain he last had it in here.'

Melissa looked at the confusion and hectic activity and felt a sense of satisfaction. Here at last was something for which she could condemn Kirkham and set her feelings for him on a nicely belligerent footing once more. Was it not typical of him to be careless enough to lose one of his possessions then create the maximum of fuss until it was found again?

'Has his lordship no other snuff-box he can use until this one re-emerges?' she asked, somewhat icily.

'Oh yes, my lady. A good half-dozen to my certain knowledge, but he would sooner have lost everyone of them plus a great deal besides than have mislaid this one.'

'Then it is the most valuable?'

'In his eyes certainly, my lady, though I fancy in terms of guineas it would be nothing out of the ordinary, for it is just a small enamelled thing and somewhat worn with age. It belonged to old Lord Kirkham, you see, his lordship's grandfather, and for his sake our present lord treasures it above all things. Desperately fond of each other, they were. It was a sad blow to the young Lord Kirkham when his grandsire died.' Fraser heaved a regretful sigh.

Melissa knew what it was to lose things of great sentimental value, and for a moment she experienced a pang of sympathy for Kirkham. A very brief pang. In a moment she had swept it away, deciding that it served him right for being so negligent. 'And what does this snuff-box look like, in case I come across it?' she asked.

'It is oval, my lady. Of enamel on gold, and with a picture of a frigate in full sail on the lid.'

Melissa suppressed a derisive snort. Fraser had become so inured to the luxuries of the life in the Kirkham household that he considered the box to be a trumpery thing in terms of cash. But enamel on gold! There were many people who could live comfortably for a year on the proceeds of such a gew-gaw. Yet Kirkham had managed to mislay it.

'His lordship used not to be so unfortunate with his possessions,' remarked Fraser, as if he could read her thoughts. 'It is only during this last two or three years. . .first it was his pearl shirt-studs, then a very fine cigar-case, and a set of seals and——'

'I will not hinder you further,' broke in Melissa, too irritated by this proof of Kirkham's laxness to want to listen further. 'Send someone to inform me when the library is habitable again, if you please. I will be in the morning-room.'

'Very good, my lady.'

She spent a boring hour trying to read a book that had long since lost her interest. The announcement of Lady Kirkham came as a great relief.

'My lady, I am glad to see you,' she exclaimed with such warmth that the old lady's eyebrows rose.

'It is not often I am greeted so enthusiastically,' she observed wryly. 'I can only assume you want some favour of me.'

'No indeed!' protested Melissa. 'Except perhaps your advice.'

'That is all right, then.' Lady Kirkham sat down and removed her gloves. 'Advice is cheap and in plentiful supply.'

'Well, it is not really advice, I suppose,' Melissa amended. 'What I am hoping is that you will make me feel comfortable again, You see, I am in some agitation over my behaviour last night. I suppose you know all about it?'

'Lord Layfield has just given me a most detailed account.'

Melissa's heart sank. 'I fear I was undignified and that I have disgraced Kirkham,' she said.

Lady Kirkham observed her keenly. 'And what does my grandson say on the matter?' she asked.

'We have not discussed it. Last night he refused to pay attention and this morning I have not seen him — not awake,' she corrected herself hurriedly.

'In that case we can assume that Kirkham is not bothered by your behaviour. But you are, and that surprises me.'

'Does it, your ladyship? Surely it is understandable that I have no wish to make a social gaffe?'

'But I thought we were talking of Kirkham being disgraced? I would not have thought you cared.'

'I do!' retorted Melissa hotly, aware she was being baited. 'He is my legal husband, no matter what you may think. Also, I promised not to do anything to bring shame to the family. Now I fear I may have inadvertently gone back on my word. It made me so angry hearing that female shouting aloud her insults. She knew Kirkham would not give her the rebuff she deserved. Some men would, but not Kirkham. He would never be rude to a woman, no matter how provoked. That was why I stepped in.'

'Was it, indeed? And did not her insults concerning yourself colour your actions?'

'Did Mrs Hurst insult me? I was not aware of it,' replied Melissa in surprise.

Again Lady Kirkham looked at her keenly. 'Is that so?' she said. 'And now you fear you will be ostracised by Society, eh? Stop concerning yourself about it. You were completely justified; as for your response you are to be congratulated. I could not have done better myself.'

'But surely Lady Pearmain must be displeased,' said Melissa, overcome by such unexpected praise.

'Not her. I have just come from Hetty Pearmain's and she is delighted. Quite apart from seeing that awful Hurst woman put in her place — and there are quite a few who applaud you for that alone—she says she has never held a ball that ended on such a lively note. Never fear, there is no need for you to withdraw to the wilderness immediately, though I seem to remember you saying that that is your ultimate intention.'

'It is, my lady, but not yet,' replied Melissa.

'You do not think my grandson has been sufficiently punished, eh? Maybe you are right.'

This had not been Melissa's meaning, or at least she did not think it had. Upon consideration she decided it was not prudent to analyse her motives too minutely. She concentrated upon offering Lady Kirkham some refreshment instead.

Kirkham was at home for dinner. To her disgust Melissa found herself glad to see him. The only antidote to this annoying state of affairs was to greet him with one of her sharp comments.

'Is the fare at your club not to your liking tonight, my lord?' she asked, hoping she had put the right amount of acid into her voice.

Lamentably, Kirkham did not seem to notice anything amiss.

'I did not enquire,' he said, stretching his hands to the blazing fire. 'I have had enough of this weather. Snow, sleet and a howling gale. It is a night when only a raving lunatic would be abroad unnecessarily. No, I decided to sample whatever delights Bertrand has to offer. He has really improved out of all recognititon these last few weeks, you know. The menus he used to provide were appallingly dull.'

Melissa suspected that the housekeeper was more to blame than the cook, but she said nothing.

'I shall have a word with Frazer to make sure we have some decent wine,' Kirkham continued. 'And then perhaps afterwards we can have a game of backgammon? What say you?'

It sounded too cosy for Melissa's peace of mind — but too attractive a proposition to turn down.

'That will be a tolerable way to spend the evening,' she said, maintaining a chilly tone with difficulty.

Her worst fears were realised. The dinner was superb, the wines excellent, and playing backgammon by a roaring fire in the withdrawing-room seemed the ideal occupation on such a blustery night.

'Is this not pleasant?' said Kirkham. 'I pity any poor fellow who does not have a comfortable fireside to sit by.'

'Yet I believe you are not renowned for staying at home,' said Melissa.

'I used not to be, certainly.' Kirkham paused thoughtfully, a backgammon counter in his hand. 'I suppose in the past there has been little to encourage me to remain within my own four walls. This house has always felt an empty sort of place to me.'

'What, with an army of servants here?'

'Especially with an army of servants. They always seemed to be much more comfortable here than I did, and to have more enjoyment. I used to invite friends from time to time, but the evening always degenerated into drinking and gaming — activities I could carry out far more agreeably elsewhere. Ah, I see a look of disapproval on your face.'

'Is it any wonder? A man of your rank and intelligence finding nothing better to occupy him than debauchery.'

'There is much to be said for debauchery,' said Kirkham, a glint of mischief in his eyes. 'It is companionable and amusing while it lasts, which is more than can be said for living alone in this house. But I fear all that might be becoming a thing of the past. I seem to be losing the taste for it; the onset of old age, perhaps.'

Although he had kept his tone light Melissa detected beneath it a sadder, more sincere note. Now that she was growing to know him better she was beginning to realise that Lord Kirkham, for all his rank, wealth, looks and charm, was basically a very lonely man.

In an attempt to drive off the sympathy that was starting to creep over her she said primly. 'Let us hope that such maturity brings wisdom with it.' Then for emphasis she added, 'Belated wisdom.'

Kirkham gave a chuckle. 'If I did not know better, madam, I would say you wished me back at my club again.'

'I have never made a secret of my opinion of you, my lord, so I do not see why you say "If I did not know better".'

'Are you sure that your opinion might not be mellowing just a little? Else why would you grind the formidable Mrs Hurst into small pieces so effectively, and in public too? Also, when I came in this evening, if I was not very much mistaken you were glad to see me.'

'You were mistaken, my lord,' snapped Melissa.

'No, I was not,' replied Kirkham imperturbably. 'It showed on your face for only the merest second, but it was there.'

'And what if it was?' retorted Melissa, uneasy at the path the conversation was taking. 'If you must know I find the evenings alone rather tedious at times. And as for Mrs Hurst, she got exactly what she deserved.'

'Bravo!' applauded Kirkham. 'We are absolutely in accord upon both points. We both find evenings alone miserable and we both consider the Hurst Dragon to be quite beyond anything. There, is it not better for us to be in agreement rather than squabbling? We are rather stuck with each other's company so let's make the best of it. Since it is far too inclement for either of us to leave home, here's to pleasant companionship by the fire.'

Melissa had never expected to hear him be so amenable. She knew she should refuse, give him a rebuff or even stalk out the room, but his glass was raised and he was smiling at her. Almost unconsciously she found herself raising her glass in reply, an answering smile lifting the corners of her mouth. One thing was certain. She was finding it incredibly hard to dislike Kirkham consistently.

The day's unpleasant weather proved to be but a foretaste of worse to come. A blizzard hit London of such magnitude that life came to a virtual standstill. Only the main streets were passable, and then with the greatest care, as the deep snow underfoot turned to first a murky brown from city dirt and then solidified into treacherous hillocks of frozen slush. Social events were cancelled wholesale, the theatres played to empty houses, and even the gaming-dens suffered seriously from a lack of clients. Certainly the ones normally frequented by Kirkham must have suffered a considerable loss, for he never went near them, preferring to stay at home and play backgammon and chess with Melissa.

While the snow endured, so did this state of near domestic bliss. Melissa was not sure she liked the arrangement. It was much easier to disapprove of Kirkham when she suspected he was out gaming or carousing instead of stretched out in front of the withdrawing-room fire. As the bitter weather continued she had to make a greater and greater effort to maintain her image of a censorious wife. Worse still, she began to forget that her position as Lady Kirkham, while legal, was not intended to be permanent.

She was quite shaken when she found herself in a serious discussion with Fraser over the arrangements for spring-cleaning the house at the end of the season. She had actually got as far as asking him to obtain some wallpaper samples before she pulled herself up short. What could she have been thinking of? After the season finished she intended to be living quietly in some country town or seaside resort, with Polly and maybe a pet dog, along with a sense of complacency that she had taught Kirkham a lesson he would never forget. New wallpaper for the house in Hanover Square did not enter into her scheme of things at all.

Kirkham certainly did not intend her to be a permanent fixture. While he was content to spend the evenings in her company, during the day he was one of the few gentlemen who ventured out of doors. He regularly braved the dangers underfoot to meet Mr O'Gallagher. The reason he sought out the Irishman was not for companionship, she was sure. It was because he still hoped to find proof that their marriage was invalid.

Well, he won't, thought Melissa to herself. Polly and I have seen to that.

But his persistence that they were not married had an increasingly upsetting effect on her temper.

'What is the matter with servants?' she demanded testily after narrowly avoiding collision with a large Chinese vase being moved by a footman. 'They are always fidgeting with the furniture and ornaments to no purpose. Can they not leave things alone?'

'It's Lord Kirkham's fault. He's offered five guineas to anyone who finds his snuff-box,' said Polly.

'Is it still missing?' Melissa forgot to be short-tempered in her surprise. 'Five guineas, you say? That is a fortune. No wonder the servants are going through the place with a fine-tooth comb. It is sure to make its reappearance with such a reward in the offing.'

'Not necessarily,' replied Polly. 'His lordship offered the same amount for the return of his riding-crop a while back, according to below-stairs gossip, but it was never found. It wasn't much of a thing for all its silver bands, by all accounts, being old and worn and having been mended more than once, but his lordship would have no other. Apparently it was given to him by his grandfather when a boy and no other riding-crop would do.'

'It sounds a similar history to the snuff-box. I never heard of a man with his wealth being so sentimentally attached to old possessions.'

'And not only possessions,' laughed Polly. 'He is attached to his old servants too. Most grow grey and toothless in his service, yet he will not put them out to pasture until they wish to leave. I've been told that the manservant he had before Pentecost was too doddery and short-sighted even to polish boots properly. His lordship used to sneak them out behind the valet's back to have them cleaned again by the downstairs boy.'

'There is no denying that his lordship is a very kind man,' Melissa was forced to admit.

'He is that,' agreed Polly. 'Too kind for his own good at times. Most of those below stairs, mainly those who have been in the service of the family for a long time, idolise him, but there are some who are trading on his good nature to line their own pockets.'

'I think I can put names to a few of them,' said Melissa, whose sharp eyes had missed no domestic detail during her stay in Hanover Square. 'Although they do not know it, they are in for a great shock presently.' Then her tone changed to one of curiosity.

'Pentecost is not one of the old family retainers, you say? You surprise me.'

'He does have an air of having been here since the Flood, doesn't he? Yet I understand he has not been with his lordship above three years. His predecessor refused to retire and quite literally died in service. He was tying his lordship's neckcloth at the time and dropped dead at his feet. He was nearly eighty.'

'The old fellow must have been very frail. I hope Lord Kirkham had the sense to have someone else shave him,' said Melissa with concern. 'Otherwise there could have been a terrible accident. . . Three years, you say Pentecost has been in his lordship's service?'

'That is what I was told. Why, is something the matter?'

'I am not sure. . .' Melissa was racking her brain for the elusive thought that persisted in evading her. It was something someone had said. . .something concerning the last three years. . .'I have it!' she exclaimed. 'Fraser told it to me: how his lordship used not to be careless with his possessions until the last two or three years, since when many of his valuables have gone missing.'

Melissa and Polly stared at one another.

'Coincidence?' Polly suggested.

'Possibly. Is there anyone else who has joined the domestic staff in that time?'

'I don't know, but I can soon find out.'

'It must be coincidence,' asserted Melissa. 'Pentecost is such a dignified fellow. To think of him stealing is beyond imagination.'

'It's not beyond my imagination,' said Polly with the voice of experience. 'His pompous, high-and-mighty sort are usually the worst, and besides. . . .'

'Besides what?' Melissa prompted.

'It may be nothing, but I happened to be standing

near him when Mr Fraser announced that his lordship was offering five guineas to whoever found the snuffbox. Mr Pentecost went so red in the face I feared he would have an apoplexy. At the time I thought it was the prospect of having a chance to gain the five guineas. Now I'm not so sure.'

'Had Pentecost been a footman or the gardener's boy I might agree with you, but I do not think five guineas would be such a fortune to him.'

'I don't know. He's always short of the ready, and since that day he has been in a foul temper.'

Again Melissa and Polly exchanged significant looks.

'I'll find out if anyone else has come to work here in the last three years,' said Polly. Then added significantly, 'If no one has, shall I make discreet enquiries elsewhere?'

'Yes, please,' replied Melissa. 'It is bad enough Lord Kirkham having his possessions stolen, but many hold sentimental value for him and can never be replaced. He is far too. . .' She almost said, far too nice a man to be so treated. Just in time she managed to curb her tongue and say quickly, 'Where did you think of starting your search?'

'At Uncle Billy's.'

'Do you really want to go back there?' asked Melissa with concern. Uncle Billy's was a pawnbroker's shop in one of the less salubrious alleys behind Newgate. Uncle Billy had a reputation for knowing more about stolen property than he should, but he also had a weakness for a pretty face and could be persuaded to give a little more than the going rate for items being "popped". In earlier, more impoverished times, Melissa's few possessions of value had found their way over his counter with a painful regularity.

'I'll be careful,' Polly promised. 'Uncle'll want paying

for any information. Have I your permission to make him an offer?'

'Yes, use your discretion. And for goodness' sake be careful. It is a very rough area.'

'You don't need to tell me.' Polly's teeth flashed white. 'And don't worry. I can take care of myself.'

But Melissa did worry. All the time Polly was away she paced up and down, condemning herself for allowing the girl to go. She did not have to wait long. In a remarkably short time Polly returned, and rummaging under her voluminous skirts, removed a cloth bag. She tipped it up and out fell a collection of studs and rings, watch-chains and other small objects, all of the finest quality. There, in the middle, looking a little shabby by comparison, was an enamelled snuff-box with a frigate in full sail on the lid.

'This was all Uncle could lay his hands on at the moment,' she said with a hint of triumph. 'He says he'll make enquiries about the rest and let us know.'

'The rest!' exclaimed Melissa. 'You mean there's more?'

'Yes, according to Uncle. Quite a bit that'll take some tracing. We owe him twenty guineas for this lot. Oh, and he begs complete discretion. Is that all right?'

'Certainly,' said Melissa without hesitation. Not so long ago twenty guineas would have been an impossible sum. Thanks to the generous allowance Kirkham insisted upon giving her, it no longer presented any problems. She had always been reluctant to use the money; now though, she felt she had a legitimate reason to spend it. 'And was it Pentecost?'

'Yes. Uncle Billy described him to a T. And no wonder he's been looking glum about the five guineas' reward. He only got one for the snuff-box.'

Chuckling at this information, Melissa gathered up

the objects. As she went in search of Kirkham she found herself looking forward to the expression of pleasure on his face when he had his possessions returned to him. She ran him to earth in the library, writing letters.

'I have something for you, my lord,' she said, and placed the snuff-box on the table in front of him.

For a long moment he gazed at it in speechless wonder, as if he could not believe his eyes.

Then he exclaimed, 'You've found it! Miracles will never cease. I had given up hopes of ever seeing it again, yet you found it. Clever, clever, Melissa!'

He had used her Christian name! While she was still transfixed by such a miracle he leapt to his feet and swept her into his arms. Taken completely by surprise, she did not protest. Worse still, she did not want to protest, not even when his lips pressed down on hers, driving away her senses as well as her breath. It was the most wonderful sensation she had ever experienced, sending a warm flood of happiness coursing through her veins. Exhilarated and intoxicated, she put her arms about his neck and kissed him back, matching his enthusiasm and his ardour. Only when sheer breathlessness forced him to set her back on her feet did she feel shocked at what had happened.

How could she have behaved in such a way? Kirkham was excited by the return of his snuff-box; she had no similar vindication. She feared her only excuse was the fact that she actually enjoyed being close to him, feeling his body against hers. It was a terrible admission. She was stunned at her own reaction, while at the same time she still savoured the warm pressure of his lips on hers. Her confusion increased.

'You clever creature, how did you achieve it?'

Kirkham's voice brought her back to earth with a

jolt. He spoke happily, excitedly, but he betrayed no sign that for him the heavens had just split asunder. His embrace and his kisses had meant no more to him than if he had bussed a pretty parlourmaid in passing. The realisation was like a douche of cold water to Melissa. She continued to remain rooted to the spot, but now it was because she was numb with dismay at her own behaviour. She longed to run from the room but her pride would not let her. To her relief she realised that she was still clutching the bag containing the other trinkets.

'It was Polly's doing mainly,' she said, hoping her voice did not sound strained. 'Do you wish to see what else she brought back?'

'You have more for me?'

He stood watching with happy anticipation as with shaking hands she emptied out the cloth bag. As item after item was revealed he exclaimed with pleasure and surprise; but nothing surpassed his delight in the return of the enamelled snuff-box. If ever Melissa had considered his attachment to his older possessions to be an affectation, such a thought was dispelled now, as his strong fingers caressed the scratched enamel surface of the box.

'But you have not told me how you came by my things!' he declared.

'It was by putting two and two together and making enquiries,' Melissa said. 'More than that I am not at liberty to say, nor is Polly. Not all of the gew-gaws you lost are here, of course, but we are hopeful of returning some of them to you presently. More to the point you are not interested in how you came to lose so much?'

'I thought I had become inordinately careless.'

Melissa raised her eyes heavenwards. 'Inordinately foolish,' she retorted, her shattered emotions forcing her to seek refuge in her old sharp-tongued tone. 'Did it never occur to you you might have a thief in the house?'

'Among my servants? Never!' Kirkham's response was absolute.

'Unpleasant as the fact may be, you must face it. One of your servants has been stealing from you. You started losing your possessions about three years ago. Who entered your service at that time?'

'I have no idea.'

'Pentecost!'

'Pentecost?' He gave a bark of derisive laughter. 'No, I flatly refuse to believe that I am employing thieves, and as for accusing Pentecost. . . That is too preposterous!'

Melissa sighed. 'Then you will have to take my word for it. If you choose to ignore the coincidence of timing, then we have an accurate identification from the fence who bought your baubles,' she said.

'How do you know of fences and such?' Kirkham demanded, suddenly suspicious.

'One cannot live in the shadow of Newgate without acquiring an uncool ventional education, and Polly's is even more varied than mine. Our informant had no reason to lie when he described Pentecost with great accuracy.'

'You are certain. . .? A firm identification, you say. . .?' He glared into space as he considered her words. 'Then I suppose I have no alternative but to accept that my manservant is a thief. Pentecost! A man who had my absolute trust! My own body-servant! The rogue! The wretch!' Kirkham had begun to stride about the room his jaw clenched, his face dark with fury as the full impact of Melissa's words struck him. 'Well, he has betrayed me for the last time. He will be away from this house within the hour, without a hint of a character.

There will be no household within a thousand miles that will touch him with a barge-pole. But first I intend dealing with Mr Pentecost personally, and when I have done he will regret he ever thought to cross me!'

Melissa had never seen him so angry. He strode from the room, looking so fierce that she felt almost sorry for the hapless Pentecost.

Doubtless it is no more than Pentecost deserves, she told herself. His behaviour is a sad betrayal of Kirkham, who does treat his servants well. Not that he will suffer much by being cast out. Probably he has a very nice little nest egg stacked way, the proceeds of his pilfering.

Unexpectedly, she spent the rest of the day basking in a glow of self-satisfaction. She told herself that it was because she had brought a thief to his just deserts. As usual she was fooling herself. Her feeling of well-being was for one reason and one reason only. She had pleased Kirkham. It came as quite a shock, therefore, when, some time later, she happened to notice Pentecost disappearing towards the servants' stairs long after he should have left the house. In some agitation she sought out Kirkham.

'My lord! I have just seen Pentecost!' she exclaimed. 'He must have crept back into the house in some way and is no doubt bent upon mischief.'

To her surprise Kirkham did not immediately leap to his feet in fury. Surprisingly, he took the news quite calmly.

'Pentecost is involved with nothing more mischievous than laying out my evening clothes,' he said.

'How can that be? You had him thrown out of the house.'

'That was certainly my first intention, but I had second thoughts. The poor fellow was most abject in his apologies. He was sadly short of the ready, and, being hard pressed by the dunners, he succumbed to temptation. He swears it will never happen again, and I believe him.'

'You let him stay?' Melissa declared, her incredulity growing. 'You must be the biggest fool in Christendom!'

'No doubt, madam.' Kirkham retorted. 'But when Pentecost told me the cause of his financial problems was gambling I could not find it in my heart to be too hard on him. After all, no one in this land knows more than myself the dreadful problems that gambling can heap upon a man.'

Melissa drew in a sharp breath as the happy glow within her was harshly extinguished. She tried to think of an acid retort, but the words would not come.

'I hope you do not come to regret your generosity,' she said quietly, and left the room.

She made her way to her dressing-room. She needed to be by herself for a while. Kirkham's words had stung her more than she expected, and she had to know why. The terrible suspicion that she might be falling in love with him was beginning to trouble her. She had some serious thinking to do. But serious thinking did little good, except to make her realise that the sooner she retired from public life as Lady Kirkham, the better. This realisation made her feel extraordinarily depressed.

In spite of her own troubles, the Pentecost affair continued to bother her.

'His lordship's too kind for his own good,' Polly had remarked when she heard what had happened. Melissa was inclined to agree with her.

'Then you do not consider Pentecost to be a poor creature who was only tempted because he was hard pressed?' she asked.

'Not him! He's out to make a fortune and he doesn't

care how he does it. If his lordship intends to keep him on he will need to have everything of value in the house bolted to the floor.'

Melissa held great store by Polly's judgement of character. The girl's time spent hiding in the Rookery had given her an insight into human nature that was fortunately denied to most people.

If it had simply been a matter of losing a few silver spoons or the occasional cruet Melissa would not have minded, but Pentecost must have known the things he stole were of tremendous personal value to Kirkham. He had taken them for no better reason than that they were easily saleable. She was not prepared to stand by and let Kirkham be distressed again.

'If he will not protect himself, someone else must do it for him,' she said. 'Send Pentecost to me, if you please, Polly. But first, tell me the names of all the fences you know, apart from Uncle Billy, of course.'

The manservant arrived promptly, looking as dignified as ever. Melissa regarded him with her iciest stare.

'I understand that you have reason to be grateful to his lordship,' she said.

'Indeed yes, my lady.' The pompous demeanour evaporated. 'I cannot express my gratitude for his exceeding kindness. I do not deserve such consideration. I am overcome with such shame I can scarcely raise my head, I swear by all I cherish that such a thing will never, never happen again.' The normally ponderous voice shook, the heavy jowls trembled, tears sprang into the protuberant eyes—and Melissa did not believe any of it. Pentecost was play-acting.

'I am glad to hear it,' she said, 'because although his lordship may be kindness personified I assure you you have a harsher adversary in me. I give you fair warning: let there be so much as one tooth lost from his lordship's comb and you will find yourself in serious trouble. I may not be able to prevent you from stealing, but I can certainly prevent you from selling your ill-gotten gains. I can ensure that no one will touch your loot. A warning will go out to everyone, from the Hatch brothers at St Giles to the likes of Silas Brook at Wapping, not to have dealings with you. Moreover, I will surely hear of it if you offer so much as a silver button for sale; and I promise you Lord Kirkham will not be lenient a second time. Steal as much as you like, it will not do you a scrap of good. You may go now.'

There was no play-acting now about Pentecost's ashen cheeks and dropped jaw as he fairly ran from the room. The startled expression in his eyes affirmed beyond doubt Polly's assessment of his character.

Melissa had the satisfaction of knowing she had protected Kirkham, but it was not enough. The earlier glow of contentment would not return, no matter how she tried. She wanted something more. The trouble was, she did not know what. At least she was spared the torment of being much in Kirkham's company, for with the increasing thaw he had again taken to frequenting his club at night. Their pleasant domestic interlude was at an end.

She was therefore surprised when Kirkham came into her dressing-room one day and said, 'Madam, I believe this is yours.'

'I think not, my lord,' she replied, regarding the unfamiliar shagreen box.

'No? Then I must be mistaken. Would you be kind enough to open it, just to make sure?' He spoke in a casual, offhand way which roused her suspicions. It would not be beyond him to be playing some trick on her. 'Go on,' he insisted. 'It will not bite.'

'Very well, my lord.' Gingerly she pressed the catch,

then stood transfixed. The box might have been unfamiliar, but its contents were not. On the white satin lining lay a gold-framed miniature edged with seed pearls. The portrait was of a young woman who bore a striking resemblance to herself, save that she was dressed in the fashion of a good twenty years earlier. Melissa was unable to speak.

'It is yours, I think?' said Kirkham gently.

She could only nod her head, as tears coursed down her cheeks.

'By Harry, I'd not have gone to such trouble if I'd known it would have this effect!' he exclaimed, with false jocularity.

Tremulously she managed to smile, brushing the tears away then wiping her hands, childlike, on her skirt before she picked up the miniature.

'How. . .how did you come by it?' she managed to ask at last.

'To be honest, I had an accomplice. I had decided to give the reward for finding my snuff-box to Polly—I knew better than to expect you to accept my five guineas—and in the course of things we got talking. What an interesting girl she is, to be sure. During our conversation she let slip that you had sold your last decent possession, a miniature of your mother, to 'buy' her from the scoundrel who insisted he was her master. You were instrumental in returning to me something I valued beyond price. I wanted to do the same for you. I was certain you would turn down my guineas but I felt sure you would not reject this miniature so readily. A request to Polly for help, plus the assistance of some mysterious uncle who preferred to remain nameless, was all it took.'

'There was no need,' protested Melissa, though her fingers lovingly caressed the picture.

'Yes, there was.' His voice had grown gentle. 'You went to much trouble to return my snuff-box to me, you identified the rogue who stole it, and what did I do? When we disagreed on how Pentecost should be treated I retorted with the first words that came into my head. Harsh, silly, hurtful words that I would have taken back the instant they were uttered if I had been able. I could not, and the knowledge has made me feel uncomfortable ever since. You returned my greatest treasure to me, the least I could do was to return something you treasured, by way of thanks and with my humblest apologies.'

So saying he bent and, taking her hand in his, miniature and all, gently kissed it. Then, before she could speak, he left the room.

Melissa did not move. She knew now, beyond any doubt, that she loved Kirkham. She also knew why. It was because beneath the raffish, rakish exterior there was a very gentle, considerate man. The gambling man-about-town she despised, but the other, sensitive, kindly Kirkham, had her heart. Two very different sides to the same person. Not that it made any difference. Although he had made his apologies in a way that delighted and touched her, she feared that his earlier words, spoken in the heat of the moment, were closer to his true feelings. Then he had made it plain how much he disliked and regretted their marriage. She might love Kirkham, but it was painfully evident that he did not love her.

CHAPTER SEVEN

How Melissa wished she could return to the early days, when she could despise and dislike Kirkham to her heart's content. It was infinitely preferable to her present state of having a constant ache inside. Not that she allowed her unhappiness to show. In public she played the devoted wife, complete with false smiles and what she wished were false endearments. At home she reverted to the sharper attitudes and acerbic tongue he had come to expect of her. She would have to leave him, and soon, that much was evident. She had come to him, albeit unwillingly, as a penniless nobody. She would leave him, equally unwillingly, as the elegant Lady Kirkham. Such a change in status made her feel beholden to him, at least enough to make sure his domestic arrangements were in order before she went.

Most of the staff were perfectly satisfactory. Fraser, the butler, for example, was both devoted to Kirkham and efficient at his job. If left alone Bertrand could be relied upon to produce superb meal after superb meal. As for Pentecost, Melissa felt she had dealt with him soundly enough. Of the senior servants this left only Mrs Hawkins.

Since their early battle of wills the housekeeper had been sullen and uncooperative. If Melissa made a request, or even an order, she could always find a plausible excuse for its not being done — there was not enough staff for the extra cleaning that Melissa deemed necessary, or the girl who had been delegated a specific task was exceptionally stupid and had misunderstood.

Mrs Hawkins might have been good at her job once, but ten years in Kirkham's easygoing service plus her greedy, slothful character had left their mark. Melissa noted the near-insolence and the ineptitude, waited until she was sure of her ground, then she pounced.

'Mrs Hawkins,' she said, 'I clearly remember ordering the upper landing to be thoroughly cleaned last week.'

'It was done, your ladyship, though not as thoroughly as I would have wished, I'll admit. But what with your ladyship's soirée on Wednesday, and two dinner parties within the week. . . The maids can only do so much, your ladyship.' As she spoke, Mrs Hawkins regarded Melissa with a contemptuous glare.

'The upper landing has been cleaned recently, has it?' Melissa replied calmly. 'Then I wonder how it comes to be infested with mice?'

'They'll have come in from the garden, my lady. The cold weather must have driven them in.' Again the glare was bold and challenging.

'Perhaps these mice were indeed escaping from the winter chills. Unfortunately it was not this winter that drove them indoors. They have taken up residence in one of the curtains, and by the looks of things have been there for several generations. I object very much to vermin considering our drapery to be their family seat.'

'I did not expect your ladyship to go looking for mice. In my experience the gentry. . .' Mrs Hawkins stopped, leaving her veiled insult unspoken but implied.

'In your experience the gentry are there to be gulled and cheated, is that not so?' Melissa continued. 'Which accounts for these.' She laid out a sheaf of bills.

Mrs Hawkins went pale. 'How did you get your hands on those?'

'That is not important,' said Melissa, not revealing that they had come to light, like the mice, during the search for Kirkham's snuff-box. 'The mice were dispatched by two junior footmen and the kitchen cat. These accounts will be rather more difficult to dismiss. I have taken days going over them and I want some explanations. Look at the quantity of venison, for example. A great amount to be consumed within one month, and by a gentleman renowned for eating away from home.'

'That's last year's bill,' declared Mrs Hawkins, pushing the paper back across the desk.

'Before I came here, therefore you consider it none of my business, eh? Well, I am afraid I disagree with you. Let us look at more. All this game consumed in one household! And such a quantity of fish! Turbot is not one of his lordship's favourite dishes, and I agree he no doubt was entertaining friends, but the whole of White's and Boodle's combined could not have consumed this amount. At first I thought the servants' hall of this house must have been keeping a table second to none, but my enquiries proved otherwise. What happened to it — the game, the fish, the shellfish? What did you do with it?'

'Me? I had naught to do with it. It was that Bertrand — devious, thieving foreigner, that's what——'

'Mrs Hawkins, Bertrand had no hand in this. I have already questioned him and I am satisfied that these are not his accounts. A few enquiries elsewhere have told me what I suspected. That this household had two lots of food bills. One ordered legitimately by the cook, and the other by you. And Lord Kirkham, who knows naught of domestic economy, paid both. What did you do with your lot, Mrs Hawkins? Did you resell the meat and fish, or were they purely mythical — a ruse cooked up between you, the butcher, and the fishmonger?'

'It was that dirty slut, your maid, who let on, wasn't it?' cried Mrs Hawkins.

Now it was Melissa's turn to glare. 'That remark alone would be enough to cost you your position,' she said. 'However, I can add dishonesty and incompetence to the list. Therefore I suggest you pack your bags and leave immediately. You will be paid a half-year's wages, in consideration of Lord Kirkham's kindness, not mine.'

'All right, I'll go!' Mrs Hawkin's eyes glittered with malice. 'I've no wish to stay where a strumpet sets herself up as gentry. Yes, I'll go! And we'll see how you get on without me to run this place.'

'Mrs Hawkins,' said Melissa calmly. 'I have already told you, my generosity is far inferior to his lordship's. Guard that tongue of yours if you do not wish to leave here without a penny. And do not set your hopes up that there will be chaos after you have gone, for I am quite capable of running the house myself.'

In fact Melissa was in control for only a few days. Fraser had a cousin in need of a situation. Mrs Cobb arrived within the week, small, bustling, and efficient. In no time at all the house in Hanover Square began to take on a brighter, cleaner, fresher air, and any mice who now considered taking up residence in the long brocade curtains quickly changed their minds. Polly was able to report that life below stairs was also more comfortable.

'Mrs Cobb is strict,' she related. 'There was a few grumbles behind her back at first, but not any more. You know where you are with her and what you're supposed to be doing. Most folks prefer that. The days are gone where there were six maids turning out a guest bedroom while one poor soul broke her back trying to get the dining-room clean before breakfast, as used to happen under Mrs Hawkins.'

'Even Bertrand was singing Mrs Cobb's praises to me this morning,' smiled Melissa. 'Apparently she told him she had never seen such well-presented food in all her experience. Yes, I think everyone is happy to have Mrs Cobb with us.'

Her statement proved not quite accurate. Kirkham proved the exception.

'Madam,' he declared one day. 'I have just encountered a little dot of a woman in bombasine bustling about the place clanking her keys. When I asked who she was, she replied she was my housekeeper.'

'Which she is,' replied Melissa. 'Mrs Cobb replaced Mrs Hawkins.'

'Replaced her? Why? Was Hawkins ill?'

'No, she was dishonest, incompetent, and insolent, therefore I dismissed her.'

'You dismissed her?' Kirkham's brows went together in a fearsome manner, clearly inherited from his grandmother. 'By what right, may I ask?'

'By the right of being your wife and châtelaine of this household.'

'You are not my wife!'

'Oh, do not sing that old song again,' snapped Melissa irritably. 'Whatever the circumstances, I did you a favour by getting rid of a woman who has been fleecing you right, left, and centre, and who has allowed your house to get in a disgraceful condition.'

'I resent you turning her off without so much as a by your leave. Hawkins has been my faithful servant these ten years, she should not have been dismissed without my permission.'

'Hawkins has been your dishonest servant these ten

years, and deserved what she got. She must have cost you a fortune, if nothing else in damaged furnishings. The upper landing curtains will have to be replaced because of her negligence. They have been chewed to bits by mice.'

'I am not concerned with furnishings. I am objecting to your taking it upon yourself to interfere in my domestic arrangments.'

Melissa opened her mouth to give a pithy reply, then unaccountably closed it again. Anger had brought colour to Kirkham's face and a brilliant glitter to his eyes. In his annoyance he had run his fingers through his dark hair, making its fashionable disarray even more pronounced. In short he looked incredibly handsome, and for a moment her breath was taken away.

'Our domestic arrangements!' she retorted, returning to her normal self with a rush. 'If I do not see to such matters, who will?'

'I repeat, they are not your concern, madam. To keep my household under control I employ a housekeeper. . .'

'Exactly,' said Melissa triumphantly. 'And who is to keep the housekeeper under control if you have made a bad choice?'

'I can control my own house,' declared Kirkham.

'If you say so, my lord. No doubt that is why you have been paying two lots of butcher's bills and fishmonger's bills these last few years. But if you are determined to be in control then I understand the scullerymaid is needed at home and wishes to leave. Perhaps your lordship will occupy yourself with choosing a replacement.'

'Sarcasm does not become you, madam,' said Kirkham coldly. 'And one of my objections to the dismissal of

Mrs Hawkins is that it is bound to cause resentment below stairs.'

'You need have no worries on that score,' said Melissa in an unexpectedly quiet voice. She was tired of the bickering between them and she suddenly longed for a return of the amicable relations that had existed during the bad weather. It had not been love but it was infinitely preferable to the eternal quarrelling. 'Mrs Cobb seems to have fitted in very well. I am reliably informed that she has the respect of the servants under her, Bertrand likes her, and as for Fraser, it was he who recommended her; she is his cousin. You see, my lord, you need have no fear of your household disintegrating.'

'That makes no difference to my original point. You have no authority to dismiss my servants. This subterfuge that we are married is no excuse. It is a state of affairs destined not to last much longer, for soon I intend to find that our so-called marriage was not legal, and I have no intention of letting you rearrange my life in the meantime.'

'It is taking you a prodigious time to find the proof, is it not, my lord?' Melissa replied, returning to her angry tone once more. 'That is because it does not exist. I keep telling you that you waste your time. I am your legal wife.'

'I will tell you what you truly are, madam.' Kirkham was fairly snorting with rage. 'You are the most aggravating, annoying, trying female it has ever been my misfortune to encounter. No wonder you needed to resort to drugs to get me to the church. Sober and with a clear head I would have shot myself sooner than have taken one step in such a direction with you!'

He turned angrily on his heel and stalked from the room. After he had gone Melissa slumped into a chair.

How she wished she could have thought of an alternative to that ceremony at Saint Willibrod's. It was causing her untold misery. Why had it never occurred to her that she might fall in love with Kirkham? Under the circumstances, she supposed, it had seemed too incredible to contemplate. Marriage did have the advantage of protecting her reputation, but considering the permanent pain she carried with her these days that was a poor consolation indeed.

Perhaps the only satisfactory solution would have been if her wretched brother had been strangled at birth. After all, it was entirely his fault. The way she felt at that moment, it was a task she would willingly have undertaken, albeit belatedly, if the rogue should ever emerge from hiding and cross her path.

It must have been thoughts of James, uncomplimentary though they were, which made Melissa certain she saw him. She was in the carriage with Polly, being driven to take tea with Lady Kirkham. They were going up Brook Street when she recognised a jaunty figure strolling along.

'Polly!' she exclaimed. 'That is my brother, surely?'

'Where!' exclaimed Polly, gazing out of the window. 'I can't see anyone resembling him.'

'Oh, he has gone. He must have turned off into Avery Row. I only caught a fleeting glimpse, yet I am sure it was James.'

'I doubt if it was, not so close to Hanover Square,' Polly remarked.

'There are certainly a few words I mean to have with that young gentleman when I finally catch up with him.'

Choosing those words occupied Melissa's thoughts until, as they were entering Grosvenor Square, a near collision with another carriage drove all else from her mind. Only the skill of Kirkham's coachman averted disaster. The cause of the trouble was a flashy equipage being drawn by a pair of showy chestnuts. They were being driven at too great a speed by a gentleman wearing a greatcoat with more shoulder capes than was either fashionable or in the best of taste. To Melissa's surprise she recognised the other occupants of the carriage; they were Mrs Hurst and her daughter. She felt sorry for poor Beth, who looked terrified at the rate they were travelling; then, to her satisfaction, she noted that Mrs Hurst's normally florid countenance was sickly pale. Suddenly she was conscious of Polly giving a shudder.

'Are you all right?' she asked in concern. 'That was quite a jolt we received, but Richards did exceedingly well to keep us upright.'

'I'm fine, thank you,' Polly replied, but in a subdued voice. 'It was the sight of that man, the one driving the other coach.'

'You know him?'

'I've come across him.' Again Polly shuddered. 'Lord Beaucombe! One of the nastiest, most evil men it's been my misfortune to encounter. Take my advice, if you ever come upon him, then turn tail and get as far away as you can.'

Melissa was astonished and startled by the vehemence in the girl's words. Polly was no tender flower, experience had seen to that, and never before had she spoken with such loathing and fear.

'I will heed your warning, I promise,' Melissa said. 'But if he is so terrible, what were the Hursts doing in his company?'

'Beaucombe?' declared Lady Kirkham when she mentioned the incident to her. 'I would entertain every cut-throat and pickpocket in the city before I would let that man cross my threshold.'

'Then you agree with Polly that he is evil?'

'Evil and depraved.'

'What can Mrs Hurst be about, driving out with him and taking Beth too?'

'Goodness knows, unless the stupid woman has her eye on Beaucombe as a possible son-in-law! Everyone knows she is mad to catch a title, and she is idiotic enough to make a play for the scoundrel.'

'But that is terrible. Beth Hurst found even Kirkham alarming.'

'Then if it proves true the chit will have something real to be frightened of,' said Lady Kirkham, not without sympathy. 'Now that is enough of the Hursts, we have our own affairs to attend to. Kirkham called on me this morning, as I had something of interest to tell him. Now I am informing you. Today I finally heard from my man of business. After making discreet and extensive enquiries, consulting the best lawyers and so on — a pretty penny this is going to cost me, no doubt — he informs me that he can find no reason to question the legality of your marriage.'

'Oh, dear,' said Melissa.

'Oh, dear? Is that all you can say? I thought you would be delighted.'

'I have never doubted the legality of our marriage, your ladyship. Your man's report has come as no surprise to me. The reason I say "Oh, dear" is because Kirkham will now be in a foul mood.'

'He certainly left this house glowering like a thundercloud,' agreed Lady Kirkham. 'And I am sorry for anyone who crosses his path today. But as I told him, things could be worse.'

'I am sure that cheered him up remarkably.'

Lady Kirkham barked a laugh. 'He came as close to using unbecoming language as any man I have seen,' she chuckled. 'There is no denying I would have organised my only grandson's marriage differently if I could, but since that is impossible we must make the best of things. And a pretty tolerable best it may turn out to be.'

'I think I should leave Kirkham and retire to the country as soon as possible,' said Melissa.

'Do not be too hasty on that score. No doubt there are things to be arranged between you and Kirkham first.'

'What sort of things? I do not want an allowance or anything like that.'

'Kirkham's wife is certainly not disappearing into the wilds to live in some cowherd's hut,' replied Lady Kirkham briskly. 'But financial considerations apart, there are no doubt other matters to be discussed.'

Melissa could not think what they might be, but she knew she would discover them soon enough.

Kirkham's first reaction was to find comfort in disbelief.

'My grandmother's man of business is a fool, a dolt. She should have put him out to pasture years since,' he exclaimed angrily, ignoring the fact that he himself frequently kept on servants who were long past their usefulness. 'Wait until O'Gallagher gets here. He will have a very different tale to tell.'

Melissa could not imagine what Mr O'Gallagher could have unearthed that had escaped Lady Kirkham's extremely able representative. Fortunately she was not kept waiting long. The very next day Shaun O'Gallagher called.

'My dear fellow! The very man I want to see!' exclaimed Kirkham when he entered. 'Come, what have you found out?'

Mr O'Gallagher looked uncomfortably from Kirkham to Melissa then back again.

'I am in a sorry quandary and no mistake,' he said. 'For I shall be obliged to anger one of you by pleasing the other.'

Kirkham lounged back in his chair, his long frame stretched out casually, but Melissa was not fooled. She could sense the tension in him. Realising O'Gallagher's information meant so much to him added another burden to her already heavy heart.

'You have no need to be distressed, Mr O'Gallagher,' she said. 'We both owe you a debt of gratitude for all your efforts. Neither of us would be churlish enough to condemn you for reporting the truth.'

'That is very kind of you, Lady Kirkham.' He gave a grateful smile. 'It is a gentle heart you have. Kirkham, you are married to an angel, you know that. . .' His voice died away and he looked miserably down at the carpet.

'Are you telling me what I think you are telling me?' asked Kirkham in a strained voice.

O'Gallagher nodded.

'But it can't be so! This marriage can't be legal!' Kirkham slammed his clenched fists on the arms of the chair.

Melissa had anticipated that when this moment came she would revel in her triumph, but she did not feel one bit like revelling.

'What can I say?' asked O'Gallagher. 'I checked everything I could think of, then checked twice over. The parson, the church, the licence, the ceremony, they are all sound and legal. I thought I had found a loophole in the fact that you remember so little of the ceremony. To that end I had a discreet word with the Bishop of Watcombe, who was dining at the club. He was scant comfort, I am afraid. He said that if the bridegroom not remembering the ceremony was grounds for declaring a marriage null and void then a good third of the unions in this country must be illegal.'

'But surely if he can see the groom is incapable...' protested Kirkham. 'What would it take for him to deny or to postpone a wedding?'

'If the groom was past everything then he said he would certainly postpone the ceremony, though in his experience ten minutes under a good cold pump usually restores most men's wits. His own rule of thumb is that the groom must be able to stand unaided throughout the ceremony. He has no objections to the groomsmen hoisting the fellow back into the perpendicular, but no holding him up. He was adamant on the point.'

'Did you have to hold me up?' asked Kirkham, though there was no hope in his voice.

O'Gallagher shook his head. 'Really things are not all that bad,' he said, trying to sound reassuring. 'I am sorry to have disappointed you, my old friend, but on the other hand I am relieved not to put Lady Kirkham into an embarrassing and indelicate situation. Besides, you were thinking of marrying, anyway, were you not? And you have got yourself the most beautiful bride in London, everyone says so. Does it matter whether it was by accident or design?'

'Yes!' declared Kirkham in a voice that made the crystal chandeliers tremble. 'A man should decide his own destiny in all things, especially in marriage. It is too important a matter to happen by chance.'

'You believe that matrimony should be carefully considered and not decided like a lottery?' asked Melissa sweetly. 'Then it is a pity you did not hold such firm views a few weeks since. It is also just as well you are not a woman. Much chance you have of deciding your destiny or aught else if you are female.'

'You seem to have managed pretty well, madam,' Kirkham snarled, then recollected with a start that his friend was still present. 'Your pardon, O'Gallagher. We should not air our differences in your presence. It is abominably rude of us.'

'I thought that airing differences was the very stuff of matrimony.' For the first time O'Gallagher smiled his normal cheery smile. 'I will leave you now so that you and your differences can have full rein.'

He rose and went to take his leave of Melissa. As he bent over her hand he gave it a conspiratorial squeeze and whispered something in a voice too low for Kirkham to hear. As he left the room she considered his words. What the Irishman had said was, 'Take heart, dear lady, I think our good Kirkham doth protest too much.'

What on earth can he mean by that? she wondered.

After he had gone Kirkham slumped back into his chair, no longer sprawled in a semblance of relaxation, but with his head in his hands, the picture of misery.

Melissa had a strong impulse to rush to him, and console him by taking him in her arms. She wanted to press her cheek against his hair and plead with him not to be miserable; if only he would let her she would make him truly happy. She did no such thing, of course. Actions of that sort were the stuff of dreams.

'Now that your grandmother's man of business and Mr O'Gallagher seem to be of the same mind, I trust you will now accept our marriage as a fact,' she said, struggling to keep her voice calm.

'I do not want to. Heaven knows I do not want to, but I fear I must!'

'Come, my lord, things may not be so bad. We deal

together tolerably enough at times. There are whole days when we scarcely exchange a cross word.'

'And many more when I wish we need not exchange any words at all,' he snapped back. 'I may be forced to accept our marriage, but nothing will persuade me to like it.'

His words stung her to the quick, obliging her to gaze intently out of the window to hide the tears that had sprung to her eyes.

'My lord. . .' she began when she was in control of herself once more, then she realised that he had left the room. Her first impulse was to bury her head in her arms and weep properly. It took an iron will not to do so. She had never been one to take refuge in tears and she had no intention of starting now.

It is your own fault, she scolded herself severely. You may have had no option but to marry the man; however, there was no need to fall in love with him. You have no one to blame save yourself.

Having given herself the berating she felt she deserved, she made for the music-room to practise on the piano. The mental exercise of coping with some of Mr Mozart's keyboard studies was just what she needed to restore her spirits. Out of consideration for the ears of the other inhabitants of the house she preferred to use the music-room rather than play on the instrument in the withdrawing-room. Her route led her towards the back of the building, along a quiet corridor that was not used much. As she passed one of the closed doors on her way she was brought to a halt by the sound of two people, a man and woman talking. It was a small ante-room that was seldom opened, and for anyone to be in there at all was surprising enough. What astonished her more was that she could recognise the voices, subdued though they were.

Flinging open the door, she demanded, 'And exactly what is going on here?'

She was met by looks of dismay from Polly's sparkling black eyes and from a pair of deep blue eyes that closely resembled her own.

'Have you nothing to say?' she continued. 'Has the cat got your tongue?'

'My dearest sister. You look more beautiful than ever.' James Daubenay took a step towards her, the look of alarm on his handsome features being rapidly replaced by a charming smile.

Melissa fended him off with an upraised hand. 'Do not try to cajole me,' she said sternly. 'You can first tell me what you are doing here, next you can tell me where you have been hiding all these weeks, and then you can remain silent while I say a few words in your ear that will be naught for your comfort, I can promise you.'

'You are not to blame Polly for my presence,' James pleaded. 'I was concerned for you. Yes, I was,' he insisted at his sister's derisive snort. 'I felt I had left you in a somewhat awkward situation. I was overcome with remorse for my part in your predicament. I still am. Then I met Polly quite by chance one day. I felt the least I could do was to find out how you were faring.'

'How I was faring? In a somewhat awkward situation? My stars, what understatements!' cried Melissa. 'What is it about you men that you can think rationally and reasonably after you have acted, yet never before? And as for your part in my predicament, as you call it, without you there would have been no predicament.'

'Yet you cannot say that I did not act with your best interests at heart,' said James persuasively. 'Look at you! Lady Kirkham, living in a fine house, with clothes and jewels and servants. It is a far cry from seeing

Newgate Gaol every time you looked out of the window.'

'True, but you forgot one thing,' said Melissa in a deceptively amenable voice. 'The title and the rest are the result of my own and Polly's conniving. If left to you I would have been back looking at Newgate after a brief, no doubt enlightening but unpleasant period as a nobleman's doxy. As it is, the price I am paying for my title, my fine gowns and my respectability is being trapped in a disagreeable marriage with a disagreeable man!' Melissa was far from sounding amenable now, and James took a step back.

'How can you say that?' he declared. 'Kirkham is a regular fellow.'

'Doubtless he is if viewed across a card-table when filled to the ears with claret. One sees a different aspect of his character from the marriage-bed and across the breakfast-table.'

She was being rather unfair to Kirkham, she knew, but the sudden appearance of James, who was the cause of her troubles, added vinegar to her tongue.

'And if you really think him such a regular fellow,' she went on 'then I suggest you quit this room and go and seek him out, face to face. I would be interested in your view of his lordship's character afterwards, supposing you were still capable of speech, for I warn you, Lord Kirkham is no more happy in this marriage than I am.'

'I did not mean to drop you in the suds, Mel, honestly.' He looked truly sorrowful, and his eyes begged for forgiveness.

Melissa had a sudden memory of him as an appealing small boy, pleading that he had not meant to break the last decent cup, had not meant to eat the apple-pie intended for supper, had not meant to lock the cat in the coal-cupboard. James never meant harm, or believed he did not. She knew well enough that his intentions were far from malicious, it was simply that he never stopped to consider the consequences of his actions. This trait, combined with a handsome face, great charm and a weak character, had added up to disaster more often than she could count, though never of the magnitude of this recent escapade. Somehow he had always managed to extricate himself, invariably with her help. Angry as she was with him, she knew that nothing had changed. She would help him avoid Kirkham's wrath because he was still her little brother and she loved him.

She turned her attention to Polly. 'I don't suppose this is the first meeting you have had with my brother since we came to Hanover Square?' she said.

'No, my lady.' Polly faced up to her bravely.

'And I suppose it was you who found him somewhere to hide from everyone's anger?'

'Yes, my lady.'

Polly's defensive stance and her frequent use of 'my lady' roused Melissa's suspicions.

'You have not been giving him money, have you?' she demanded.

'I say!' protested James indignantly.

Polly said nothing. She did not need to.

'Oh, Polly,' sighed Melissa. 'The five guineas Lord Kirkham gave you for returning his snuff-box. . . Can I guess where they have gone?'

'They were mine to do with as I pleased,' countered Polly.

'Indeed they were, but they will be repaid. I have no intention of letting you subsidise this reprobate of a brother of mine.'

Melissa was so touched she gave the girl a hug. She

did not bother to ask why Polly had gone to such bother to help James; she knew they were both in the same situation. They both adored him, and for better or for worse, they would always protect him.

'As for you, James, the sooner you are out of this house the better,' she said, reverting to her crisp, authoritative tone. 'Polly will take you through the garden and out by the side-gate. You have not told me where you are hiding. Perhaps that is as well. I can contact you through Polly. Above all things, do not visit this house again. If you come up against Kirkham in a good mood he will merely call you out. If he is in an ill temper, such is his fury against you, he is capable of horsewhipping you right through the town, and that would be the end of any hopes of your rejoining polite society. Now go.'

'You are the best sister a fellow ever had.' James made to kiss her goodbye, but she avoided him. She was already a long way along the road to forgiving him, but she had no intention of letting him know it yet.

Now she no longer needed to worry about James her mind was free to dwell upon other things. Kirkham, for example, and how much longer she would stay with him. Whatever she decided, while she remained under his roof she had to go on playing the devoted wife in public. When they visited the theatre at Drury Lane together she felt there was almost as much acting going on in their box as there was on the stage. But that was only at the beginning of the play. Once they were settled and the curtain rose she was free to relax and let herself be absorbed by the dramatic art of Shakespeare and the superb acting of Edmund Kean.

Kirkham, too, seemed to have been totally engrossed in the play. Certainly he had not been so affable for days.

'A magnificent performance. I have never seen better,' he said enthusiastically, as they made their slow exit from the theatre.

'Nor I,' agreed Melissa. 'I have thoroughly enjoyed this evening.'

'Have you? Good. So have I. I see from the playbills over there that Mr Kean is to perform again in *The Merchant of Venice*. We must bespeak seats as soon as possible though I cannot quite see the date from here, can you?'

Pushed along inexorably by the crush, Melissa craned her neck to see if she could make out the details on the poster, loosening her grip on Kirkham's arm as she did so to get a better view.

'I think it is some time next month,' she said, turning back to him. Only it was not Kirkham she was addressing but a haughty-looking lady, a complete stranger. Then she saw Kirkham's dark head above the crowd. He was being carried to the right by the press of bodies, while she was being carried forcefully to the left. There was nothing for it, she just let herself be carried along.

Near the street entrance she saw a small haven of tranquillity, a space behind the main door. She forced through purposefully in that direction, intending to take refuge there until the crowd cleared a little, and Kirkham could make his way towards her.

She was busy adjusting her dress, which had become somewhat rumpled in the chaotic exit, when a shadow fell across her.

'There you are. . .' she began, looking up, but it was not Kirkham. She found herself gazing into the hard features of Lord Beaucombe.

If she had not already been told what sort of a man he was she could have guessed his character. Every line of his face betrayed a life of depravity. His pink mouth, with its thick moist lips, was disturbingly sensual. But it was his eyes that caused a *frisson* of alarm to trickle down Melissa's spine. They were of pale opaque blue. Never in her entire life had she seen a gaze so predatory nor filled with such blatant carnal lust. It did not make her feel any more comfortable to smell the heavy brandy fumes on his breath.

'What is a pretty creature like you doing hiding in corners?' he leered. 'Here, let me help you.' And he stretched out a hand towards the crumpled corsage she had been rearranging.

Melissa's reaction was to slap his hand away promptly.

'Kindly go away, sir,' she snapped.

'Ah, the pretty creature has pretty claws, and can use them. I like that.' His leer deepened, and even in the shadowy light Melissa could see the spark of interest gleam in his eye. 'No, I will not go away. Not now when we are just getting acquainted.'

'We are not getting acquainted, sir,' insisted Melissa. 'I have no wish to know you. My husband will be here presently. I suggest you remove yourself before he arrives.'

'And what sort of a husband is it that leaves a beauty like you hiding in corners? Not one that deserves such a gem.'

Beaucombe was grinning a wide, wet-lipped smile. Melissa felt her fear intensify as she realised he was pushing her further into the corner, deeper into the shadows. It seemed foolish, being afraid when there were dozens of people swarming about only feet away, yet there was something about Beaucombe's presence and the way his burly figure blocked out the candlelight that terrified her.

'Move aside and let me leave,' she declared, determined not to betray her nervousness. 'If you do not then I will call for help'.

'Who would hear you?' asked Beaucombe, backing her further into the darkness. 'Who knows you are here?'

He had a point. What with the chatter of voices in the foyer and the clatter of carriages in the street outside it was doubtful if her voice would be audible. Also, no one leaving the theatre would be aware of her presence in the sinister gloom behind the door. Worse still, Kirkham would not be able to find her.

'Besides,' went on Beaucombe with self-satisfaction, his hands pawing at her slender waist. 'Besides, I flatter myself that such is my reputation there are few men who would dare to cross me—and even fewer husbands!' He began to laugh at his own so-called wit but his laughter was cut off abruptly as an arm came about his throat, wrenched back his head and dragged him off Melissa.

'There you are sadly mistaken!' exclaimed a familiar voice. 'Here is one man, one husband, who will only be too happy to give such a cur the thrashing he deserves.'

'Oh, Kirkham!' cried Melissa with relief, escaping from her darkened prison with all the speed she could manage.

In the comparative brilliance of the candlelight she saw Beaucombe rising to his knees, with Kirkham, his face white with fury, towering over him. Beaucombe was on his feet now, nursing his bruised throat.

'You will pay for this, Kirkham!' he snarled, his face suffused with angry blood. 'My seconds will call upon you tomorrow.'

'Tell them not to bother,' Kirkham retorted. 'I would not waste good steel nor a decent bullet nor yet my time upon the likes of you. I will deal with you now once and for all.'

So saying he side-stepped the lunge Beaucombe made at him, grasped him by the collar and the seat of the breeches and flung him bodily out of the door and down the steps. Beaucombe landed face downwards among the mud and filth of the street.

Kirkham turned to Melissa. 'Are you all right?' he asked urgently, grasping her gently by the arms. 'That animal. . .he did not harm you, did he? Because if he did I will go after him and——'

'No, he did not harm me,' cut in Melissa swiftly, afraid he would indeed go after Beaucombe and get hurt. 'I was a little alarmed, nothing more.'

'I blame myself. I should have taken greater care of you, and not let us get separated.'

'You cannot be blamed. . . In such a crush these things occur. . . And I was much at fault, I should not have let go of your arm.'

Melissa was suddenly finding it difficult to express herself, not because of the aftermath of her recent experience, but because of the look on Kirkham's face. He was extremely concerned, more so than she would ever have expected on her behalf. This was none of his play-acting in public, this was genuine anxiety lest she had been hurt. And there was something more. An intensity and urgency in his eyes, along with an expression that set her blood racing.

'You are safe. . .that is all that matters.'

He continued to gaze at her. For one long, incredible moment Melissa thought he might be going to kiss her. Then a mass sigh of approval brought her swiftly to her senses. For the first time Melissa realised that people had stopped and were watching events with fascination.

Kirkham became aware of their presence too. Swiftly

recovering himself, he bowed with dignity towards their audience.

'My sincere apologies if I have alarmed any of you ladies by causing a fracas in your presence,' he said calmly. 'I am afraid I had to teach a rogue a lesson, which, while unpleasant and undignified, was nevertheless urgent and necessary. You have my utmost regrets if I have caused distress to anyone.'

'With the exception of Beaucombe, eh?' someone called out.

A ripple of laughter went round the crowd, and the last vestige of tension went out of the situation. The stream of bodies resumed its way towards the street.

'Come, let us go home,' said Kirkham to Melissa. 'You have had shocks enough for one night.'

But for Melissa the encounter with Beaucombe was already fading from her mind. It was being driven away by the gentle, elusive expression in Kirkham's eyes when he looked at her, and by the secure warmth of his arm about her waist as he led her to the carriage.

CHAPTER EIGHT

SPRING seemed to have arrived in Hanover Square unaccountably early. It was cold as ever, no flowers brightened the window-boxes, the sparrows had not even begun sparring for nesting sites, yet Melissa felt that spring was in the air. She had been convinced of it ever since the evening she and Kirkham had spent at Drury Lane.

That visit to the theatre had brought something unexpected to her life. She hardly dared to recognise it as hope. Yet surely she had not imagined Kirkham's reactions? He had shown care and concern for her. And had there not been something else in his expression besides anxiety? A warmth? A tenderness? Or was she letting her imagination run rampant?

For the first time Melissa allowed her dreams to have full rein, going about in a happy stupor like a green girl. But only for a while. Although she was attentive to his every mood and emotion she never again saw anything like tenderness in Kirkham's expression. Her hope, being a young and tender plant, shrivelled and died.

It was about this time that Melissa noticed they had a new manservant. Whether he was a groom or a footman she was not sure; the only certainty was that he was built like a house-end, had hands as big as York hams and a nose that had long since deviated from its natural shape.

'I do not wish to have my footsteps dogged by a prize-fighter,' she complained. 'There's no getting rid of the man. When I try to send him away the only answer I get is, "It's his lordship's orders, my lady.".'

'The fellow is absolutely right,' said Kirkham. 'Those are my expressed orders.'

'Oh, really!' protested Melissa. 'Surely we can find more fitting duties for such a hefty fellow other than trailing about after me. Why is there this sudden need for me to have a permanent manservant, anyway?'

'I merely consider it prudent. Town is becoming appallingly rowdy these days.'

'I had not noticed it.'

'Then maybe you are particularly unobservant. I deem it wise for you to go abroad properly escorted. Let that be an end to the matter.' Kirkham turned his attention back to his newspaper.

Melissa was not prepared to let the matter end there. 'But why a prize-fighter?' she protested. 'Why can I not have one of the regular menservants who. . .' Her voice tailed away as she suddenly saw the significance of her new retainer. 'Beaucombe!' she exclaimed. 'You think I need protecting from him?'

Kirkham laid aside his newspaper with a sigh. 'I think it is something we must consider,' he said. 'It is unfortunate that you are so sharp; I had hoped to keep such a possibility from you. Fox is fearless and dependable, which is why I have employed him. Beaucombe will think twice before tackling him.'

'Surely Beaucombe would not attempt anything! Not in London!'

'Who would have expected him to foist his unwelcome attentions on a lady in the foyer of Drury Lane? I regret to say Beaucombe is capable of anything. Therefore you will oblige me by never venturing out of doors without protection.'

'Will he want to wreak vengeance on you?' Melissa

demanded. 'Surely you need Fox more than I do, since you are Beaucombe's most likely victim.'

'Madam, I thank you for your concern, but I have no intention of reordering my life because of that rogue. You will keep Fox. As my wife it is only fitting that you are properly protected — yes, as my wife,' he added dourly. 'It goes against the grain but I fear I must accept that legally you are my spouse. As such you will be treated according to your rank.'

'This is a change of tone for you, my lord, to finally accept that we are married,' she said. 'May I ask what brought it about?'

'The force of the evidence. After much consideration I have reached the conclusion that there is nothing to be gained by continuing to fight the validity of our union.'

Melissa felt the faint stirrings of hope once more. Did this mean that he was growing fond of her? His next words crushed her sudden surge of happiness.

'However, madam, I must tell you emphatically that although I am now forced to accept you I don't like the arrangement any better,' he said brusquely.

'Then how do you intend that we order our lives, my lord?' she asked icily, swallowing her disappointment with difficulty.

'For the moment we will continue as we are. Our charade seems to be working tolerably. Most of Society appears to be taken in. As for the future, I am giving that much deliberation. To remain bound together for the rest of our lives would be intolerable. Unfortunately there are certain matters which must be given careful thought before I reach any conclusions.'

Melissa's disappointment grew increasingly bitter. There was no hint of warm or growing interest here.

'What certain matters?' she demanded.

Kirkham did not reply. He was already engrossed in his newspaper again.

How foolish she had been to imagine, even for one minute, that he was coming to care for her. By such idiotic fantasies she was only making things worse for herself. In her anger and distress Melissa was sorely tempted to walk out on him there and then. Let all of London hum with the news that Kirkham's new bride had deserted him. Let him be the butt of every gossip-monger and vicious tongue. What did she care? Then she remembered the promise she had given to Lady Kirkham. Much as she was tempted, she would not go back on her word, although she knew it was bound to cost her dear.

The hectic activity of the London Season continued unabated, with Lord Kirkham and his new wife drawing everyone's eye. There were times when Melissa wondered how long she could continue playing the part. As if she had not enough to bear, there was now the impending danger from Lord Beaucombe. Gradually, however, when nothing untoward happened, she ceased to be conscious of any threat, and no longer even noticed the heavy-footed tread of Fox as he followed behind her.

Musical soirées were extremely popular that Season, and the one held by Lord Layfield, at his home in Portland Place, was superb. Melissa revelled in the music.

There was only one thing which marred her enjoyment of the evening, and that was the sight of Beth Hurst sitting with her mother at the other side of the room. The poor girl looked desperately unhappy. Melissa was not the only one to be concerned on Beth's behalf. Gerard Woodley was among the guests, and

Melissa saw him glance frequently in Beth's direction, his anxiety plain to see.

It was not until the interval immediately before supper that Melissa got a chance to speak to Miss Hurst.

'Why, Lady Kirkham, how delightful to meet you again.' Beth's small face lit up with genuine pleasure, but Melissa was distressed to note that the girl looked terribly pale and the shadows beneath her eyes were dark as bruises.

'You will pardon me for saying so, Miss Hurst, but you do not look well,' said Melissa bluntly.

'Oh, I am well enough. I never ail anything,' was the swift reply.

'Then is something troubling you? Look, let us stroll about, then we can talk more freely. Something is wrong, I can see it. Will you not confide in me?'

'Wrong? What can be wrong?' There was a note bordering on hysteria in Beth's soft voice. 'I am the happiest girl in the world, for I am shortly to be betrothed. You may give my your congratulations betimes, Lady Kirkham, for I shall soon be Lady Beaucombe.'

Melissa drew in her breath sharply. So it had not been an idle rumour.

'My dear Miss Hurst. . . Beth,' she said sympathetically. 'Can you not object?'

'Object? To one of Mama's schemes? She will get a lord for a son-in-law and Beaucombe will get my considerable inheritance. An estimable exchange in the eyes of the world, no doubt.'

'And what will you get?'

'A husband who is cruel and lecherous, and a deal more besides. I beg your pardon, Lady Kirkham, for once having said I found Lord Kirkham alarming. I was a fool. I know now what alarming truly means.'

Melissa was startled at how much Beth had grown up since they had last met.

'Will not your father intervene?' she protested.

'He must know nothing of this,' said Beth, with unexpected firmness. 'He has given his written consent to the marriage, but he knows naught of the sort of man Beaucombe is. If he did he would certainly object most strongly, and he must not be agitated, his health is too precarious. He is never to know.'

'Surely something can be done,' declared Melissa. 'Can't I help in some way?'

'Dear Lady Kirkham, you have helped me already, by letting me unburden myself to you.'

'That is little enough. . .' began Melissa, but already Mrs Hurst was glaring round the assembly, looking for her daughter. With a reluctant farewell Beth hurried away.

Melissa felt most distressed and also somewhat guilty: if she had not tricked Kirkham into marriage Beth Hurst would probably be Lady Kirkham by now. She felt she had to make amends by helping Beth in some way. Her eyes lit upon the unmistakable auburn hair of Gerard Woodley. She had no idea how she was to help Beth Hurst, but if she did it could only be with the assistance of Mr Woodley. She sought out the company of her host.

'My lord,' she said smiling. 'Will you be kind enough to come to the rescue of a poor hapless wretch deserted by her husband?'

'Now that is the sort of request I have long awaited,' beamed Lord Layfield. 'In what way can I be of service?'

'By introducing me to Mr Woodley; I fancy we have a mutual friend.'

'Is that all?' Lord Layfield pretended to be disappointed. 'I had hoped for something much more romantic. Never mind, perhaps being called out by a jealous husband is too much to hope for at my time of life. Come along, my dear, and we will find your new chevalier.'

If Mr Woodley was surprised at being sought out by Lady Kirkham he was too well bred to show it. He was also too polite to demur when she asked him to escort her through Lord Layfield's long gallery to look at the paintings, though she could not help noticing a certain reluctance.

'Mr Woodley, you can relax,' she said, after they had scrutinised several Layfield ancestors. 'I did not ask you to accompany me out of caprice, nor yet to carry on a flirtation. When I said we had a mutual friend I spoke truthfully. That friend is Beth Hurst.'

Gerard Woodley stiffened. 'I did not know that your ladyship and Miss Hurst were acquainted,' he said.

'It is not a long acquaintanceship,' admitted Melissa. 'That does not mean I am indifferent to her happiness. She is in trouble and it is my fault. But for me she would doubtless be planning to marry Lord Kirkham by now, not Beaucombe... Your pardon, Mr Woodley. That was not very tactful of me.'

'You have no need to apologise, my lady,' said Gerard Woodley grimly. 'You speak only the truth. I wish she had married Kirkham. Then she would have been safe. He would never have ill-treated her.'

'That answers a very personal question I was reluctant to ask.' Melissa spoke gently. 'You do love her very much, do you not?'

'I do.' There was no mistaking the sincerity in the brief reply.

'And are you willing to do your utmost to help her?'

'I would willingly lay down my life for her.'

For a brief moment Melissa was disappointed in his answer. It sounded over-dramatic, smacking too much of the opera they had just enjoyed. She feared Mr Woodley was not the young man she had thought him. Then she looked into his grey eyes and changed her mind. There was nothing undependable or over-dramatic about Gerard Woodley. He meant every word.

'Then we are both agreed she must not marry Beaucombe?' she said briskly.

'Of course! Do you imagine I have not tried to devise a scheme?' declared Mr Woodley hotly. 'But it is not easy. I refuse to do anything that would harm her reputation.'

'Naturally,' agreed Melissa. 'Let me put my brains to the matter too. I may be able to think of something.'

'You would do this for Beth?' Woodley sounded surprised and touched.

'I would,' Melissa replied. 'I feel I owe her my help as well as my friendship. If I get any good ideas I will let you know. Therefore, I beg of you, if you receive a clandestine letter from a married lady suggesting a rendezvous please do not get the wrong idea. It will be from me.'

'I promise not to be shocked. I assure you I will come running at your ladyship's command.' For the first time he smiled, making his pleasant face look unexpectedly boyish. Melissa agreed with most of London in thinking Mrs Hurst a fool for not snapping up young Woodley for her daughter while she had the chance.

Kirkham was not in the best of moods when she rejoined him

'I have been looking for you everywhere,' he grumbled. 'Where have you been?'

Melissa wondered if she should tell him of her intention to help Beth Hurst. Then she decided against it. If he disapproved of her plans it would only make any further action much more difficult.

'I have been about the place,' she said vaguely. 'Chatting and such.'

'You women, when you get gossiping!' Kirkham raised eyebrows in exasperation. 'Now for pity's sake stay close to me! It will soon be time to leave, and if you wander off again we will be an age waiting for our carriage.'

Melissa forebore to mention that he had been chatting to a couple of his acquaintances from White's for a good half-hour before she had 'wandered off'. Instead she smiled sweetly and said, 'I will stay as close to you as a shadow, husband, dear. And tomorrow I will have Fraser send out for a leg-iron and a length of chain, then you will be certain to have me to hand.'

Kirkham assumed a sickly smile of mock devotion. 'Do not tempt me, madam,' he said. 'Only the fact that my house in Hanover Square is sadly devoid of dungeons prevents me from finding the idea quite delightful.'

They had returned to their habitual squabbling again. Melissa's heart sank at the prospect. She was finding their bouts of perpetual quarrelling harder and harder to bear. Why was she falling deeper and deeper in love with him when it was obvious he was disliking her more and more? She wished she could leave him, not out of pique but to give her bruised heart some respite. She could not, though. Not only had she to keep her word to Lady Kirkham, she now had Beth Hurst to consider.

How to help Beth occupied her thoughts considerably. The obvious solution would be for Beth to elope with Gerard Woodley, of course. But how? Not only was Mr Woodley very protective towards Beth's reputation, she knew that neither Mrs Hurst nor Lord Beaucombe would abandon their mutual bargain easily. They would be certain to pursue the young lovers with great determination. There was no denying it, this elopement would have to be meticulously planned down to the last detail.

It became increasingly obvious that soon she must meet up with Gerard Woodley again. There were things she wished to discuss with him, details she wished to find out. . . It was too early to suggest a meeting, but if they chanced to encounter one another somewhere then that would be most fortuitous.

Good luck was on her side, for one afternoon as she was being driven in Hyde Park she encountered him.

'Mr Woodley, I think a little exercise would be most beneficial,' she said, after they had exchanged greetings. 'May I request you to escort me for a short stroll?'

'Nothing would give me greater pleasure, your ladyship.' He handed her down and offered her his arm.

'There,' she said with satisfaction as, with Fox plodding behind at a discreet distance, they set off beneath the bare trees. 'We can have a good chat, for there are a dozen things I wish to discuss with you. One thing is so obvious it requires no discussion. You must elope with Beth.'

'I agree with you, my lady. The problem is how to do it respectably.'

Melissa gave a chuckle. 'A respectable elopement sounds to be a contradiction in terms. I know what you mean, though, and that is why I offer myself as chaperon.'

'As chaperon?' Gerard was astounded at such generosity. 'Lord Kirkham would not object?'

'I am sure it could be arranged,' said Melissa vaguely. 'I have no definite plans, you understand. Just one or two unformed ideas. How would it be if Beth and I, suitably escorted, travelled together to Gretna Green, while you travel the same route but independently? That would be perfectly respectable.'

'That would be capital!' he exclaimed. 'And if we took a devious route then that would confuse any pursuers.'

'It would be even better if we laid a false trail. Fortunately your colouring is distinctive. Could we not find a young man with red hair who, for a few guineas, would impersonate you and drive at great speed towards Gretna Green taking an alternative road? Perhaps with a lady companion?'

'That is a masterly scheme! You have my deepest admiration, my lady.' Gerard Woodley was beaming with delight. 'But we can do better than one false trail. We can lay two. I have a pair of young cousins. They do not resemble me except that we all have the Woodley colouring, but that is the important part — people remember the red hair.'

'You think they would agree?'

'Agree? They would both revel in such an adventure.'

'Then we would need two lady companions for them. Their sisters, perhaps?'

'I think we can safely leave my cousins to provide their own companions,' said Gerard with a twinkle in his eye. Then he grew serious. 'There is one major snag to our schemes that we have not considered. Beth herself. She is such a timid creature, and so used to obeying her mother absolutely. I fear she will not agree to this elopement.'

'Mr Woodley,' said Melissa gravely, 'have you spoken to Beth recently?'

'Unfortunately no.'

'I have. Beth has few illusions about what marriage to Beaucombe will entail. She is afraid, Mr Woodley. Really afraid, not just her natural timidity. And she loves you very much. She will agree to the elopement. Have no doubts about it.'

They walked on in silence for a while, both with their thoughts preoccupied by Beth.

'The sooner Beth knows what we plan, the better,' said Melissa suddenly. 'There is a concert next week. Lady Bedthorp is giving it in aid of something or other. You will be there?'

'Certainly. And you?'

'Yes. Now we have to ensure that Beth and her mother will be there.'

'That is easily done.' Gerard smiled his gentle smile again. 'Lady Bedthorp is an old family friend. I merely have to persuade her to send invitations to the Hurst household. It always works. Mrs Hurst can never resist an opportunity to mix with the *haut ton*.'

'You mean you have done this before?'

'Of course. How else would I ever get to see Beth? Even though I am often prevented from speaking to her we usually manage to exchange messages. Leave the arrangements to me. I can almost guarantee that the Hursts will be at Lady Bedthorp's concert.'

'I had not thought you to be so devious, Mr Woodley,' said Melissa approvingly. 'It is an excellent quality in a fellow conspirator. Now, perhaps you would be kind enough to return me to my carriage. And be in good heart. I think we are well on the way to arranging a most successful elopement for you and Beth.'

When they reached the carriage Gerard Woodley

bowed over her hand. 'Lady Kirkham, I have no words to express my gratitude for all you are doing.'

'Gratitude is unnecesary. As I have said, I feel partly responsible for the predicament that your Miss Hurst is in.'

'You cannot blame yourself for Lord Kirkham's falling in love with you,' he protested.

Melissa could not explain that her responsibility for their marriage went far beyond coquettishness, so she merely smiled and said, 'You are most gallant, sir, but I do feel under an obligation. And even if I did not I would still want to help Beth.'

'My darling girl is lucky indeed to have a friend like you, my lady.'

Gerard Woodley handed her back into the carriage and doffed his hat in farewell. Melissa observed that he looked considerably happier than when she had met him.

She had offered to act as chaperon on this elopement, but how to do it she had no idea. Two young ladies could not travel about the country without a male escort, even if one was married to a lord. Again she considered letting Kirkham into their plans, and again she rejected the idea. She was far from being in his favour at the moment, and she dared not risk him prohibiting her from taking part. Too much was at stake.

They had scarcely gone a quarter of a mile before the solution to the problem appeared strolling nonchalantly across the grass. Melissa ordered Richards to stop the carriage, then she lowered the window.

'James,' she ordered. 'Get in!'

'How could I refuse such a charming invitation?' Her brother grinned back at her, his blue eyes gleaming.

'Do not even consider it,' she said sternly, and to add emphasis to her words she held open the carriage door.

Still smiling, James climbed up beside her, kissed first her cheek then Polly's.

'And you need not try to get in our good books,' declared Melissa. 'What on earth can you be thinking of, walking abroad in Hyde Park like this! What if Kirkham had been driving with me?'

'Is he not attending the prize-fight at Jives Court today?'

'You seem remarkably well informed about his lordship's movements,' said Melissa. She looked sharply in Polly's direction and was not surprised when the girl avoided her gaze.

'Oh, come, Mel, I cannot skulk about the back streets forever. A fellow's got to get out and about some time,' James protested.

'You sound very brave. I wonder if you would sing the same tune if Kirkham were closer at hand. However, I do not intend to scold you. I have a better use for you. I am going on a journey, and you will act as my escort.'

'A journey? Where?'

'I have not decided.'

'When?'

'I do not know.'

'This sounds a very vague sort of journey.'

'It is merely that I have not yet made my final arrangements. It is not important, is it? You have no other schemes in hand?'

'No...except that you know how I hate leaving London during the Season——No, I have no plans,' he added hastily, catching sight of his sister's ominous expression. 'I am completely at your disposal.'

'Good. I will let you know as soon as I need your

services.' She rapped for Richards to stop the carriage. 'This is where you get down.'

'What, here? This is miles out of my way,' objected James.

'It is a nice quiet spot where as few people as possible will see you descend from my carriage. Of course if you want Kirkham to know you are back in Society again we could always drive on further...'

'No, this will do fine. The exercise will be good for me.' James began to scramble out, then he stopped. 'Sis,' he said in a persuasive way. 'I don't suppose... I mean could you...?'

Melissa gave a sigh and reached for her reticule.

'Ten guineas. It is all I have about me. And this is to be the last time,' she said decisively.

'You are a sister in a million. I swear I will not ask again...'

As they drove away, leaving an effusive James at the roadside Melissa caught Polly's eye.

'And you need not look so knowing, miss!' she exclaimed. 'That is the last money Mr James will ever get from me.'

Polly said nothing. She just grinned, then Melissa began to grin too. They both knew there would be no more money...until the next time.

If Melissa had any serious hopes of keeping her meeting with James from Kirkham she was destined to be disappointed. Next day, as soon as he returned from his club Kirkham confronted her in the library.

'Well, my lord, and what are we to quarrel about today,' she asked wearily, deducing the worst from his grim expression.

'I am sure you can guess, madam,' he retorted. 'I had barely set foot in White's this morning before two people informed me they had seen you out driving with your brother.'

'White's must be singularly short of gossip these days if a lady's being accompanied by her own brother excites comment.'

'The information was passed on by way of conversation, not gossip, but that did not make it any more palatable to me. You know my opinion of that wretch. How dare you consort with him?'

'How dare I?' repeated Melissa in a voice low with anger. 'How dare I meet my own brother? My own flesh and blood? I was not aware that you had forbidden such a rendezvous; and if you had I would certainly not have agreed.'

'He may be your own flesh and blood but he is not fit company for Lady Kirkham. I am surprised he summoned up the courage to crawl out of whichever rathole has been his refuge of late. He frequents unsavoury places, mixes with the lowest of the low.'

'I agree that his acquaintances are mostly unsuitable, and I sorely regret the fact. They are mostly people he encounters during his visits to gaming-hells. I believe that was where he met you, my lord?'

Kirkham's brows went together angrily. 'Do not prevaricate with me, madam,' he snorted. 'I will not have you consorting with your brother and there's an end of it.'

'No, it is not!' retorted Melissa. 'I flatly refuse to abandon James. I agree he is weak and unreliable, but that is all the more reason why I will not cast him off. I am the only family he has. Left to own devices, there is no knowing what terrible trouble he would get into.'

'The trouble he causes to himself does not concern me. It is the trouble he has caused to me that makes me want to throttle him. It is no exaggeration to say that because of him all hope of happiness in my life is gone. Therefore I command you never to see him again.'

'And I refuse!' she snapped.

Kirkham's eyes were glittering with fury. 'Madam, I presume that somewhere in that travesty of a marriage ceremony of ours there was something about you obeying?'

'There was also mention of love and comfort and honour,' snapped Melissa. 'Are you being selective in the upholding of your vows, or is it that, since you can remember so little of the ceremony, none of them signifies?'

'Love? Comfort? Honour?' he roared. 'Where you are concerned, madam, that is expecting the impossible of any man. How can anyone love, comfort and honour a nightmare? It is certainly beyond my capabilities!'

Melissa had been stung before by his words, but never like this. For a terrible instant she feared she was going to be overwhelmed by tears. It took all her self-control to hold them back.

Shaking with the effort, she said evenly, 'I have always known that you were unhappy in our marriage. Until this minute, however, I do not think I appreciated the depth of your suffering. Since we are both miserable it seems pointless going on with the charade simply for the sake of public opinion. I confess it was never my intention to remain hanging about your neck. From the first I planned to leave you and live quietly somewhere in the country. Only a wish to torment you further kept me silent. Now I think the torment has gone on long enough, therefore I will leave your house within the hour. As soon as I am settled I will let your man of business know my address. Otherwise we need have no other contact with one another.'

Her head high, her back ramrod straight, she would have left the room if Kirkham had not called her back. There was no softness in his voice, nor regret, only the sharp bark of command.

'Hold, madam! You are too swift!'

She turned back to see him looking at her as grimly as ever.

'My instincts are to greet your departure with intense relief,' he went on. 'Unfortunately you cannot go just yet. There are other matters to be considered.'

'If they are financial then please understand I will not accept any money or allowance from you.'

'They are not financial.'

'Then what. . .?'

Kirkham, too, now straightened himself to his full height. His eyes still glittered angrily as he glared at her.

'First and foremost, you may live where you please when we part. You will accept an allowance from me, I will brook no argument on that point. I am not having it said that my wife lived in penury — for make no mistake about it, you will continue to be my wife. I will not countenance a divorce. If you have a lover waiting for you somewhere then you must make your own arrangements, for you will continue as my legal spouse until death releases us. Is that clear?'

'Yes, my lord.' Melissa would have left the room, too dispirited to argue about the allowance, if he had not called her back again.

'Pray do not be so impatient! I have not finished!' The anger had not lessened in his voice. 'Once we separate you will be able to live comfortably with no interference from me. I am no more eager to keep in contact with you than you are with me. However, there is one obligation that must be fulfilled before we can reach that happy state. As you know, I am the last of the Kirkhams. Therefore it is my responsibility not to let our ancient and honourable line die out. . . I think you can guess what I am going to say.'

'No, I cannot,' said Melissa, trying to ignore the dread that was beginning to beset her.

'Then for pity's sake think on it!' he snapped irritably. It was the first hint he had given that he was finding the speech difficult. 'I am the last Kirkham, you are my wife. You may leave this house, I will support you in luxury for the rest of your days, you may do as you please without let or hindrance—once you have given me an heir.'

'You are joking!' gasped Melissa.

'Would I joke about such a subject?' he retorted. 'Do you think I like the idea any better than you? Unfortunately I regard it as my duty. Knowing what a low opinion you have of me, you will no doubt be surprised to learn that I am extremely proud of my lineage. For generations the Kirkhams have been brave and honourable and served their country well. The idea that the line will die out with me cannot be tolerated, not if it is within my power to prevent it. Unfortunately, if the heir is to be legitimate, you are also involved.'

'No!' said Melissa appalled. 'No, I will never agree!'

'At least give the matter some thought. You are not going to go all simpering and romantic, are you? It is not necessary to like one another to beget an heir. Hundreds of people achieve it every year with never a thought of love and all that nonsense.'

Melissa could not bring herself to reply. It could not be easy for people who were not fond of each other to beget children, but what if one partner loved while the other hated? That was more than difficult, it was appalling in its torment.

'No,' she whispered eventually. 'I cannot do it.'

'Think on it,' he insisted. 'Consider it part of the marriage contract. That is what most folk do.'

'No,' she repeated.

'Then I must appeal to your honour. One thing I have learned about you is that you have a strong sense of duty. I did not force you to marry me. As I know to my cost you did the arranging, aye, and the marrying. Oh, I accept that you had your reasons, but in protecting your honour did it never occur to you that you might be putting an end to a family that can record its lineage back a good three centuries? If the Kirkhams die out the responsibility will be yours alone.'

'I cannot,' she said.

'The idea is new to you,' he said suddenly, almost kindly. 'You need time to think.' He stretched out his arms to her as if to grasp her hands. Melissa shrank away from him. 'You have no need to fear me,' he protested, misunderstanding. 'I would never force you, I swear it. Is your opinion of me so low? All I will do is to implore you to consider the matter seriously. It is of great importance to me.'

For a long time after he had left the room Melissa sat stunned and immobile, not knowing what to think. Such a development had never occurred to her. It was stupid and naïve of her perhaps; she should have expected such an eventuality and been prepared for it. But she had not, and now the whole business horrified her. In other circumstances nothing would have pleased her more than to give Kirkham a child. In other circumstances! As things were, she could think of nothing more distressing than to have him possess her body with no more emotion than the coldly calculated intention of producing an heir. The thought made her shudder.

Yet he had been right when he had pointed out that her intervention had upset his more conventional marriage plans. Even if he had not wed Beth Hurst he would have found some other suitable bride to produce a nursery full of little Kirkhams for him. But she, Melissa, had stepped in and spoiled all that. Falling in love with him had not helped, it had merely complicated matters. The responsibility for the continuation of the Kirkham family lay with her and she did not know what to do. She only knew she had never been so unhappy in her life.

CHAPTER NINE

MELISSA spent a long miserable day trying to decide what to do. Yet the instant she reached a definite conclusion she knew she had never had any choice. However much her brain might have anguished over the problem, in her heart she had always known that she would abide by Kirkham's conditions. Not because of the promise of a good allowance for life, nor yet the prospect of spending the rest of her days in peace and security It had been the deep throb of sincerity in his voice when he had expressed his fear that the Kirkham line would finish with him.

How to tell Kirkham her decision proved almost as difficult as reaching the conclusion itself. That evening they had guests to dine, preventing any private conversation. And afterwards Kirkham had disappeared into the library with the determined air of a man who did not want to be disturbed. The book he was reading, plus a decanter of brandy, kept him occupied until a late hour.

The waiting stretched Melissa's nerves until they felt like bowstrings. She wanted the matter done with as soon as possible. Finally, convinced that she would have to leave it until next day before she could have a serious conversation with Kirkham, she went to bed. The thick bolster, as usual set down the middle of the great bed looked most reassuring. Once Polly had gone she tried to settle but sleep would not come. Then she heard the click of Kirkham's dressing-room door and the rumble of voices as he talked to Pentecost. She sat up in bed and relit the candle. A few minutes later Kirkham entered, clad in his brocade dressing-robe.

'You are still awake, madam?' he said formally. 'I had thought you to be asleep long since.'

'I cannot sleep,' she said. 'I have too much on my mind.'

'Ah...' said Kirkham. He seemed uncertain what to say next.

'My lord, we have things to discuss,' she said briskly. 'Is this a convenient moment?' How absurd and formal her words sounded, but only by adopting such a manner could she speak at all.

'You are right, we do have things to talk about. And, yes, this is as good a time as any.' He hesitated for a moment then sat down on the bed beside her. 'Am I to assume that you have thought over my proposition?'

'I have. There are, however, some matters we must sort out. For example, what if I give you only female children, or if I prove barren? What happens then?'

'I think that after the tenth girl we might give up,' he said. Then as Melissa winced he added hurriedly, 'Your pardon, I should not have made a joke of it. This is no laughing matter. You are right, these are eventualities we must consider. What say you? If we have no male heir within two years then we stop trying? Does that sound reasonable?'

'Very reasonable.' She heard her calm reply, scarcely believing her ears. How could she be responding in this rational matter-of-fact manner when her heart was breaking?

'Am I to assume, then, that you are willing to try to give me an heir?' Kirkham asked, just as formally.

'Yes.'

'In that case all the other conditions pertain. A generous allowance will be yours; you will be free to go where ever you like and do whatever you please without hindrance from me.'

There was an awkward pause.

'If we must be about things then I suggest that there is no time like the present, madam. If it is convenient to you, of course.' He sounded absurdly hearty.

'It is convenient,' said Melissa in an almost inaudible voice.

'You are sure you would not sooner wait until I have spoken to my lawyer and had the proper papers drawn up?'

'There is no need for that.'

'Perhaps you are right. He would want to take time over the wording, otherwise I can see some of the phrases proving a bit tricky.' Again his inappropriate joke fell flat. He was ill at ease.

Melissa realised that Kirkham was as uncomfortable in this situation as she was.

In a sudden gesture he reached across, and snatching up the bolster threw it across the room. 'We may as well dispense with that,' he said.

Then he removed his dressing-gown and was about to get into bed when he stopped. Taking up her hand he ran his thumb gently across her fingers. 'I am sorry to put you to this, Melissa,' he said softly. 'Truly I am. I would have spared you if there had been any other way.'

'I know,' she said. The gentleness of his touch and her own state of nervous tension made her voice tremble. He had chosen this moment, of all times, to address her by her Christian name. It did nothing to help her composure.

'This is a sorry pickle and no mistake,' he said, sounding regretful rather than angry. 'However, we must make the best of things.'

With this singularly unromantic remark he blew out the candle.

Melissa had often wondered what it would be like to have Kirkham's arms properly about her. Now he carefully removed her nightgown and enfolded her in an embrace. She was taken by surprise at the sensual pleasure the closeness of his body, hard and muscular, afforded her. It was far more than anything she had anticipated. Her instinct was to melt against him, flesh against flesh, until they became one being. But she did not. This was no act of love, this was the begetting of an heir. Her role was to be submissive and unresponsive. It was very difficult. She would have found it easier if Kirkham had been rough or selfishly demanding. He was not. He proved to be a kindly lover and this nearly overset her. Experienced and gentle, the softness of his caresses against her skin would have given her such pleasure if she had allowed herself. He knew how to arouse and how to give enjoyment which, combined with his consideration, made it all the more difficult for her to bear.

It should not be like this, she cried to herself. This is all wrong. We should be experiencing nothing but love and beauty and pleasure. That would have been the most wonderful thing imaginable. Instead everything is ordered by duty. Why, oh, why could things not have been otherwise?

But it was no use having dreams. This was reality, where obligation ruled.

Afterwards when passion and duty had both been expended, Melissa lay in a crumpled heap, determined not to betray her misery. The tears that soaked her pillow fell silently, she bit her lips to hold back the sobs which threatened to choke her, but there was nothing she could do to mask the spasms of despair which racked her body. At one point she thought she felt her hair being gently smoothed away from her brow. At another she fancied a sympathetic hand stroked her tear-stained cheek in an effort to give comfort. But in her emotional state she was not sure. It might just have been the overwrought imaginings of her unhappy mind.

The bed was empty when she awoke next morning. His lordship had risen early and gone riding in Rotten Row, she was informed. She was glad of the respite; she sorely needed time to compose herself. She and Kirkham did not meet up until almost dinner-time. They were engaged to dine with friends. The only opportunity they had for conversation was in the carriage.

'You are in good health and spirits, I hope, madam? You are not fatigued?' Kirkham asked.

'I am in excellent spirits, I thank you, my lord,' she replied.

It was the only oblique reference either of them made to the change in their relationship. Within minutes they had arrived at their hosts' house and the chance for private conversation was at an end.

Melissa was thankful she had Beth and Woodley's elopement to arrange. If she tried she could concentrate upon it fully, to the exclusion of all else. At times she had to remind herself forcefully that Beth had not yet agreed to the scheme. When she had proposed the idea to Gerard Woodley Melissa had been absolutely convinced that Beth would agree. Now that the date of Lady Bedthorp's concert drew nearer she was not so sure. The girl was such a timid creature she was quite likely to refuse point-blank from sheer panic.

By the time the evening finally arrived Melissa was thoroughly restless and unable to settle. Upon finding her fully dressed and actually waiting for him Kirkham's eyebrows rose.

'I had not realised I was tardy,' he said. 'I apologise. Is there any particular reason for us being so prompt?'

'I just thought it might be a good idea to get there before the street is completely jammed with carriages,' said Melissa with a casual shrug of the shoulders. She could hardly explain that she was impatient to get there to promote an elopement.

'That is prudent thinking,' said Kirkham. 'Richards will appreciate it if no one else.' But although he spoke jokingly there was puzzlement in his eyes as he looked at her.

They made a handsome couple as they entered the grand salon at Lady Bedthorp's house. Melissa had given up her protestations at every new gown that was thrust upon her, and now she wore one of Madame Elise's latest inspirations. It was a creation in bronze satin embroidered with pearls. Loops of pearls were woven into her golden hair, and with the Kirkham pearls adorning her throat the effect was both elegant and striking. Melissa scarcely noticed the admiring glances as she moved through the crowd that was already beginning to gather.

The looks of approval bestowed upon her husband, usually by female eyes, were harder to ignore. He did look extremely handsome, his superbly cut coat covering his wide shoulders with scarcely a wrinkle, his breeches an impeccable fit over his muscular thighs, his neckcloth a snowy masterpiece of ingenuity. Melissa tried to ignore the feelings of unease which such frank ogling of her husband always provoked in her. Surely it must only be a matter of time before he accepted some of the favours openly yet silently offered to him. The fact that he may have already done so did nothing to promote Melissa's happiness. It was no consolation to appreciate that, if so, he was being particularly discreet.

The arrival of Beth Hurst, with her mother, brought a welcome diversion from her uncomfortable thoughts. Less pleasing was the sight of their escort. Lord Beaucombe ushered his charges somewhat impatiently into their seats, then looked round the assembly with a sneering arrogance. To her discomfort his gaze settled upon her. The expression in his eyes was carnal and challenging. She refused to let him see her disquiet and returned his stare with cold hauteur, then she deliberately turned away. Not quite quickly enough, however, for she saw his glare move on to Kirkham. At once it turned into a blatant hatred.

Kirkham was not aware that he was under scrutiny. He was occupied with greeting his grandmother, who had just arrived, and in settling her comfortably. Melissa felt very afraid for him, yet there was nothing she could do. He was adamant that he was a match for Beaucombe. She hoped he was right.

Little of the concert, excellent though it no doubt was, registered with Melissa. She was too occupied with the twin problems of worrying about Kirkham's safety and the daunting task of luring Beth away from her mother. Once more the ladies' retiring-room proved the solution.

'Lady Kirkham, I am so glad to see you here,' Beth greeted her as she entered the room. 'I am desperate to talk to someone and you are the only friend I have.' She looked more pale and anxious than ever. 'What am I to do? I cannot—I will not marry that man!'

'Nor shall you,' said Melissa briskly. 'You are going to elope with Mr Woodley and I am to help you.'

Beth gave a long sigh of relief. 'Oh, yes, please!' she breathed.

Melissa was taken aback by such an immediate response. She had been prepared to persuade.

'You agree?' she said in surprise.

'Oh, yes, yes, please! Can it be soon?'

'As soon as possible. Mr Woodley and I have both been concerned for your future; we have drawn up a rough plan. He said he would be here this evening, though I have not seen him yet.'

'I have,' said Beth with a happy smile.

'Good.' It occurred to Melissa that this was an extraordinary way for a young girl to hear of her impending elopement. She did her best to make amends. 'I know that Mr Woodley would wish to tell you all this himself,' she said, 'along with his declarations of how much he loves you and wishes to protect you. Sadly, because of the unfortunate circumstances he cannot. I understand that you and he are able to exchange messages sometimes; but in case he is not able to communicate with you I must be his inadequate substitute.'

'I appreciate that we have little time,' said Beth. 'And as for my dear Woodley's declarations, once we are married I shall have the rest of my life to listen to them.' And she smiled again.

Relieved that Beth's sensibilities had not been hurt, Melissa said, 'Our idea is that you and I, escorted by my brother, shall travel towards Gretna Green by some devious route — a small family party touring the country, exciting no comment. At the same time Mr Woodley will take the same road but travel independently. Meanwhile, he has persuaded two of his cousins. . .'

If Beth had any objections to having her elopement organised for her and only being informed of the event somewhat belatedly then she gave no sign. Her small face lit up with delight and evident relief.

'And when will this be, dear Lady Kirkham?' she asked.

'I fancy at the end of the Season would be a good time, when the roads are better.'

'There is one thing that troubles me. Please do not take offence, Lady Kirkham, but I am convinced my mama would never give her permission for me to go travelling with you.'

'That troubles me too. You cannot be taken up from your own home, that is certain. Have you no relative whom your mother would allow you to visit alone? That might make things easier.'

'I have an aunt who lives at Epsom, my father's sister. She is always delighted to have me to stay.'

'That would be ideal. And Epsom, too, the perfect place for you to rest after the rigours of the Season. Could you persuade your mother, do you think? Convince her that you are feeling jaded and need to restore your strength and looks before your wedding.'

At this reminder of her possible future with Lord Beaucombe Beth shuddered.

'I will try,' she said, then with unexpected determination she added, 'Nay, I *will* persuade Mama.'

'Splendid.' Melissa had to lower her voice because other ladies had entered the room. 'As soon as we hear you are visiting your aunt — and that should be easy to ascertain — we will act. In the meantime you must convince your mama that you are going into a decline: refuse food, pretend to swoon, weep a great deal — if the tears will not come then read sad poetry or think on sad things. If you do all this, then any doctor worth his fee will order you into the country forthwith.'

'I will do it, I promise,' said Beth.

Noises outside warned them that the interval was over and the second part of the concert was about to commence. As she rose to leave Beth leaned over and whispered into Melissa's ear, 'Mrs Angelica Thomas, Ivy House, Epsom.'

Melissa was perplexed, until Beth whispered again more urgently, 'My aunt's address, Lady Kirkham. You must have it else how will you know where to come?'

Melissa could not help smiling as she went to rejoin Kirkham. There she had been, convinced that she was the driving force in the arrangements, and she had forgotten such a vital detail. So much for her self-esteem. It was reassuring, though, to know that Beth had her wits about her. After a lifetime of being browbeaten by her awful mother it showed remarkable spirit.

Melissa wished she could see Gerard Woodley, to tell him how well things were going. Unfortunately she had only glimpes of him. It was not until the end of the concert, when people were making their way from the grand salon, that she caught his eye. He was on the other side of the room, too far away for them to speak, even if Kirkham had not got a firm hold on her arm. As well as she was able she tried to pass on the good news to him, inclining her head and smiling. To her satisfaction he beamed back and bowed with a delighted flourish. He understood!

She had not thought Kirkham observed their little pantomime, not until they were back at Hanover Square.

'I did not realise that you are acquainted with Woodley,' he observed.

'Mr Woodley? Yes, we are slightly acquainted.'

'Slightly? From the way the fellow was doing acrobatics to attract your attention you would appear to be particular friends. Who introduced you, for I certainly did not?'

'It was Lord Layfield, I believe,' said Melissa, knowing full well that it was.

'Oh, the other evening, when he trailed you past his lordship's works of art. Your acquaintanceship has certainly blossomed in a very short time.'

Melissa was tired, and the conversation seemed to be heading down an all too familiar path.

'My lord,' she said, 'you appear to be objecting to something but I do not know what. Would you be kind enough to be specific, so that I can know what I have done wrong?'

'I am asking you, madam, to be more discreet in your dalliances. How you amuse yourself is your own affair but only up to a point. If you are considering presenting me with a cuckoo for an heir then think twice.'

He stalked away angrily. Melissa was stung by his behaviour, as well as bewildered. He had been far more angry than such a minor incident warranted. Looking back, she recalled that he had been very quiet and preoccupied in the carriage coming home. The fact that Gerard Woodley had bowed enthusiastically to her hardly seemed to justify his moodiness. Then she remembered another detail of the homeward journey. Sitting on the box beside Richards had been the hugely muscled figure of Fox. That was unremarkable, but now she recalled the two grooms who had been up behind. They had been of similarly huge proportions and she had not recognised them. Beaucombe! What a stupid fool she had been! Kirkham had expected retaliation from the blackguard somewhere along the route. Was it any wonder that he had been preoccupied and his temper short?

For once Kirkham was already in bed when she

entered the bedchamber. He lay with his eyes closed and the covers up about his ears. Melissa was not taken in.

'I know you are still awake, my lord,' she said. 'And if you could postpone going to sleep for a few minutes I would like a word with you.'

Kirkham rolled over with a groan. 'If you must, madam,' he said, propping himself up on his elbow. 'What is so important it cannot wait until morning?'

'The fact that you did not tell me you suspected some move from Beaucombe.'

'Oh, that!'

'Yes, oh, that! Did you think I would not notice that we are now served almost entirely by prize-fighters? Any more and we could set up in opposition to Gentleman Jackson.'

'Merely a precaution.'

'You really think it is necessary?'

'Would I employ them otherwise? Apart from the money I pay them, Fraser informs me they are eating me out of house and home below stairs.'

'But Beaucombe has shown no inclination to get even.'

'So far! Having been reliably informed that I should be on my guard I would be foolish to ignore such a warning, especially against a devious individual like Beaucombe.'

'But who gave you this information?' she demanded, intrigued.

'Madam,' said Kirkham with some exasperation, 'could this inquisition be delayed until tomorrow? I am tired and I would like to get some sleep. I assure you there is nothing to fear. I know more of Beaucombe's movements than he does of mine, therefore I have made sure we are well protected. You have no need to worry, you are perfectly safe.'

It was on the tip of Melissa's tongue to protest that she was worried for him, not for herself. But this came uncomfortably close to betraying her true feelings for him. 'Just one more thing, my lord,' she said, ignoring his groan. 'I merely wish to assure you that I have no intention of cuckolding you, with Mr Woodley or anyone else. . .' Then an imp of irritation made her add, 'At the present!'

Kirkham gave a snort of annoyance. 'Perhaps you would be kind enough to inform me when such an event might occur,' he said. 'I would prefer to be the first to know, not the last, as I believe is usual!'

So saying he turned over, thumped his head on the pillow and hauled the bedclothes back over his head. Only a few locks of dark hair were visible above the counterpane and the sight of them moved Melissa in an extraordinary way. How she wanted to stroke them gently, to feel their springy softness in her fingers. But she blew out the candle and got quickly into bed.

She lay awake for a long time, her mind preoccupied not with any potential danger from Beaucombe, but with the tantalising proximity of Kirkham beside her. She allowed herself a wonderful dream in which he took her in his arms and called her his only love. Sadly it was only a dream. In reality Kirkham lay on the far side of the great bed, not moving, although Melissa sensed he was still not asleep. The bolster was absent, but it might as well have remained in position. Dared she move closer to him? she wondered. Maybe even enfold him in an embrace? No, it was too great a risk. He was certain to rebuff her and she knew she could not bear to be rejected. There was no alternative but to remain awake and miserable at her side of the bed, while he remained at his. They might have been a world apart.

'How goes it with you, madam?' demanded old Lady Kirkham when she arrived for tea one afternoon.

'Very well, I thank you,' replied Melissa.

'Humph!' Lady Kirkham did not look convinced. 'Then it must be my imagination that you are looking somewhat down.'

'It is the Season,' Melissa put in quickly. 'Everyone finds it wearing.'

'I do not,' stated the old lady. 'But then few people have my stamina. How do things stand between you and my grandson? That is what I really want to know. We do not seem to have had a private talk this age.'

'We are dealing well enough.' Melissa hoped she was putting conviction in her voice.

'He is not happy.' The words came unexpectedly.

'I know.' Melissa pushed her teacup away. 'Oh, how I wish I had never got into this tangle! I have never been so miserable in my life. And nor, I fancy, has Kirkham.'

'That is the way of things, is it?' said Lady Kirkham with surprising sympathy. 'I had hoped you would be dealing together rather better by now, but clearly that is not the case. Certainly in public you are to be congratulated, for you are both most convincing.'

'Yes, in public!' said Melissa bitterly. 'We can be like two turtle-doves when the eyes of the world are upon us. That is the easy part.'

'And could not some of this billing and cooing stray over into your private life?'

'No!' Melissa's reply was emphatic.

'Ah,' said Lady Kirkham knowingly. She went on, 'In that case I presume you will soon be leaving Kirkham's house?'

'Not as soon as I would wish.'

'And why is that?'

'Kirkham has laid down conditions.'

There was a pause, with Lady Kirkham clearly waiting to hear what those conditions were and Melissa equally reluctant to give details. Then Melissa felt a desperate need to confide. She had no one else who was older and more experienced with whom to share her troubles, and she sensed that Lady Kirkham would not be totally unsympathetic.

'He wants an heir first,' she said.

To her dismay Lady Kirkham gave a beam of satisfaction. 'I was wondering when he would get round to that,' she declared.

'You cannot approve?' exclaimed Melissa.

'Of course I do. It has troubled me much to think that the Kirkham family might soon become extinct. Now, because of you, it will not.'

'You do not consider the possibility that I might refuse his conditions?'

'No,' said Lady Kirkham flatly. 'You are Kirkham's legal wife, and I have judged your character too well to think you capable of denying your duty.'

'You see nothing distasteful in such an arrangement?'

'Good heavens no! That is what marriage is for, to beget heirs. At least, it was in my day. You youngsters have mollycoddled yourselves with too many romantic thoughts and such nonsense. It only complicates things. A man and a woman in a bed, set upon creating a child, they are the essentials. Nothing else is necessary.'

'Yes, it is!' cried Melissa, bitterly disappointed at the older woman's lack of understanding. 'There is love. That is the greatest necessity of all.'

Lady Kirkham shook her head. 'It can come later, once you have a thriving nursery.' She paused and looked shrewdly at Melissa with eyes surprisingly like Kirkham's. 'It is your tragedy, my dear, that you have chosen to put love in the wrong order. Ah, you did not think I had guessed?' she said as Melissa drew in her breath sharply. 'Surely you know by now that nothing pertaining to my grandson escapes my notice. Having weakened in this way, I only hope you do not let your feelings cloud your judgement. You must do your best to discount your own emotions and think only that you have entered into a contract: a marriage contract that has the begetting of an heir as its principal clause.'

'You ask the impossible!' cried Melissa.

'I ask the very difficult,' corrected Lady Kirkham. 'And I ask it for your own happiness as well as for the furtherance of my family. If Kirkham has an heir he has a future. You would not deny him that, would you?'

'I suppose not, but what if I cannot have a child?'

'That is something beyond our control. My grandson would never blame you for it. Whatever their faults, the Kirkham men are compassionate.'

Suddenly the old lady took Melissa's hand in hers and said in a voice that was strangely soft and wistful, 'Six children I bore Kirkham's grandfather. Only one survived, and he had to die in an accident before his own child was born! There is nothing you can tell me about the responsibility for furthering an ancient line, my dear. For fifty years I have watched the Kirkham family totter on the brink of extinction, knowing that my failures played their part in bringing it about.'

'But it was not your fault,' protested Melissa indignantly. 'You could not help it.'

'No, but that is no consolation when duty is tempered with love. Which is why I advise you for your own sake to put your emotions behind you and think only of your duty. It will make your life much easier.'

Lady Kirkham seemed to give herself a mental shake. She released Melissa's hand, returned to her usual ramrod posture and barked out, 'And I hope my grandson is doing his duty regularly by you. If not I shall have something to say to him.'

'Oh, please no,' begged Melissa, horrified at the idea of the old lady lecturing Kirkham on his duties as a husband.

'Perhaps you are right,' agreed Lady Kirkham. 'These men, they get so offended if they imagine their manhood is in question. Best let nature take its course. You are not breeding yet, I suppose?' Then she noted the expression on Melissa's face and declared, 'No, of course not. Far too soon. Wait until Kirkham takes you to the family home in Devonshire. That should do the trick!'

Melissa had a deal to think about after the old lady had departed. At first she had thought Lady Kirkham unsympathetic to her plight. Now she knew better. Kirkham's grandmother understood only too well. Melissa was not certain she could follow her advice no matter how kindly it was offered. But if she produced an heir it would mean a great deal to Lady Kirkham too, that was obvious. Melissa uttered a sound that was half sigh, half groan. No matter which way she turned it seemed that she could not escape having to do her duty.

In truth Lady Kirkham would have had no fault to find with her grandson as a husband. He carried out his marital duties meticulously. He was unfailingly kind — as the old lady had said, the Kirkham men were always compassionate — but there were times when Melissa felt that his compassion would break her heart. He was always gentle, never aggressively demanding. Sometimes she could almost believe that he meant the tender caresses he bestowed on her and that he delighted in the sensual fondling as much as she did. For she did delight in it! No matter how she tried to restrain herself, there were times when she could not help but respond. Then afterwards she would be full of bitter regret, for with Kirkham it was merely a means to an end, while she had made a fool of herself.

Time and again she turned to planning Beth's elopement as a relief from her unhappiness. It was becoming increasingly obvious that she must arrange final details with Gerard Woodley. She hoped for a chance meeting, but as luck would have it a convenient encounter never materialised. There was nothing for it, she would have to send him a message.

Polly's brow frowned with apprehension when Melissa put the letter into her hand.

'I hope you know what you're doing,' she said. 'This could mean trouble.'

'Only if you are not discreet,' Melissa retorted. 'It is a perfectly innocent note.'

'You and I know that, as does Mr Woodley, presumably. But would his lordship take the same view?'

'His lordship would not even be interested,' said Melissa.

Polly's reply was an impolite snort as she set off for Gerard Woodley's town house.

Melissa had requested a 'chance' meeting in Hyde Park, and true enough there was Gerard Woodly strolling along as she approached in her carriage.

'Why, Mr Woodley, how fortuitous!' she exlaimed loudly enough to be heard by interested passers-by. 'I was longing to take the air for a little while.'

'Then may I have the pleasure and honour of offering you my arm and of being your escort?' he asked, courteously handing her from the carriage. Once they had begun walking he said in a low voice, 'Was that not splendidly done? Who would believe that we are a pair of conspirators?'

'You are enjoying this!' accused Melissa, half laughing.

'To be honest I am, Lady Kirkham. I am quite surprising myself. I had always thought I was a dull sort of fellow, but now I find I have a positive talent for intrigue.'

'I am glad to hear it. I hope you understood from my demeanour on the night of the concert that we are to go ahead with the elopement?'

'I did, I thank you. And Beth and I were able to exchange short messages. We have to use a cypher as a precaution, which is rather limiting, but she was able to tell me how happy she is at the prospect.'

'Good. We have established that Beth is to persuade her mother to let her stay with her aunt in Epsom. It will be easier for me to collect her from there — I will think of some tale to prevail upon the aunt to entrust Beth into my care. Then we will set out upon this devious route we mentioned. I thought of going westwards first, instead of the more usual direct route.'

'Capital! My thoughts exactly. I suggest we make for Bath.'

'Why Bath?'

'Firstly no one will remark upon your going there to take the waters, not after the Season. Secondly it is not an obvious stop on the route to Gretna Green. And thirdly my maternal grandfather lives there, giving me an excellent reason for travelling there.'

'Yes, I like the idea.' Melissa nodded approvingly. 'And only after Bath do we head northwards. We must work out a route.'

'I have already done so, my lady,' said Gerard,

slipping a folded paper into her hand. 'You can examine the details at your leisure. My suggestion is that you do not take too obvious a road northwards but make detours to various watering-places — Malvern, Droitwich, maybe even Buxton. That should put any pursuers off the scent. I have also included rough details of my cousins' routes. One has decided to dash up the Great North Road exciting as much notice as possible by his speed. The other will take the country roads but behave in a more furtive manner, which will naturally excite just as much interest as his brother. They will both make sure everyone is aware of their red hair and that they are each travelling with a lady. We mean to ensure that they are noticed. Needless to say, neither of them will finish up at Gretna. They intend to lead their pursuers a merry dance. My cousin, Robin, is even talking of travelling to the far north, beyond Aberdeen.'

'I fancy anyone trying to follow them will be fit for Bedlam by the time this is all over,' chuckled Melissa, then she had a sudden spasm of misgiving. 'You think our plans will succeed?' she asked.

'They cannot fail. My only anxiety is for you. Lord Kirkham will not object to your going touring? And you have got someone to escort you?'

'My husband will not object,' said Melissa with more conviction than she felt. 'And as for an escort, my brother James will accompany us.'

'I am glad to hear it. I would not have you inconvenienced for anything. What is to be done now?'

'Nothing except be prepared to embark upon the elopement swiftly, as soon as we hear that Beth is safely in Epsom with her aunt.'

'And do we go there together? Not to her aunt's

house, obviously, but I could await you outside the town?'

Melissa thought carefully. 'Better not,' she said. 'It is too risky. James and I will collect Beth, then we will have no more contact with you until. . .until. . .'

'Bath?' suggested Gerard.

'The ideal place,' beamed Melissa. 'No meetings, though! I care not how desperate you are to be with your beloved. We will exchange messages, nothing more, and so it must be at all our stopping places until we get to Gretna itself.'

'I can see you are a hard taskmistress,' smiled Gerard. 'However, I am happy to abide by your rules, strict as they are.' They had returned to the carriage now, and he prepared to help her in. As he took her hand to do so he raised it to his lips. 'Dear Lady Kirkham,' he said, 'Beth and I will be forever in your debt. Without you we would have had no chance of happiness.'

'Yes, you would,' replied Melissa firmly. 'All I am doing is ensuring the respectability of this enterprise. I am the chaperon.'

Gerard shook his head in smiling disagreement as he eventually aided her into the carriage. As she drove off she could see him standing, looking after her, his hat removed in salute, his red hair gleaming in the late winter sun.

She had been home barely quarter of an hour when Kirkham returned.

'Did you enjoy your afternoon's entertainment?' she asked.

'Not as much as you enjoyed yours, evidently,' he replied.

She looked up at him, puzzled by his abrupt tone. His face was grim, his lips tight with anger.

'What do you mean?' she demanded. 'And what has put you in this tantrum?'

'A tantrum! Is that what you call it?' he demanded with increasing fury. 'Do you not think I am justified?'

'Not until I hear the cause of all the fuss.'

'The fuss, as you deign to call it, madam, was caused by my being where I was not expected. You thought I had gone to the prize-fight, did you not? You depended upon it. Sadly your hopes were disappointed. An unlucky slip and a broken arm caused the fight to be abandoned early, so early I decided to while away the time in Hyde Park.'

'Why!' exclaimed Melissa. 'I was there too!'

'I know,' snapped Kirkham. 'I saw you. What is more I saw your paramour, your Woodley.'

'Mr Woodley is not my paramour. He is an acquaintance, nothing more. I have already told you so.'

'And I have already told you, madam, that I do not care about your amours. What I do care about is if you flaunt them in public. For heaven's sake show more discretion or——'

'Or?' demanded Melissa, incensed at his attitude.

'Or I will insist that you stop seeing him.'

'And if I refuse?'

'Then I will close this house, even though the Season is not over, and we will remove to my estate in Devonshire.'

'We?'

'Yes, we! You and I and the whole household!'

'Poof, I would refuse to go!'

'You would go, madam! Make no mistake about that!' From the way his eyes glittered with anger she had no option but to believe him.

'Goodness, I had no idea that jealousy could make you so fierce,' she taunted him.

'Jealous? Of you, madam?' His voice was heavy with sarcasm. 'You sadly overestimate your charms. I am concerned with preserving my family honour, nothing more. If you think otherwise then you are a bigger fool than I took you for.'

Melissa could think of no reply. She stalked past him and hurried up the stairs. Tears streamed down her cheeks as she ran. What had she hoped to achieve by provoking him? To hear a declaration of love? For her pains she had heard nothing but the truth. If she was now deeply hurt she had no one else to blame but herself. Yes, she had to agree with Kirkham — she was a fool indeed!

CHAPTER TEN

KIRKHAM'S temper did not improve much over the next few weeks. He was not alone. As the days grew warmer and the Season drew to a close everyone, including Melissa, seemed to become jaded. It was as if the bright spring sunshine was showing up the shabbiness of the ceaseless round of routs and balls and entertainments, making everything appear dingy and stale. These days Melissa and Kirkham scarcely exchanged one civil word in private. Melissa knew she was beginning to suffer from the strain, and she fancied Kirkham was feeling it too. It was a stupid, complex life they led—acting the perfect couple in public, squabbling in private, and being forced to behave like lovers in bed. No wonder there were times when they were reduced to exchanging silly insults.

'Why are you always like a bear with a sore head?' she protested after one verbal skirmish.

'Put it down to marriage, madam!' declared Kirkham bitterly.

'You make such a drama of it. How was I to know that you were reading Mr Southey's *Life of Nelson*? It was lying on the library table with no sign of anything to mark the pages.'

'That is because it fell out when you moved it!'

'Oh, for pity's sake!' It was all so petty. Suddenly she was moved to offer an olive branch. 'Perhaps I should have realised. It was on the table where you always leave your current book—I just did not think. Here, you take it.'

'No, thank you. I would not deprive you of the pleasure.'

She refused to give up. 'Can we not share it, as we used to do? We had some very agreeable evenings reading together.' Recollection of those pleasant interludes swept over her with happy longing.

'Thank you, but no. Our reading styles would not be compatible. You have the book. I will read it when you are done.'

She realised she had come close to pleading with him. That would never do. With a nod of agreement she took the volume and settled herself in her favourite library chair. There she remained for several hours, staring uncomprehendingly at the pages of the book, not taking in a word.

Melissa continued to be wary of Kirkham's threat to move the household to Devonshire. If things had been different she might have enjoyed the prospect. At the back of her head there lurked a crazy notion that if she and Kirkham were together somewhere quiet, away from the giddy social whirl, then maybe they would grow closer. She had no grounds for such an extraordinary idea, merely a persistent hope. Besides, although London born and bred, she found the idea of getting away from the stuffy city very agreeable — at the proper time. Kirkham's threat to leave before the Season ended was one she dared not take lightly. Therefore she had to be careful not to give him any provocation by meeting Gerald Woodley, or else the whole elopement would be in jeopardy.

It was very difficult arranging an elopement when the participants could not get together. A brief message exchanged during a chance encounter, perhaps at the opera or some other function, was the best she and Woodley could manage.

This is ridiculous, thought Melissa to herself. It is worse than poor Beth trying to avoid her mother, and without the justification.

It was no use, though. They had to go on being cautious. As for Beth she continued to attend the various social functions under the stern eye of her mother, and invariably escorted by Lord Beaucombe. She was beginning to look so worn and desperate that Melissa wondered at the heartlessness of Mrs Hurst in persistently denying her daughter a visit to the country. The waiting was an added strain to Melissa's nerves, and she pitied Beth and Woodley who, she felt, must be suffering even more. Then something happened that made her forget such anxieties for a while.

Kirkham had been away all day. It was no novelty. Of late he had taken to absenting himself from the house for long periods. This time he had mumbled something about a steeplechase having been arranged and the prospect of capital sport, confirming what she had long suspected — that he had returned to his old gambling ways. She tried to censure him in her mind for going back to such low pastimes, but somehow she could not summon up the earlier condemnation. The gambling she disapproved of as much as ever, it was towards Kirkham that her attitude had changed.

It was almost dark when a stirring in the hall announced his return. They were engaged to attend the theatre with friends that night, and Melissa, who had been waiting in the withdrawing-room with growing impatience, hurried out. At the sight of him her words of reproof died on her lips, for his broadcloth sporting-coat was torn and muddied, and on his cheek he sported a fine multicoloured bruise.

'What have you been up to?' she demanded. 'Are

you hurt? You were not foolish enough to ride in the steeplechase, were you?'

'No, I was not, madam. There is no need to berate me,' he retorted.

She knew his testy reply was in response to her own tone, for in her anxiety at his dishevelled appearance her voice had been sharp.

'I did not mean to scold,' she said more calmly. 'Seeing you in such a state startled me, that is all. You are sure you are not hurt?'

'Nothing the application of a little witch-hazel cannot ease.'

'But what happened?'

'A minor fracas, nothing more.'

'You have been brawling?' she asked incredulously.

'Not from choice.'

'Then for pity's sake tell me what happened!' she persisted.

'I can see I must, or I will get no peace. We tangled with a gang of highwaymen.'

'How terrible! Did you drive them off? Was anyone injured?'

'Of course we drove them off! We were more than a match for them.' Above the livid bruise his brown eyes sparkled with enthusiasm.

'You enjoyed it!' Melissa declared. 'You were in danger yet you enjoyed it!' Then she looked at him cautiously 'You speak of "we". Who else was with you? Mr O'Gallagher?'

'Of course Shaun was there. Trust him never to miss the chance of a decent mill.'

'You speak as though you were expecting to be attacked,' she said accusingly.

Kirkham shrugged his shoulders casually. 'We had some inkling,' he said.

'But who. . .? Of course! Lord Beaucombe!' Then suddenly a terrible anger swept over her, borne of her fear at the risks he had run. 'Of all of the stupid fools! Had you no more sense that to provoke a man like Beaucombe? Knowing that he was likely to attack, any sane man would have avoided the area, but not you! Oh no! You had to prove how brave you were by deliberately crossing his path. You might have been killed, don't you realise that? And——'

'Hold, madam! Hold!' Kirkham interrupted, taking her by the shoulders and giving her a gentle shake. 'I was in no real danger. Having been forewarned I made sure to have plenty of stout fellows with me—and I do mean stout!' He gave an unexpected grin. 'You should try sharing a carriage with Fox and a few of his friends; it is a crowded experience, I can promise you. There they were, fully armed and eager to try their mettle. Poor old Beaucombe and his brutes had a sad shock. They did not even have surprise on their side, there being few places on the Kent Road these days that afford cover to footpads and their sort. We had worked out where they would most likely be lying in wait.'

'Beaucombe knew where you would be and which route you would take!' exclaimed Melissa, unmollified. 'How did he find out?'

'That would take no great intelligence. Word of the proposed steeplechase has been abroad this fortnight or more. It was no secret that I meant to attend. Since the race was being held in the country south of Bermondsey it was most probable I would take the Kent Road. A little information and some guesswork was all Beaucombe needed. He was not to know that my sources of information were far superior to his.'

'And Beaucombe? What of him?'

Kirkham gave a satisfied chuckle. 'He will be quite

incapacitated for the next week or two, I made certain of that.' And he flexed knuckles that were swollen and bruised.

'Your poor hands!' cried Melissa, catching sight of them. 'What can I be about, questioning you when you are hurt? I will tend to them for you.'

'Thank you, but no,' he replied. Then, as if he sensed her feeling of rebuff, he added kindly, 'Fox will attend to me. He is much skilled in the treatment of cuts and bruises, it is part of his trade. You will see, by the time we are due to leave for the theatre he will have me as handsome as ever.'

'You cannot mean to go to the theatre after this!' protested Melissa.

'Certainly I do,' replied Kirkham, making for the stairs. 'Beaucombe may hope to disrupt my life but he will not succeed. His interruption on the Kent Road provided an enjoyable diversion. Now I intend to divert myself further with a pleasant evening at the theatre.' Part-way up the stairs he paused and, looking down over the ornately carved banisters, said, 'My one regret is that this incident has upset you. If I had used my common sense I would have entered the house by another door, so sparing you the distress of seeing me like this. It was never my intention to alarm you.'

It had been a long time since he had spoken to her in such a way, in a tone that was soft, almost tender. Melissa stood rooted to the spot, watching his tall figure continue to stride up the curving staircase. He had been gone from her sight for several minutes before she recollected herself enough to follow after and dress for the theatre.

The removal of Beaucombe from the social scene allowed Melissa to relax a little. His absence may have had another, unlooked for benefit. Although Mrs

Hurst, resplendent in burgundy velvet, was present at the next soirée, there was no sign of Beth.

'She was definitely invited,' breathed Gerard Woodley to Melissa as their paths crossed near the supper table. 'Can she be ill, do you think? Or. . .?'

His unspoken question was answered, thanks to the unwitting assistance of a stout dowager with an abiding curiosity.

'Your daughter is not with you, ma'am,' she asked of Mrs Hurst. 'Not indisposed, I hope?'

'She is a little under the weather, nothing more,' boomed Mrs Hurst. 'I have sent her to her aunt in Surrey for a short stay to take the country air. We cannot have her going into a decline with her wedding pending, can we?'

Melissa and Gerard exchanged delighted glances.

'I think it is time for me to go into a decline too,' Melissa breathed. 'I will let you know when I am ready to leave.'

'I will be ready,' he whispered in reply.

'I did not know Woodley was to be here tonight,' remarked Kirkham when she returned to him. 'Did he have much to say to you at the supper-table?'

'A mere exchange of pleasantries. There is nothing for you to look disapproving about, my lord.'

'I am glad to hear it.' Kirkham's reply was abrupt. 'To tell the truth I am finding this evening exceedingly dull. Would you have any objection to leaving now?'

'None at all,' replied Melissa honestly. Her swift response prompted him to look at her sharply.

'You are feeling well?' he asked. 'You look somewhat pale.'

'I am fatigued, nothing more. I shall be glad when the Season is at an end, it is exceedingly wearing.'

'I agree. I will tell you what! The Season has but a

short time left to run and we do not need to witness it to the bitter end. Why do we not leave London and go home to Devonshire?'

This was the last thing Melissa wanted just then. But she dared not show her true feelings.

'It sounds delightful,' she said, summoning up a smile. 'In the past I have had no opportunity to travel so I do not know that part of the country but I hear it is extremely beautiful.'

'It is,' responded Kirkham with enthusiasm. 'Nowhere is its equal in my estimation. You have not seen Kirkham Hall, either, have you? That is another treat to come. It is a fine place; my family have lived there since before Queen Elizabeth's time. It borders the sea, you know. Have you ever seen the sea?' Melissa shook her head. 'Then I quite envy you,' Kirkham declared, his enthusiasm increasing. 'To see it all with fresh eyes! That will be an experience indeed.'

He spoke with such emotion that for the first time Melissa regretted her involvement with the elopement. How wonderful it would have been to travel to the Devonshire countryside with Kirkham. More than ever her instinct suggested that once they were alone, away from the hurly-burly of the city, then their relationship might mellow. But she was committed to helping Beth and Woodley; they were relying on her.

'It seems I have a rare pleasure in store,' she said. 'Though I wonder if perhaps it could be postponed for a very short time?'

'For what reason?' asked Kirkham, his agreeable manner fading.

'I thought to spend two or three weeks at Bath. I am feeling distinctly jaded after these last months—you must remember I am not used to such high living, and my digestion has suffered. A short time taking the waters should set me up to enjoy the summer at Kirkham Hall.'

For a brief moment Kirkham looked quite disappointed. 'Sea-bathing!' he declared. 'That is what you need to set you up, and there are excellent facilities at Kirkham. . . But if you are set upon pouring spa water down yourself then I suppose we could go there *en route*. It means a detour, but nothing to signify.'

It had never occurred to Melissa that he might offer to come too.

'I could not drag you all that way!' she exclaimed, hoping she did not sound as alarmed as she felt. 'I know your opinion of Bath. You were only saying the other day how much you disliked the place.'

'That is true,' Kirkham admitted. 'There is no getting any peace in the place for the squeak of Bath-chair wheels and the rumble of disordered bowels. It is not a place I would go from choice.'

'Then you need not come. I am sure James could be persuaded to escort me.'

'Your brother? I would not trust him to escort a cart-load of hay safely!'

'Maybe not, but a cart-load of hay has no say in the matter. I have, and I will keep him up to the mark. Besides, did you not mention that Fox is to take part in a prize-fight soon? I could not tear you away from that.'

'On the contrary, that is one reason why I should come with you. If Fox is fighting he cannot be guarding you. The other fellows are excellent in their way, but I know Fox to be totally reliable.'

'Surely there can be no danger from Lord Beaucombe at the moment?' Melissa was feeling more and more desperate. 'Did you not say he would not be fit to appear in Society for some time? All the more reason for me to partake of the waters now, while you enjoy your prize-fight. After all, I am only proposing to go to Bath, not to Outer Mongolia. And James, with all his faults, would never leave me unprotected.'

The indecision on Kirkham's face made her hold her breath. Then, to her intense relief, he relaxed and said, 'Oh, very well. You go to Bath to take the waters if it amuses you. Personally I would pay good money not to contaminate my inside with the stuff, but you must please yourself. In due time I shall come to fetch you and we will drive to Devonshire together.'

Melissa held back a sigh of relief with the greatest difficulty. If she timed things properly she would be able to go to Gretna Green with Beth and be back at Bath before Kirkham arrived. Then, and only then, would she tell him of her part in the elopement.

'I do make one condition,' he said suddenly in a voice that made her blood run cold.

'Which is?'

'Upon no account is that brother of yours coming to Devonshire with us. He may go to perdition if he chooses, but he stays well away from Kirkham Hall. Do I make myself clear?'

'Perfectly, my lord,' said Melissa, her renewed relief making her feel quite faint. Evidently she was more in need of the Bath spa water than she had realised.

For the next few days she was in a turmoil of anxieties and anticipation as the day of departure drew closer. A reluctant Polly took the final message to Gerard Woodley, and brought back the tidings that he was departing for Bath that very day and would rendezvous with her there.

On the day of Melissa's own departure she could scarcely speak for nervousness. So much could go wrong.

'Are you sure you want to go?' demanded Kirkham.

'You look quite done up already and your journey has not yet begun.'

'It is merely excitement,' Melissa assured him, almost truthfully. 'I cannot recall ever having been on such a long coach journey before.'

'Then I hope that wretch of a brother of yours takes care of you,' Kirkham stated. 'I only wish it were Richards who was driving you. Perhaps I should come myself after all. . .?'

'No, there is no need, I promise you,' said Melissa hastily. 'Goodness, you have provided me with grooms and attendants enough. And I am sure Perkins will do very well. He is an experienced fellow.'

Melissa had considered it a stroke of good luck when Richards had sprained his wrist. He was an excellent coachman but absolutely devoted to Kirkham. How she was to persuade him to drive her to Bath via Epsom, and thence on to Gretna Green promised to be no easy matter. Now, because of Richards's minor accident, she had only Perkins, the under-coachman, to contend with. He was younger, livelier, and altogether more malleable. Melissa foresaw no problems with him.

She was right. Once it had been explained to him that they were taking part in an elopement—and he had been convinced it was not Lady Kirkham who was eloping—Perkins entered into the spirit of things with gusto. After being Richards's shadow for so long he relished a chance to show his prowess, and brought the elegant equipage to a standstill outside the Epsom home of Beth's aunt in record time.

'Lady Kirkham! You have no idea how delighted I am to see you!' Beth greeted her excitedly. 'Please permit me to present my aunt, Mrs Thomas, to you. Aunt dear, this is my very good friend, Lady Kirkham, and her brother, Mr Daubenay.'

'It is kind of you to honour us with a visit, Lady Kirkham, and you too, sir.' Angelica Thomas regarded Melissa with eyes that sparkled with intelligence. 'Will you both honour us further by taking refreshment with us after your long journey?'

'Nothing would be more delightful nor more welcome, ma'am,' said James, bowing extravagantly low over her hand. He was rewarded by an amused smile.

Mrs Thomas was an older version of Beth, small, trim-figured, and neat. What hair showed beneath her widow's cap was still predominantly glossy brown, like that of her niece. The only difference was in manner, for there was no trace of nervous diffidence about Mrs Thomas. She was all alert brightness, her demeanour kindly yet assured. No one would ever have described Angelica Thomas as a mouse. Observing her Melissa's heart sank. It was going to be no easy task persuading this self-possessed lady to let Beth come away with her.

'You would like Beth to be your travelling compaion?' said Mrs Thomas when, after the tea-tray had been removed, Melissa finally broached the true reason for her visit. 'That is extremely gracious of your ladyship. I am sure my brother, Beth's father, will give his permission immediately.'

'Beth's father?' repeated Melissa with dismay. 'Cannot you give your consent? Time is of the essence, you see.'

'I regret disrupting your ladyship's arrangements, but I am sure you appreciate my situation. I am merely Beth's aunt, responsible for her happiness and her welfare while she is in my charge, but that is all. It is for my brother to say whether or not she can accompany you.'

'But, Aunt, dear, you know Papa trusts your discretion entirely,' protested Beth. 'He would be perfectly happy for you to give your consent on his behalf.'

'I dare say he would,' replied Mrs Thomas, clearly surprised by this show of spirit from her timid niece. 'Nevertheless I would prefer it if we awaited his permission.'

Although Melissa, assisted with unexpected persistence from Beth, did her best to persuade Mrs Thomas to change her mind the elderly lady remained steadfast. Time was getting on, and it looked as though the elopement was doomed before it had begun. Two things had become evident during the course of the conversation. One was the genuine affection Angelica Thomas felt for her niece. The other was the equal contempt she had for Beth's mother. In desperation Melissa felt she had only one course open to her.

'Mrs Thomas,' she said. 'I will tell you the truth. There is far more behind this excursion than a wish to have Beth as my travelling companion. Are you acquainted with Mr Gerald Woodley?'

'I am not, though I know of him,' replied Mrs Thomas, ignoring Beth's alarmed gasp. 'My brother often mentions him in his letters. He thinks very highly of the young man, who is his neighbour.'

'The true purpose of our journey is to enable Beth to elope with Mr Woodley.'

'Oh, Lady Kirkham! How could you?' exclaimed Beth, bursting into tears.

Mrs Thomas did not react immediately. 'An elopement, you say,' she said at last with icy calm. 'Would you be kind enough to explain further?'

'Mr Woodley and your niece have long been in love,' began Melissa, above Beth's increased sobs. 'I understand him to be an excellent choice save for the fact that he has no title, which sadly in Mrs Hurst's eyes is an essential requirement for any suitor.'

'I know my sister-in-law's foolish ambitions well enough, thank you,' retorted Mrs Thomas.

Her tone of voice encouraged Melissa to continue.

'Unfortunately, it looks as though Mrs Hurst will have her way. . .' Melissa embarked upon a description of Beaucombe's character, leaving out nothing.

'Surely you can understand, dearest Aunt, how I could not bear to be the wife of a man like that?' cried Beth.

'I do indeed.' Mrs Thomas's mouth was a grim line. 'Your father would never stand for it, though.'

'But I could not appeal to him, could I?' said Beth softly.

'No, indeed.' The concerned expression on Mrs Thomas's face betrayed how fond she was of her brother. 'Ill as he is, he would come dashing to your defence, although it would cost him his life. Therefore you have settled upon elopement as a solution to your problems, eh? You realise that your reputation will be irrevocably lost.'

'That is where I will be of service,' said Melissa. 'I am to be Beth's chaperon.'

'And I am most grateful to Lady Kirkham for her help!' cried Beth. 'Mr Woodley is most careful of my reputation. Why, although he will be travelling the same route, we shall not even meet until we reach Gretna Green, all to protect my honour.'

'Ah, I see. I wondered at the absence of the young man at his own elopement,' commented Mrs Thomas drily. 'I was beginning to think that Mr Daubenay here was destined to play a greater part in the drama than he was admitting.'

'Who me?' declared James in some alarm. 'Madam,

I assure you I am simply here on escort duties. Can you imagine Lord Kirkham allowing my sister to travel the high road without some reliable male in attendance?'

'And that is you, sir? The reliable male?' The corners of Mrs Thomas's mouth twitched as she regarded James. Melissa realised she had summed up her brother's character pretty quickly.

'There is no one better!' James declared.

'There was no one else available!' amended Melissa, and was rewarded by a full-blown chuckle from Beth's aunt.

The laughter faded swiftly from Mrs Thomas's expression.

'I will admit I am in something of a quandary,' she stated. 'If I do nothing then it would appear that my beloved niece is destined to marry a monster. If I let her go with you I have no means of knowing where she will end up. I hear good reports of this Mr Woodley, but I would have to assess his character myself before I handed Beth over to him. There is only one possible solution. I must accompany your party! I realise it is an imposition, foisting myself uninvited upon someone of your rank, Lady Kirkham, but without me Beth does not leave this house. Furthermore, if I do not like the look of this Woodley fellow then I bring my niece back here unwed.'

Mrs Thomas sat very upright in her chair, as if braced for opposition. A stunned silence reigned in the elegant withdrawing-room.

'Will it take you long to prepare yourself, madam?' asked Melissa when she had recovered from her astonishment.

'We can be off within the hour,' said the intrepid Mrs Thomas. 'Beth, my love, please go and help Kitty with the packing. It is to be done decently, mind. None of this romantic nonsense of setting off with naught but a hairbrush and a clean pair of stockings. If you are to wed it will be as stylishly as conditions permit.'

Once the delighted girl was out of earshot she turned to Melissa. 'Now, my lady, I have a question which will seem impertinent but which must be asked. Why are you going to such trouble to help my niece?'

A dozen half-true excuses filtered through Melissa's mind, but she discarded them. Only the absolute truth would be accepted by those sharp eyes.

'In a way I am partly responsible for Beth's predicament,' she said. 'My marriage to Lord Kirkham is quite recent and was—er—somewhat unconventional. I did not know it until after the wedding but if it had not been for my intervention she would most likely have married Kirkham.'

'For someone who married her sweetheart Beth seems exceedingly fond of you.'

'Oh, Beth was not attached to Kirkham, but she would have been happy with him eventually, I am convinced of it—she could not have helped herself, for Kirkham is the kindest of men and would have treated her extremely well. You can see that I had to intervene since I was the unwitting cause of her being sacrificed to that Beaucombe brute.'

'I can see that Lord Kirkham made his own choice well,' replied Mrs Thomas knowingly. 'If this Woodley matches his reputation then maybe everything will turn out for the best. Now if you will excuse me. . .'

Mrs Thomas was as good as her word. An hour later they were on the road once more; the necessary hiring of another carriage to take the extra baggage and Mrs Thomas's maid, with Polly as well, did not delay them. As they rode out of Epsom Melissa decided that the unexpected addition of Beth's aunt only added to their credibility. Even the elderly carriage rumbling on behind played its part, for who in their right mind would embark upon an elopement so encumbered, and minus the potential bridegroom?

The journey to Bath went smoothly, so smoothly that Melissa gradually relaxed and began to enjoy the scenery. Since she had never travelled it was all new to her, and she was hard put to it to remember her dignity as a member of the aristocracy and not enthuse over every novelty. All that was missing was Kirkham. His presence would have enhanced her enjoyment, and somehow she was certain he would not have minded how much she exclaimed with delight along the way.

At first the possibility of pursuit seemed remote. Only when they rejoined the busy Bath road were their nerves stretched by the rapid approach of some speeding curricle or a dashing coach and pair. The inclination to hurry too, to get as much of their journey over as speedily as possible, was very tempting. However, upon the advice of Mrs Thomas, volubly supported by Perkins, they broke their journey at a tolerable inn and reached Bath without too much fatigue.

'Mr Woodley does know the address of our lodgings?' seemed to be Beth's only worry.

She had no need to be anxious. A message from Woodley awaited them, suggesting that they visit the Pump Room that afternoon.

'He will be there but he will not greet us or anything,' said Beth, who had had her own private correspondence in the same hand. 'He merely wishes to be assured that we have arrived safely.'

'He is cautious and discreet, I will give him that,' said Mrs Thomas, then she chuckled. 'I wonder what he will make of my presence in your midst? If he is not up to much I may frighten him off. I am only funning, you silly miss,' she added, laughing at Beth's indignant expression.

A day's rest was all they permitted themselves in Bath. Melissa was sorry. She liked what little she saw of the elegant city and would dearly have loved to stay longer.

I shall come again on the way back of course, when Kirkham comes to meet me, she comforted herself. And no doubt I can make a longer stay at some other time, though knowing Kirkham's opinion of the place any prolonged visit would have to be alone.

Then she remembered that any future visit to Bath would be alone, anyway, since she did not intend to remain with Kirkham any longer than was necessary. The thought was a depressing one.

Their small cavalcade travelled northwards at a leisurely pace, breaking their journey at preordained places of interest. At every stop Gerald Woodley announced his presence by a discreet letter, nothing more.

'I must say this is a most well-organised elopement,' said Mrs Thomas approvingly. 'Our route has been carefully worked out, and at every stop we have had excellent lodgings awaiting us.'

'That was Mr Woodley's doing,' replied Melissa. 'See, here I have the instructions he sent me for our journey. It was he who decided which roads to take, he who chose our lodgings for us. And a very good choice he has made thus far.'

'I only hope he had found comfortable accommodation for himself,' declared Beth with concern.

'From what I hear of your Mr Woodley I am sure he will cope,' said Mrs Thomas. 'I am beginning to be most impressed by that young man. He is discreet and thoughtful, as well as having spirit. A rare combination.'

'He is certainly not one who ignores attention to detail,' smiled Melissa. 'This itinerary. . .' and she waved the sheaf of papers in her hand '. . . has been amended more than once because he was not satisfied.'

'I fancy the organisation of this elopement did not fall to Mr Woodley alone,' Mrs Thomas stated. 'I am sure you had a major part in it, Lady Kirkham, and you are both to be congratulated. Certainly the idea of setting a false trail — nay, two false trails — has worked particularly well. We have had no hint of pursuit. A masterly stroke!'

'I would love to know how Mr Woodley's cousins are faring,' Melissa chuckled. 'One had declared his intention of pressing on to the northern limits of the land, the other prefers to go round in circles.'

'Then I am almost sorry for any representative of my sister Hurst who has the luckless task of trying to follow either of them,' said Mrs Thomas, laughing too. 'Now where is it we lie tomorrow? Buxton, did you say?'

So far the elopement had gone with scarcely a hitch. It was at Buxton that their plans came nearest to encountering trouble. The others had gone walking, attracted by the superb scenery, but Melissa had remained behind. She was finding the excessive coach travel upsetting, something she had never anticipated. It was as she rested in their private sitting-room that she overheard voices. Two gentlemen, obviously acquaintances, were sitting in the garden below her open window.

'You are newly up from Town then,' said one. 'And what is the latest *on dit*?'

'Precious little,' replied the other. 'The only gossip I

heard was that young Woodley had eloped with some heiress or other.'

At once Melissa stiffened, her book falling unnoticed onto the floor.

'Young Woodley? Not Gerard Woodley?'

'The very one.'

The first gentleman gave a snort of laughter. 'Well, I can give the lie to that piece of news,' he said. 'What need has Woodley to run off with any heiress? He is very plump in the pocket himself. Besides, I assure you I saw him in Bath with my own eyes but a few days since. He was visiting his maternal grandfather, General Hardcourt. A martyr to the gout is the poor old gentleman.'

'You are sure you were not mistaken?'

'Absolutely certain. Why, we had a long conversation. He mentioned doing a little touring when his visit to his grandfather was done, the Welsh Borders perhaps, then maybe across to Malvern. I was able to give him directions to some excellent places of interest. He was most grateful. Took notes. . .' The first gentleman gave another snort of laughter. 'Young Woodley cannot be a very ardent lover if he prefers to push his grandsire about Bath in his chair rather than be with his beloved. No, you may depend on it, someone remarkably short of gossip has noticed that he and this Miss Whatever-her-name-is were absent from Town at the same time and tried to make mischief. Eloping indeed!'

There was the crunch of boots on gravel and a faint whiff of tobacco, then the voices faded as the two gentlemen moved away.

Melissa was both shaken and elated. Elated at the success of their carefully planned subterfuge, yet shaken that they had come so close to ruin. There had always been a chance that they would encounter some acquaintance. It was a risk that could not be avoided. Now she hoped that Gerard had already left Buxton and did not meet up with the unknown gentlemen.

The others greeted her account of what had happened with interest.

'That was a close shave,' observed James. 'Not that it would have signified. Woodley need only have said that he had changed his plans and wandered further than he had originally intended, or something of that sort. In the absence of any lady no doubt they would have laughed over the so-called elopement.'

'It certainly shows the prudence of us travelling in two parties,' said Mrs Thomas. 'And it also reminds us not to get careless. Perhaps we should not wander abroad too much, where we are likely to meet people. And we should insist upon dining privately.'

James looked rather downcast. His behaviour on the journey had been impeccable, but Melissa suspected that being the perfect escort was proving something of a strain.

'Bear up,' she said in his ear. 'There is not much further to go now. Then when you and I return alone there will be twenty guineas in your pocket to spend.'

'You would bribe your own brother?' He tried to sound indignant.

'Yes.'

'Good. I accept the offer.'

When they reached Carlisle Beth was thrown into an agony of anticipation. She could not believe that soon perfect happiness would be hers, and she kept imagining every disaster, conceivable and inconceivable, which might prevent her from marrying her Woodley. Only when they reached their lodgings in Gretna and the young man himself enfolded her in his arms did she agree to stop worrying.

'I understand you wish to marry my niece!' stated Mrs Thomas bluntly, once the lovers had disentangled themselves and the introductions had been made.

'Yes, if you please, ma'am.'

'I do not know whether or not it does please yet.' Mrs Thomas regarded him with a stern eye. 'Perhaps you will be kind enough to spare me an hour of your time after we have dined. In this instance I stand for my brother and therefore I must inform you, sir, that if I am not completely satisfied with you then there will be no marriage.'

Gerard, looking somewhat taken aback by this ultimatum, managed to reply, 'Certainly, madam.'

During the interview it was Melissa whose nerves were on edge. Could they have schemed so hard and come so far to end in failure? Oddly enough Beth sat contentedly with her embroidery.

'I do not know why you are in such a pother, dear Lady Kirkham,' she said. 'Of course my aunt will approve of Gerard. How could she help herself?'

She proved to be right. Gerard emerged from the interrogation looking rather wan but triumphant.

'I have passed with flying colours,' he said. 'Your aunt approves of me as your prospective husband.'

'I never doubted it for a minute,' said Beth happily, kissing him on the cheek.

'At times I felt it was a close-run thing,' grinned Gerard. 'Mrs Thomas has no connections with the Inquisition, I trust? If not then she has missed her vocation.'

'Where is the good lady?' asked Melissa, much relieved.

Gerard gave a laugh. 'She has commandeered your

brother as escort, Lady Kirkham, and is now on her way to beard the minister in his own manse.'

'To make arrangements for the wedding?' asked Beth and Melissa in unison.

'To confirm that he is fully qualified and licensed to perform the ceremony,' laughed Gerard. 'My love, it is as well I had not planned a fake wedding. Against your aunt I would have stood no chance.'

Having given the bridegroom her approval Mrs Thomas returned to announce that the minister, too, would pass muster.

'All is arranged,' she declared. 'The wedding will be tomorrow afternoon. In the smithy!' She gave a little shudder at such informality. 'However, despite the circumstances this wedding shall be as stylish as we can manage. There is a tolerable florist in the town—I think decent bride-flowers are so important! And I have bespoke an elegant repast for afterwards. Now I suggest that we all get some sleep. Tomorrow will be a busy day.'

To the very end everything about the elopement went well. True, the minister did regard Mrs Thomas somewhat warily, and remarked that the number of witnesses was uncommon in a fugitive marriage. But the blacksmith, who had been denied neither his traditional role nor fee as witness, remarked, 'Och, the more the merrier!'

For all its unconventionality the wedding proved to be charming. Beth looked delightful in a fine pink silk gown sprigged with white, a chaplet of pink rosebuds on her glossy brown hair, a posy of the same blooms in her hand. As for Gerard Woodley, he stood so proud and handsome beside his bride that Melissa felt a lump rise in her throat. She feared she was something of an expert in unconventional weddings; memories of the dank musty church where she had become Kirkham's wife flooded into her mind. How she wished she had some pleasing memories of the occasion to cherish, as Beth and Woodley would cherish their recollections of this day.

First thing next morning the newly-weds, along with Mrs Thomas, prepared to journey south.

'We are eager to return to Mr Hurst as soon as possible,' Gerard said. 'Our great fear is that he may have heard rumours and become agitated. We wish to set his mind at rest.'

'And I want to reassure him that everything was managed with the greatest decorum,' added Mrs Thomas. 'For all this was an elopement, he need not fear the slightest stain upon his daughter's reputation.'

'That will mean much to him,' said Beth. 'And it was all due to you, dear, dear Lady Kirkham.'

'Indeed it was. I do not think we can ever thank you enough,' agreed Gerard. 'Are you sure you do not wish to travel with us? It seems most churlish, leaving you and Mr Daubenay behind.'

'I promise you we are quite content,' Melissa assured him. 'To be honest I would rather relish an extra day's rest; then we will make our way south-west, for I go to my husband's estate in Devonshire.'

'And Mr Daubenay?' enquired Mrs Thomas.

'I fancy he will eventually look for a more lively venue,' smiled Melissa.

The wedding-party departed with smiles and tears, thanks and fond farewells. Melissa found it very quiet and peaceful after they had gone, for James had wandered off on some pursuit of his own. She tried to read, but such a lot had happened in the last two or three weeks that she could not concentrate. It seemed incredible that the elopement had gone so smoothly. Only one minor alarum at Buxton and not a hint of pursuit. She could hardly believe their luck. Anyone who came after Beth now would be too late.

Scarcely had the thought crossed her mind than there was a commotion below as a vehicle came thundering in at great speed, with a tremendous rumbling of wheels and pounding of hooves. Squawking hens fluttered out of the way, while every dog in the place began to bark. Intrigued, Melissa looked out of the window. She could see little more than the roof and the steaming team, who were already being unharnessed by the ostlers, but she could make out that it was a light, stylish conveyance, built for speed. Below stairs everything was in uproar because of this new arrival. Melissa wondered if perhaps their pursuers might have belatedly caught up with them. Her suspicions were confirmed by the sound of booted feet running up the stairs and hurrying along the corridor towards her sitting-room. She braced herself as the door was flung open, expecting to see a stern stranger, some relative of Mrs Hurst. Instead she found herself confronting Kirkham. A white-faced, grim-visaged Kirkham.

'Well?' he demanded in a voice that was no more than a snarl. 'Where is he? There is no point in lying, madam. I know you are not here alone. Where is he, I say? Where are you hiding your lover?'

CHAPTER ELEVEN

THE situation was so ludicrous that Melissa almost burst out laughing. To be accused of having a lover! Mirth bubbled up inside her at the idea; but one look at her husband's angry face and she controlled herself.

'I have no idea where you got such a Gothic notion, my lord,' she said. 'I have no lover. I am here alone with James.'

'And you expect me to believe that? You came all the way up to Gretna with your brother for the delights of the scenery, I suppose?'

'No, I——'

'Do you deny that Gerard Woodley is here?'

'Yes, I do! He——'

'It will not profit you to lie, madam. I know you came with Woodley. Where is he hiding? Or has he deserted you already?'

'Of course he has not deserted me——'

'Ah, the steadfast lover to the end. Where is he, then? Do not try to deny that he is about the place somewhere, or that you and he have eloped together, for I have written proof.' He flung a bundle of papers into her hands.

The first she recognised at once as the rough copy of the itinerary for their journey, much crossed out and altered, but quite legible. The final piece was a torn portion of letter in Gerard Woodley's hand. The message was incomplete. It said, '. . .will await you at Bath . . .we will be together. . .complete happiness. . . Your devoted and grateful servant. GW.'

'Where did you get these?' Melissa demanded.

'Do you deny that they are yours?'

'No, I do not! These are my private papers! How dare you take them? It is despicable!'

'More despicable than for a married woman to besmirch her husband's honour by running off with another man? How careless of you to leave such incriminating evidence behind. It told me exactly where to find you. But why Gretna? That is what puzzles me. Were you intending to add bigamy to your other infamies?'

'No, I was not——'

'Then you were merely indulging some romantic fantasy? I could almost pity Woodley; he has no idea what he has taken on——'

'Do you intend ever to let me speak?' demanded Melissa angrily. 'Or have you made your mind up to condemn me out of hand?'

'If you would cry mitigating circumstances, I warn you, you are wasting your breath.'

'Will you hear me out?' Melissa cried, thoroughly exasperated. 'Firstly, yes, Mr Woodley was here, but he left this morning. By now he is somewhere on the road between here and Carlisle with his wife.'

'His wife?' For the first time Kirkham's anger faltered.

'Yes, Gerard Woodley did elope—with Beth Hurst, not me. I came merely as Beth's chaperon.'

'Beth Hurst? Chaperon?' Kirkham sank on to the nearest chair.

'It was the only hope they had. Mrs Hurst was planning to marry Beth off to that monster, Beaucombe. Did you not know? Such a terrible thing could not be allowed. To elope was the obvious solution.'

'I do not understand why you were involved. You say you acted as chaperon, but why you?'

'I like Beth, we have become good friends. Besides, if I had not married you she would most likely have become Lady Kirkham in my stead, and at least have been safe.'

'How I wish she had!' exclaimed Kirkham, suddenly leaping to his feet again. 'She would have been a much less bothersome wife! It is no use, madam, you almost had me persuaded by your Banbury tale. Almost but not quite. You forget I know how glib your tongue can be. Travelling all this way to be chaperon to Beth Hurst! It is too preposterous.'

'It is the truth, I tell you——' Before Melissa could say more she was interrupted by a knock at the door, and the landlady entered.

'Your pardon, my lady, my lord.' The woman bobbed a curtsy. 'I've had his lordship's valise put in your ladyship's room. I hope that was right? And since your lordship hasna brought a manservant would you like my Dougie to unpack and attend you? He's fair experienced in such things.'

'That sounds very satisfactory,' put in Melissa before Kirkham could speak. The mood he was in he was likely to roar forth some angry oath, and she had noted the look of eager inquisitiveness on the landlady's face. 'And would you be kind enough to send up some wine for his lordship? He is in sore need of refreshment, having come here with all haste in the hope of offering his congratulations to Mr and Mrs Woodley, only to miss them by an hour.'

'Oh, what a shame!' The landlady's curiosity melted into sentimentality. 'A rare wedding it was that you missed, my lord. I tell you frankly I worry about some of the marriages we see here, for I fear the poor brides have not a shred of reputation left. It was a rare treat to see a ceremony where all the proprieties were observed and everything done with such decorum. Why, Mrs Woodley—Miss Hurst as was—had not one chaperon but two. Och, I'll fetch your lordship's wine myself. The finest our cellars can offer,' she added, departing hastily in the face of Kirkham's growing impatience.

There was a long silence after she had gone.

'Two chaperons?' Kirkham said at last.

'Yes, Mrs Thomas, Beth's aunt, was with us. Did I not mention her?'

'You did not. This aunt, she was with you all the time?'

'Yes, from the moment I fetched Beth from her house at Epsom.'

'And Woodley—where did you meet up with him?'

'Not until we reached Gretna. He is a very proper young man, determined not to harm Beth's good name in any way. That was why he travelled separately.'

There was another silence, more prolonged than the first.

'It would seem that apologies are necessary,' said Kirkham at length. 'I most humbly beg your pardon for my harsh insults and for having mistrusted you. You were speaking the truth. I should never have doubted your word.'

'You should never have doubted my integrity,' retorted Melissa. 'And your apologies do not include these.' She waved a hand at the papers strewn on the table. 'You went through my private things! How could you have stooped so low!'

'I did not!' Now it was Kirkham's turn to protest indignantly. 'They were found by one of the servants, and passed to me for safekeeping.'

Melissa considered his words carefully.

'No,' she said. 'That cannot be. This copy of the elopement plans was locked away in my bureau, I am sure of it.'

'Are you now doubting my word?' demanded Kirkham.

'Of course not, though I have my suspicions about this servant. Who was it? One of the maids?'

'No.'

'Then who? And how did they come by this letter? I was always careful to tear up my correspondence on the elopement and burn it in my dressing-room fireplace.'

'You did not trust me enough to confide in me?'

'I did not trust your temper,' replied Melissa. 'I could not take the risk. You were quite likely to forbid me to help Beth and Woodley out of pique.' She sniffed at the fragment of letter. 'There, it still smells slightly of burning. I thought it did. And look! The edges have been cut with scissors, when I know I tore them roughly. Someone did not want it known that they had been rummaging about in my fireplace. And going through my bureau,' she added. 'Who was this servant, and what sort of a story did he or she spin you?'

'That he had found the papers in the garden.'

'Stuff and nonsense. So it was a male servant! And one adept at undoing locks without a key... Was it Pentecost?'

'Yes,' admitted Kirkham, looking uncomfortable. 'He will be turned off without a character the instant we get back to Devonshire. I should have listened to you and dismissed him months ago, when you first discovered his dishonesty.'

'He cannot have discovered these papers by chance,' said Melissa thoughtfully. 'I fear he must have often gone through my things in the hope of finding something incriminating. What a grudge he must have borne against me for all these months.'

'How am I ever going to apologise to you?' uttered Kirkham suddenly. 'I have mistrusted you and insulted you. As if that were not enough my own manservant, someone whom I should never have kept in my service, has behaved disgracefully towards you and tried to stir up trouble between us. What on earth can I say. . .? What can I ever do to make amends?'

He looked so distressed that Melissa's heart went out to him in an instant. 'You have no need to be despondent,' she said softly. 'I should have confided in you about the elopement. Now I consider the matter I see how it must have seemed to you, especially when supported by Pentecost's contribution. Apologies are not necessary. We will forget the whole incident.'

'You are too generous; when I recall some of the things I said to you. . . I will make it up to you, I promise.' He paused. 'If you want the plain truth, I was convinced that you really had eloped with Woodley, and I did not like the idea. I did not like the idea at all.'

Melissa drew in her breath and waited. Was he going to say he cared for her? Was now the moment when he would declare his love?

No declaration came.

'Is there anything you would like to have?' he asked. 'Anywhere you would like to go? You have only to name it. You expressed an interest in Bath. I do not suppose you had much chance to see the place on your travels? Shall we go there? We could take a house and spend as long as you like.'

For a moment Melissa felt only disappointment. Then the tone of his voice registered upon her senses. He sounded ardent and tender and—yes, relieved—as if he were glad that things had turned out well in the end. In addition he was standing very close, close enough for her to feel the beat of his heart.

'I—I think I have had enough of journeying for the present,' she said unsteadily. 'Do you know what I would really like?'

'No.' His lips were so near she felt the soft fan of his breath on her cheek.

'I would like to go to Kirkham Hall.'

'You could not have said anything that would have pleased me more.' His arms came about her, holding her closely. 'Oh, Melissa, how much better it is when we do not quarrel.'

She never got a chance to answer, for his lips pressed down on hers, warm and demanding. Her response was immediate, clinging to him as if she would never let him go, her mouth hungrily taking all the kisses he had to offer. The recent miseries and uncertainties faded away as if they had never existed. She was in Kirkham's embrace. She wanted nothing more. Eventually they were forced to part, but only to the distance of a loving whisper.

'How could you imagine that I cared for Gerard Woodley,' she said softly. 'What sort of competition is he for you?'

'None, I hoped. But jealousy makes uncertain fellows of us all.'

Jealousy? He had been jealous of Woodley? Melissa caught her breath with sudden happiness. This was what she had wanted to hear. Before she could speak he said, 'What an inconsiderate fellow I am. Here I am holding you and kissing you with the dirt of the roads still upon me.'

'I do not mind,' said Melissa. 'Providing you continue to hold me and kiss me.'

'I have married a hussy!' exclaimed Kirkham delightedly. 'I thought I knew all about you yet still you continue to surprise me.'

'No one could ever consider our marriage to be dull.'

'True.' Kirkham gave a chuckle, then with one finger proceeded to follow the line of her cheek. 'There is one thing I said earlier that I wish to disclaim.'

'We said we would forget about our earlier words. It was all a misunderstanding.'

'Maybe, but this I must take back. I would not rather have Beth Hurst as my wife. Delightful biddable girl that she is, I fear I would have found her too quiet. I have grown accustomed to a marriage filled with the unexpected. Anything less would be tame by comparison.'

Melissa scarcely knew how to reply. It was the first time he had ever expressed contentment with their marriage. More important, it was the first time he had even intimated that he was happy she was his wife.

'Kirkham. . .' she began, trying to find the right words to express the depth of her emotion. 'Kirkham——'

She got no further, for lively footsteps and a cheery whistle warned them that they were about to be disturbed.

When James saw Kirkham his expression grew decidedly wary.

'I did not know you were here, my lord,' he said in an artificially hearty voice. 'If you were hoping for a share of the wedding meats I am afraid we've guzzled the lot.'

'It serves me right for being johnny-come-lately,' said Kirkham, matching him for false bonhomie. 'Now if you will excuse me, I have not long arrived and must rid myself of all this dust.' In the doorway he paused. 'Your sister and I are going down to my estate in

Devonshire. We would be delighted if you would care to accompany us for a visit.'

James was too taken aback by the invitation to do more than splutter a response. 'Kirkham's in a dashed good mood,' he said as the door closed behind his brother-in-law. 'I expected him to give me a taste of his boot at the very least, yet he invites me to stay. Do you think he meant it? You see, there is this fellow I know in Brighton. . .'

Remembering Kirkham's dire threats against James and his refusal to have him on the premises, Melissa smiled. 'I am sure he will not be offended if you give him your excuses,' she said.

'Splendid. And, Mel, you said something about twenty guineas if I was a good boy, and I have been good, haven't I?'

'Exemplary,' replied Melissa. 'And the money shall be yours when we part. That way,' she went on, laughing at his frustrated groan, 'that way it will remain in your pocket a little longer. Who knows, it might even last until you reach Brighton.'

That evening she and Kirkham dined alone. He had been so attentive to her, so charming and affectionate, that she feared such a state of affairs could not last. But no, throughout the evening he was as charming as ever; and later, in the big feather-bed they shared, he made love to her in a way that drove away all bleak memories of her earlier experiences.

This is how it should be, she thought to herself afterwards as she lay in his arms, happily drowsy. And she felt terribly sorry for those unfortunate people who had never shared her experience.

Next morning they set off for home. Home! Melissa had never set eyes on Kirkham Hall, yet already that was how she thought of it. Kirkham travelled in the coach with Melissa, while a delighted James was entrusted with the stylish chariot. Soon after they set off Kirkham began to have second thoughts.

'I hope that brother of yours will go carefully. Perhaps I was foolish to entrust him with such a speedy vehicle. I fear he will run my poor beasts into the ground.'

'Do not worry, your horses will get plenty of rest,' Melissa assured him. 'We will find them waiting at every turnpike — James will be relying upon you to pay the tolls.'

'Good,' said Kirkham with evident relief. 'I never thought that having long pockets would turn out to be a blessing. Now we can relax and enjoy our travels.'

And enjoy them they did. Without the tensions and restraints of the elopement preying on her Melissa found even more things in the passing countryside to interest her. Her earlier instinct had been right — Kirkham did not mind how much she enthused. In fact he seemed to take delight in encouraging her.

At Bath James reluctantly handed over the reins of the chariot to one of the grooms, discreetly and gratefully accepted the twenty guineas — now swelled to fifty thanks to Kirkham's generosity — and bade them goodbye.

'Now home,' said Kirkham thankfully.

As they travelled further west Melissa was forced to admit that he had not exaggerated about the beauty of the landscape. They travelled through lush meadows, orchards in full blossom, and between high hedges coloured with the flowers of late spring. Her first sight of the sea reduced her to an awed silence. Nothing of her life in London had prepared her for anything so vast or so beautiful.

Her contentment faltered when she first beheld

Kirkham Hall. Its size was daunting, much larger than the house in Hanover Square.

'That is because we have been adding on bits for the last three hundred years,' said Kirkham, proudly regarding his home.

Melissa had certainly never seen anything to equal it for elegance and beauty. Her early fears that she would never find her way about soon faded. Kirkham's knowledge of the history of the Hall was extraordinary, and he took real pleasure in showing her round.

'My grandmother is coming in a month's time; she always passes the summer here,' said Kirkham. 'Until then let's spend our time pleasurably together.'

The next few days were blissfully happy, as they explored the house and grounds. Melissa liked it best when they went down to the cove on the fringe of the estate.

'You are a true sea-urchin,' Kirkham would laugh as she gathered shells and coloured pebbles, not caring how much the waves soaked the hem of her dress.

Melissa had instinctively felt that all would be well if only she and Kirkham could be alone; and now it had happened exactly as she had dreamed. More than that, she was growing increasingly certain that her hopes would soon be fulfilled.

One morning they went for a stroll through the park and came to a halt beside one of the paddocks.

'It is high time you saw more of the estate,' remarked Kirkham, casting a practised eye over the splendid horseflesh that happily grazed on the rich grass. 'We must see about getting you a decent mount. Now which animal would be suitable? Ah, I think she has chosen herself. She will be ideal for you.' He stretched out a hand and patted the flanks of a pretty dappled mare that had approached.

Melissa laughed as she stroked the soft grey muzzle. 'But will I be ideal for her?' she asked.

'She seems to have taken a fancy to you already, therefore I foresee no problems. It is lovely riding weather. Shall I order her to be saddled up, along with my Zeus, so that we might go for a canter?'

'The idea is an excellent one. There is only one snag. I cannot ride.'

'Not ride?' Kirkham looked astounded.

'I have never had the opportunity to learn. Besides, in the region of Newgate horse-riding is not a popular pastime.'

'Of course not! Your pardon, it never occurred to me. . . Not that it is important. I shall teach you. You would like to learn?'

'Certainly, but. . .'

'That is settled, then. I shall enjoy teaching you, and Shadow here is patience itself. You will learn quickly, I am sure of it. How can you help it with such a mount and such a teacher? Shall we have our first lesson this afternoon?'

'That is very kind, but I think I would like to postpone learning to ride for a while.'

'I do not understand why. You are not afraid of horses, are you? Because I promise Shadow is the gentlest creature blessed with four legs.'

'No, I am not afraid. How could I be?' Melissa continued caressing the mare's velvety nose. 'I do have a sound reason for the delay, though. You see, it may not be a wise thing to do at the moment. I was not going to mention it yet, not until there was no possibility of doubt, but I suspect—nay I am almost certain—that I am with child.'

'What!' Kirkham stared at her incredulously.

'I am expecting a child, my lord. Therefore I think I should postpone horse-riding until after the event.'

'A child, you say. . .? A baby. . .? You are expecting a child. . .? But when. . .?'

Melissa laughed at his bemused expression.

'Yes, my lord, a child! Surely you have no cause to be so surprised? If my calculations are correct it should be born in December.'

'But this is wonderful!' The bewilderment left his expression, to be replaced by delight. 'It is what I want above everything! The best news a fellow could have!' He flung his arms about her and would have swung her off her feet in his excitement, but thought better of it just in time. 'You are happy about it?' he asked softly. 'I know that the begetting of this child. . . Well, the circumstances could have been better, but I would be extremely sorry if you found the prospect distasteful.'

'I promise you I am very happy,' she assured him. 'To be honest, in the beginning I was not sure what my feelings would be. As you say, circumstances were not ideal. But since the first moment I began to suspect I was pregnant there was no doubt. I want this child as much as you do.'

'I am glad. Very, very glad.' Kirkham's relief was heartfelt as he took her hand and kissed it tenderly. Then his tone became brisk. 'There will be no riding lessons for you this afternoon. We will send for the doctor instead, to make sure you are given the best possible care Here I have been dragging you about the place when you should have been resting.'

'I promise you I am not an invalid,' said Melissa with a smile. 'Having a baby is a perfectly normal function. I have no intention of spending the next few months lying on a sofa, not when I feel perfectly well.'

'You are really in good health? You are not saying it just to reassure me?'

'I feel splendid. I do have occasional feelings of nausea, but I understand that is perfectly usual.' She gave a chuckle. 'There were occasions on the road to Gretna when I wondered whether I was suffering from my condition or from the bumpy ride. However, I did not disgrace myself. . . What is the matter?' she asked, for his face had grown suddenly grim. 'What have I said?'

'Are you telling me that you knew you were already pregnant when you embarked upon this journey to Scotland?' he demanded. There was no laughter or joy in his expression now.

'I did not know. I suspected it certainly, but it takes a time to be absolutely sure.'

'You had a strong suspicion, though. Knowing how much it meant to me you still risked my unborn child by travelling the full length of the country in a jolting carriage, along rutted roads? What were you thinking of, madam? Tell me that!'

The swift change of mood stunned Melissa. 'It—it was too early. . . I—I did not think there would be a risk. . .' she stammered.

'Aye, that is the truth! You certainly did not think! Why was it so imperative that you should go to Gretna! Had not Beth Hurst enough chaperons with her aunt that you should chance miscarrying?'

'We did not know that Mrs Thomas was coming with us, not until we got to Epsom,' cried Melissa. 'I had to go.'

'You felt you had a greater obligation to Woodley and his bride than you had to me or our child, is that it? Yet not two minutes since, you were telling me how happy you were at the coming event and how much you wanted the babe. And, like a fool, I believed you. I even believed that your attitude towards me had changed, that you had begun to care——' he broke off. 'I can scarcely credit my own stupidity.'

'But I do care for you!' cried Melissa. 'I lo——'

'Do not make things worse!' he interrupted harshly. 'You certainly did not behave as if you cared, either for me or the child.'

'You do not understand,' she protested.

'Yes, I do,' snapped back Kirkham. 'It is painfully simple. When you embarked upon the trip to Gretna either the welfare of your unborn babe was a matter of complete indifference to you or else you hated the idea of bearing my child so much you deliberately set out to lose it.'

'That is a terrible accusation!' exclaimed Melissa in horror. 'They both are!'

'I agree.'

'And they are untrue. I thought there would be no risk. It was such early days, and your coach is extremely well sprung. . . I did not think that anything could go wrong.'

'How extraordinarily remiss of you.' His voice was now heavy with sarcasm. 'You can organise an elopement for two acquaintances with commendable forethought and attention to detail, yet where your own child was concerned you could not see the risks. Apart from the arduous journey, have you never heard of carriages overturning or horses bolting? Have you never heard of poor and insanitary lodgings? Have you never heard of highwaymen and robbers frequenting the roads? In short, madam, have you not the slightest knowledge of the perils attendant upon modern travel?'

'Do not let us begin quarrelling again,' protested

Melissa in desperation. 'Everything was wonderful. Please do not spoil it.'

'I have not spoiled anything. My attitudes are exactly what they have always been. You are the one who is difficult to fathom. I notice you have said very little in your own defence. No doubt because you have none. I have my suspicions about your ulterior motive, but I will give you the benefit of the doubt. Indifference towards the unborn child is quite a bad enough accusation.'

'I was not indifferent! And I certainly did not act with deliberate malice!'

'You hardly behaved like a devoted mother, did you? However, from now on all that will change. The doctor will be summoned this afternoon. He will be asked to draw up the best regime for furthering the welfare of the child, and you will follow it to the letter. I will oversee you myself. The poor babe may have a callous mother, but no one will ever say that, be it boy or girl, it lacked any attention its father could provide. Now kindly wait here; that tree-trunk will afford you a reasonable seat.'

'Where are you going?' demanded Melissa, as he began to stride away.

He turned. 'I am off to summon a groom to harness up the governess-cart. You are not to walk back to the house. Oh, and in future you are not to step beyond the doors without at least one servant in attendance.'

Melissa awaited the arrival of the governess-cart in the depths of despair. How quickly her life had switched from unbelievable happiness to the deepest misery. She was forced to admit that part of her present anguish was rooted in her own guilt. She should have taken more care, but it had been so early, the prospect of a coming babe so indefinite, that it had not seemed real.

Now Kirkham was angry with her once more. More angry than at any time since their marriage. His fury she could tolerate, if only he had not returned to distrusting her again. Furthermore — and this tormented Melissa more than anything else — beneath his rage and his mistrust she had detected a deep hurt. He honestly feared she disliked him enough to want to destroy his child. She would have given everything to be able to persuade him otherwise, but try as she might she could not think how. Whatever she said he would not believe her.

Sitting bolt upright, she maintained a rigid dignity until the governess-cart delivered her to the main door. She greeted the servants graciously and climbed the staircase at a leisurely pace. Each polite smile, each measured tread, cost her dear. When the door of her room closed behind her she collapsed on the bed and wept as if the end of the world had come.

The doctor arrived promptly that afternoon, and announced Melissa to be in excellent health and the pregnancy to be progressing exactly as it should. At being asked to draw up a strict regime for Melissa to follow he said nothing until Kirkham had left the room, then a broad smile spread across his face.

'For every mother-to-be who needs my reassurance I swear I have two prospective papas in a ferment of worry,' he said. 'My advice to you, my lady, is to lead as normal a life as possible with sufficient exercise and plenty of rest. However, I can see that such simplicity will not satisfy Lord Kirkham, therefore I will draw up for you a list of directions couched in medical language. I can also give you the name of an excellent *accoucheur* for when your time comes. Do not fear that because you are in the depths of the country that you are far from competent aid.'

'You seem to assume that the baby will be born here.'

The doctor looked surprised. 'The child will be the hope of the Kirkhams. Where else should it be born?' he asked.

'Where else indeed?' said Melissa. She could not tell him that during her first few days at Kirkham Hall it had seemed an earthly paradise. That experience had been all too brief, and now she wondered how she could bear to stay and nurse her disillusionment. Not that she had any option. She was bound to remain with Kirkham until the child was born. After that she did not know what would happen.

Next morning a letter arrived from Beth Woodley. She wrote of her happiness, and of how her father, far from being agitated, had been delighted at the marriage and given them both his blessing. Beth had also written, 'Mama is most displeased, I fear.'. That sentence was the one gloomy note in a letter full of high spirits and joy. Melissa was overcome with envy. How she wished she could equal Beth's light-hearted contentment.

Instead she was forced to tolerate Kirkham's surveillance. His constant reminders of 'Madam, is it not time for your rest?' or at table, 'That dish is not suitable for you. Dr Adams advised you to avoid spices,' got on her nerves to a surprising degree. It was not that he was truly heavy-handed, but more the reason behind his supervision that aggravated her spirits. So much so that she, who had looked forward with such anticipation to them being alone in the country, was quite thankful at the arrival of old Lady Kirkham.

'I am informed that you are increasing,' stated Lady Kirkham, regarding Melissa approvingly through her quizzing-glass. 'Splendid news! My grandson is no doubt overjoyed?'

'Yes, overjoyed,' Melissa replied.

'But you less so, judging by your voice? Never fear, the early months are always somewhat trying.' Lady Kirkham went over to the open window and took a deep breath. 'London has nothing to compare with this,' she said. 'I think I will drive out to fill my lungs with decent air. Will you come with me?'

'Thank you, my lady, but it is time for my rest.'

'I only intend to be gone an hour. We will be back in ample time for resting.'

'I wish I could, but Dr Adams has set out a strict course of action for me.'

Lady Kirkham's eyebrows rose. 'Dr Adams is not usually such an old woman. You are not well?'

'I am in excellent health, thank you. It is Kirkham who insists I follow this regime.'

'Does he indeed?' Lady Kirkham's eyebrows rose even further. 'Ah, well, no doubt he is considering the welfare of the next generation. It means much to him.'

She was less tolerant by dinnertime, having watched her grandson in his new role as expectant father. 'For pity's sake, Kirkham, hold back!' she exclaimed, after Kirkham prevented Melissa from eating a dessert. 'What is wrong with your wife's having gooseberries? If they are a mite acid, as Dr Adams says, then at worst she will suffer indigestion. You have twice sent back the portion of meat she was served, then insisted she must have Madeira not claret. Really, Kirkham, let the girl breathe. Would you wrap her in lamb's wool?'

'I am merely trying to ensure that everything possible is done for the health of the child,' said Kirkham.

'Well, driving his mother mad will do naught to help. Let nature take its course.'

'You do not understand, Grandmother,' said Kirkham coldly.

'I understand that other people have had children before, aye, and with half the fuss.' Then Lady Kirkham's sharp gaze went from her grandson to Melissa, who was steadfastly staring at her plate and not taking part in the conversation. 'Do you know there is a pack of prize-fighters staying at the village inn?' she asked, changing the subject with marked deliberation.

Melissa looked up sharply.

'I do. They are here at my invitation,' said Kirkham.

'I hope you are not intending to set up a stable or a troupe or whatever it is called when a number of these fellows gather together,' said Lady Kirkham.

'No, they are merely here to further their training.'

'Oh, then that means you have a financial interest in their welfare.'

'There is no need to sound disapproving, Grandmother. They are all excellent men and should earn me a fortune. There is good money to be had in prize-fighting if you back the right ones.'

'That is the cry of all gamblers,' said Melissa disparagingly.

The look of cold reproof Kirkham gave her made her regret the remark. It had only made things worse. Then she pushed away her remorse. Why should she not say what she pleased? It was the only respite she had in a life that was rapidly becoming intolerable.

But after dinner, when she and Kirkham were alone for a few minutes, she had a serious question to ask him.

'The prize-fighters, I presume they are Fox and his friends?'

'Yes,' said Kirkham.

'Were you being truthful? Are they really here to train?'

'Do you doubt my word?' he demanded haughtily.

Then evidently regretted his sharp response, for he added more gently, 'They are indeed here to gain the benefits of the sea-bathing and country living. I thought the change of air would set them up for their next round of prize-fights.'

'Oh. I wondered if you were afraid Beaucombe might come here.'

'Let me assure you I am not afraid of Beaucombe, here or anywhere else,' he retorted, once more showing his irritation. 'But knowing how devious the man is I would have been a fool not to take precautions against him in London. However, here at Kirkham such measures are not necessary. In this countryside he would stick out like a sore thumb and I would be alerted to his presence immediately.' Then once more he seemed to relent and added more quietly, 'You can relax and forget all about Beaucombe. Here at Kirkham you are safe.'

She wished she could tell him it was not her own safety that concerned her but his; she wished also that he would go on talking to her in that gentler tone. Unfortunately it was not to be, and he maintained the chilly edge to his voice with which he seemed always to address her these days.

It was unfortunate that Lady Kirkham chose to talk about Beth and Gerard's elopement after dinner.

'The whole of London — or at least what is left so late in the Season — is agog with the tale,' she declared. 'You must give me every detail in order that I may make Lord Layfield green with envy at being so well informed. What commendable spirit to help the youngsters.'

'Sorely misplaced spirit, in the circumstances,' growled Kirkham.

'You must not be disgruntled because your wife took

part and you were left out,' replied his grandmother reprovingly.

'I hope that all has gone well for Mr and Mrs Woodley since their marriage,' put in Melissa swiftly, noticing Kirkham's mounting annoyance.

'It has. Angelica Thomas saw to that! She made sure that everyone was convinced of the propriety of the whole enterprise, and woe betide anyone who expressed any doubts. Not that many did,' chuckled Lady Kirkham. 'There are too many who have comtempt for Mrs Hurst and a dislike for that scoundrel, Beaucombe. The general opinion is delight that the Season finished on such a satisfactory note.'

'Good,' said Melissa with relief. 'It is splendid that Beth and Woodley have begun their marriage without any stain upon their reputations.'

'Thanks mainly to the aunt, it seems,' snapped Kirkham. 'You see, there was no need for you to have taken part.'

Melissa said nothing. There was nothing she could say without provoking a quarrel.

Lady Kirkham could not help but notice the strained atmosphere, though she did not remark upon it until she and Melissa were alone next morning.

'I confess I see no improvement between you and my grandson,' she remarked. 'I would have thought the coming babe to have made a difference.'

Melissa opened her mouth to make some non-committal reply. But, to her mortification, she burst into tears and unable to stop herself sobbed out the whole sorry story.

'The fellow's a fool!' declared Lady Kirkham. 'I shall have something stern to say to that grandson of mine.'

'Please do not,' begged Melissa, mopping her eyes. 'I

fear it would not improve matters. I do apologise for my weakness. I do not usually behave so foolishly.'

'The fault is with your condition,' said Lady Kirkham quite kindly. 'Increasing often makes women prone to tears. And I will not say anything to my grandson if you do not wish it.' She paused and then said in an unexpectedly hesitant voice, 'In turn I must ask a favour of you. Do not judge Kirkham too harshly. I agree he is behaving unreasonably and being most irritating, but try to see things from his point of view.'

'I have tried,' cried Melissa. 'It does no good. He thinks I am a callous creature who is not fit to be mother to his child.'

'There is more to it than that,' said Lady Kirkham. 'Remember, he was a solitary boy who grew into a solitary man — aye, for all his reputation as a rake and dashing blade about town I fancy there are few who have ever got truly close to him. Perhaps it is my fault, for I had the chief raising of him. Perhaps it was circumstances. Whatever the reason, I fear he has always had exaggerated hopes of domesticity, expecting it to bring him everything he has ever lacked — a sound close-knit family. Fond as I am of him I could never provide such a home, it was not in me. And his mother was a fond and foolish creature who lacked any hint of stability. My husband, the late Lord Kirkham, came closest. I know the lad was heartbroken when he died. I think that was why he considered marrying the Hurst girl, you know. For all her timidity she is a warm-hearted little thing, and once she had settled down I am sure she would have made him a devoted wife, if...'

'If I had not intervened.'

'I was going to say, "if things had been different". You are his wife, and I suppose that, despite your differences, deep down he hoped for the wedded bliss he had always dreamed of. For make no mistakes about it, my Kirkham is a romantic.'

'And now I have ruined everything for him.'

'No, you have not,' said Lady Kirkham sternly. 'He only thinks you have. The coming child will make all the difference between you. You must have patience with him. He is not used to being. . .being. . .'

'Being what, my lady?'

'To being a husband and a prospective father,' said Lady Kirkham in an uncharacteristic rush. 'He needs time.'

Before Melissa could speak the old lady rose and departed from the room swiftly, announcing she had talked enough nonsense for one day and was in need of air. Melissa understood her actions well enough. It was her way of covering up her embarrassment at betraying how much she loved her grandson.

Melissa thought on Lady Kirkham's words and began to see the wisdom in them. As a result she resolved to be more understanding of Kirkham. She would tolerate his unreasonable behaviour. To please him she would try to keep the regime set down by Dr Adams. She had an ulterior motive, she admitted. It was to try to make Kirkham trust her. To gain his love was beyond her reach, she was certain, but she was prepared to settle for second best.

Sadly her efforts did not last long. She was walking along one of the wooded paths in the park with Polly when she slipped and had to be carried home.

Kirkham came hurrying into the withdrawing-room where she was reclining on a sofa.

'Are you hurt?' he asked anxiously. 'Dr Adams has been called? What does he say?'

Melissa noted his concerned expression and for a brief instant her heart lightened. Then commonsense told her he was more likely to be worried about the child, not her.

'Dr Adams had diagnosed nothing more than a slightly sprained ankle,' she replied. 'He has prescribed a day's complete rest.'

Kirkham's face lost its distraught look. 'You slipped on the woodland path, I hear,' he said. 'I would have expected you to be more prudent, madam. It was not exactly an ideal route to take.'

'The sun was so hot I preferred to wander in the shade.'

'Aye, it is hot now, yet you can hardly have overlooked the fact that it rained all day yesterday. Why on earth did you choose such a dirty path?'

'I did not think it would be excessively slippery.'

It was the wrong thing to say. The words were barely out of her mouth before she regretted them.

'You did not think!' he said scornfully. 'If you ignored the risks to yourself, could you not have considered the child? Perhaps not! You certainly seem to forget your condition with disturbing ease.'

'What do you mean by that?' demanded Melissa.

'Make of it what you will. All I am saying is that with such a mother it will be a miracle if this child survives full term.'

'It will survive!' declared Melissa furiously. 'Because I want it to! But I swear that as soon as it is born we will leave both this place and you, and go somewhere where we can live together in peace.'

'Now there you are mistaken,' said Kirkham in an ominous voice.

'No, I am not. It was part of our agreement. . .'

'That you could go where you chose. I do not argue with that. But you cannot take the child.'

'What?' All the anger went out of Melissa's voice.

She was overwhelmed with sudden dismay. 'But I cannot leave my babe!'

'Why not? You have proved remarkably indifferent to it thus far.'

'You cannot mean it! You would not be so cruel.'

'I am not being cruel. The babe is not part of our agreement and never has been. You may leave and set up home where you will—alone. The Kirkham heir will be brought up here, as all the Kirkham first-born have been for generations. The continent, Scotland, the coast, the country—choose your spot, but make no mistake, madam, the child stays here with me! If you would keep the babe then you must stay too!'

CHAPTER TWELVE

THE pain in Melissa's ankle kept her immobile, adding to her anguish. She longed to pace back and forth, to give some relief to her feelings. Instead she had to remain on the sofa. Kirkham's ultimatum had caught her distressingly unawares, as had his cruelty. How could he demand such a thing of her? She had never thought he had it in him to be so harsh and unfeeling. This new appraisal of his character did nothing to stop her loving him. She wished it did. If he had begged her to stay, or simply asked her, how happy she would have been. That it would have been for the child's sake, not for his delight in her presence, would have made no difference. She would have been happy to remain with him. But he had offered her the harshest of alternatives — either to remain where she was not wanted or to abandon her baby.

'I cannot understand why you are so surprised and upset,' said Lady Kirkham, when she heard the latest development. 'Surely you must have realised my grandson would never let the child leave here?'

'No, I did not,' said Melissa. 'I thought. . . I thought. . . I do not know what I thought; but it never occurred to me that he would be cruel enough to take my baby from me.'

'Only if you leave him,' said Lady Kirkham shrewdly.

'What sort of a choice is that?' cried Melissa.

'The sort that you alone can make,' was the reply. 'You alone know which would present the greater sacrifice. Have you tried talking to my grandson?

Quietly and reasonably, I mean, not shrieking insults at one another. It might be worth the effort. Maybe you could reach a compromise.'

Melissa doubted it. She was disappointed, she had hoped for some sort of sympathy, yet Lady Kirkham seemed to regard the situation as quite logical. Might it be possible to reach a compromise? She would try it. There was no alternative.

Catching sight of Kirkham crossing the lawn outside the withdrawing-room window, she hobbled out after him.

'My lord,' she said, 'we must talk.'

'Here?' He looked quizzically at the surrounding garden.

'Where better? I never see you anywhere else to have a private conversation; and one thing is certain, a discussion between us is a matter of great urgency.'

'If you insist.' He did not sound enthusiastic. 'Should you be walking on that ankle?'

'Yes, it is almost better. I can use it normally providing I do not walk far.'

'Indeed, you should not walk far in any case.' He regarded her figure, which was growing increasingly rounded these days. 'Take my arm. We will go over to the arbour. That is no distance and should be private enough.'

He held out his arm to her. Her first reaction was to reject it, but there seemed no point in antagonising him by rudeness. She took his arm and let him lead her to the arbour.

As the setting for a romantic rendezvous the wide bench, overhung with late honeysuckle and tangled jasmine, could not have been more ideal. But there was nothing romantic about the occasion when Kirkham and Melissa sat down there together.

'You have something to say to me, madam?' he asked coldly.

'Yes. You know what I want to discuss — the child.'

'There is nothing to discuss. The child will be brought up here.'

'Surely there is some other way. What if I settled somewhere in the near vicinity? You could see the child frequently, have complete control over its education and upbringing——'

'No!' Kirkham's reply was so fierce the spaniels at his feet stirred uneasily. 'I can see what you are about. You are trying to get the best of both worlds, deserting me yet retaining your influence over the child. Very clever. But it will not do. No Kirkham heir will be raised anywhere but here, at Kirkham Hall.'

'You seem determined the child is a boy. It might prove to be a girl. What then? Will you still be so determined to keep possession?'

'The situation will not arise, madam. Had you forgotten our agreement? If we have a girl this time then we have time to try again. Two years, we said.'

'Oh, no,' protested Melissa in distress. 'When I agreed I did not realise the harshness of your conditions. I could not go through this again knowing I would be likely to lose the child.'

'Then the choice is yours.'

'What choice have I? You know there is only one decision I can make.'

'And what is that?'

'You can ask such a question?' Melissa cried distractedly. 'Do you want me to inscribe it in letters a yard high? Did you honestly think I could carry a child, grow to love and cherish it long before its birth, and then callously walk away from it once it is born, never to see it again?'

'Does this mean you intend to stay?'

'Of course I must stay! What sort of a monster do you think I am?'

Kirkham bent swiftly and stroked the ears of one of the spaniels. 'So be it,' he said, suddenly rising to his feet.

His voice sounded strangely unsteady, but Melissa did not see the expression on his face. She had turned her head to prevent him noticing the tears streaming down her cheeks. For a few minutes she was aware of him standing beside her. Then he strode away. At least, she thought he did. The sound of his footsteps on the grass stopped abruptly, and she got a definite impression that he had turned and come back towards her, but she may have been mistaken. She was weeping too bitterly to be certain. When at last she had composed herself enough to dry her eyes and look about her she was alone.

'I gather you intend to remain with my grandson,' said Lady Kirkham.

'I intend to remain with my child, which amounts to the same thing,' replied Melissa.

'Good, I am glad you have reached such a sensible decision. Separation in marriage, legal and otherwise, is always a messy affair. No good ever comes of it, that has been my experience.'

'And what is your experience of people forced to live together in something far removed from conjugal bliss?'

'You are letting your romantic notions take over again,' reproved the old lady. 'You and Kirkham, what a pair you are for such ideas. They only complicate matters. Once you permit youself to look rationally at the future there is much cause for hope. You are both intelligent; I notice you have many interests in common, and although I know you are not accustomed to country living you seem to have taken to it well. Above everything else, despite your differences, you both have the interests of the coming child very much at heart. If that is not a recipe for a tolerable life together in the years ahead then I do not know what is.'

A tolerable life together. How cold and unsatisfactory it sounded. Yet Melissa knew she must grow to endure it somehow. She consoled herself with the thought that she could focus all her love and affection on the child. That, at least, would give her life some meaning. Perhaps in time she might grow to love Kirkham less. Perhaps! She did not hold out much hope.

The evenings of late summer were too beautiful to stay indoors. Even Kirkham relented enough to agree that a gentle stroll after dinner could only be of benefit to her. Melissa's favourite route was across the park, then along the cliff-top path above the cove. Looking at the sea was one of the few things that soothed her frayed nerves and gave her some comfort.

'I shall never tire of this view,' she remarked to Polly. 'Look, the sky and the sea might be made of mother-of-pearl, there is no dividing them.'

'Will you say the same come winter, I wonder?' said Polly. She had yet to be convinced that life in the country was superior to a London existence. 'The storms we had last month were bad enough. Goodness knows what they will be like in November or January!'

'I dare say the sea will have a different kind of beauty then, more dramatic. . .' she paused. 'That is unusual! There is a boat on the beach, and some men. Whoever can they be?'

'His lordship doesn't mind the locals coming ashore here occasionally,' said Polly. 'Though I can't say I recognise anyone.' She peered through the furze thicket that protected the path from the cliff's edge. 'Does anything strike you as odd?'

'No, not in particular. . . Unless you mean that they are extraordinarily quiet.'

'That's it. They've just taken in their sail and we scarcely heard it, almost as if the blocks or whatever they're called have been heavily greased. When you think of the racket down at the harbour. . .'

'And the men are silent too. From here we could easily hear them talking, but there isn't a sound. They must be whispering; but why?' Then Melissa remembered that she was now living on the coast, where the locals had alternative and often illegal ways of earning extra money. 'Oh, how foolish of us. Of course! They are night trading. We had best withdraw, and let them land their brandy undisturbed.'

'They won't be doing any trading with the hall. We had our delivery of such things the night before last.'

'How do you know?'

'I caught Mr Fraser and a couple of the menservants taking the barrels down to the cellar. And another thing, the local men would be landing their cargo at dead of night, not when there was still a good hour of daylight left.'

'Are you sure?'

'Yes. One of the menservants was grumbling about the weight of the barrels and he said, "I don't know how the village lads get these tubs up the cliff, never mind landing them in the pitch dark. They must know this bit of coast like the back of their hands.". Then he saw me and went quiet.'

'These men can't be local, in that case. That must be why they are landing their cargo before dark.'

'They're risking a serious set-to with the Kirkham

lads, then. I've heard tales below stairs of the last time some "foreigners" tried to work this stretch of the coast. There was battle royal—blood flowing, bones broken and all.'

'What can they be about?' Unconsciously she and Polly had sunk further behind the furze bushes, where they could see yet not be seen. 'There are no signs of tubs, or bundles or packages. If they have landed anything it must be extremely small.'

'Now what is happening?' demanded Polly, her voice low despite her excitement. 'Look, they're manhandling the boat to behind the rocks over there. They are pushing the boat out of sight, yet most of the men are still on the beach. Oh my lor'!'

At the same time as Polly's exclamation Melissa gave a gasp of dismay as simultaneously they recognised a stocky figure directing operations on the beach.

'It's him!' Polly declared.

'Beaucombe!' exclaimed Melissa. 'What on earth is he doing here?'

'Something evil, you can be sure.'

'I agree. Polly, have you noticed that every man is armed? They have all got clubs or knives. Oh, heavens! Some have pistols too, do you see? Get back to the house as quickly as you can! You must inform Lord Kirkham what is happening.'

'And leave you here? Certainly not!'

'Go, I tell you. His lordship must be informed immediately, and you know perfectly well that in my condition I am not as agile as you. While you run back to the house I will keep an eye on things for a time, then I will creep away too. I am in no danger,' she insisted, seeing the doubtful look on Polly's face. 'Beaucombe and his men are showing no signs of moving from the beach, and even if they do I will have plenty of time of get away. Apart from anything else the furze bushes up here are thick enough to hide an army, Beaucombe would never find me. Now for pity's sake go!'

At last, and looking most unhappy, Polly did as she was told, making her way swiftly along one of the innumerable tracks that cut through the furze and elder bushes, bent almost double in order to avoid being seen.

From her hidden vantage point Melissa eased herself forward to see more. On the beach below the men stood in a group, listening intently to Lord Beaucombe. Although he gestured a great deal, and seemed to be making drawings in the wet sand, she could hear no word of what he said. This in itself was ominous, for Beaucombe's voice was normally loud and bombastic even in the confines of a social gathering. Under the circumstances, for him to speak quietly had to have some meaning. Yet even without overhearing his words it was only too evident that he was giving explicit orders about something. Once or twice he swung his arm towards the cliff path, and then in the direction of Kirkham Hall, causing Melissa to duck in alarm, although she knew he could not possibly see her.

Looking down on him, Melissa decided that Beaucombe seemed for all the world like a commander briefing his troops before an attack. Then she was sorry such an idea had come to her, for the only place in the vicinity ripe for attack was Kirkham Hall. She came to the conclusion that it was time for her to withdraw, yet even as she began stealthily to rise there was a sudden activity on the beach.

Sinking back on to her knees, she watched as the men moved purposefully across the sand and shingle. For one heart-stopping moment she feared they were coming towards her, but then she realised that not one of them was heading towards the path. They spread out, some going towards an overhanging cliff, others settling behind rocks. Beaucombe himself found a niche in the granite that was almost a cave. In a matter of minutes the beach seemed empty again. Only a keen observer such as Melissa would have noticed a prone body here, the outline of a shoulder there, particularly in the fading light.

But why were they hiding? Melissa feared she knew the answer. They were waiting until dark, when they intended to attack Kirkham Hall. The audacity of the plan almost took her breath away. She would have considered it preposterous if she had not known the evil character of Lord Beaucombe. He was capable of anything. Now was definitely the time for her to leave, but once again, even as she tried to move she was startled by a rustling in the bushes nearby. Fear rooted her to the spot and her mouth went dry. Could it be one of Beaucombe's men coming towards her through the undergrowth? Suddenly an animal sprang at her from the tangle of furze roots and bracken, leaping upon her in an ecstasy of happy recognition.

'Gyp, you naughty creature!' she gasped, as the dog leaped up to lick her face.

Then her initial relief gave way to realisation, and she groaned with alarm. Gyp was one of the spaniels that invariably accompanied Kirkham when he went out of doors. A youngster, little more than a puppy and still not fully trained, he was liable to dash away from the others in a fit of exuberance — but he would not be out alone. His presence meant that Kirkham must be somewhere in the vicinity.

Too late she remembered her husband mentioning something about going down to the village and calling in at Home Farm on the way. She had sent Polly on a wild-goose chase. Kirkham was not at the Hall, he was almost certainly approaching on this very path — the shortest route between Home Farm and the village. Help would come from the Hall, she did not doubt it. Fraser would organise something in his master's absence. But when? And how effective would a gang of grooms and footmen be against Beaucombe's armed thugs?

Swallowing her panic, Melissa looked down at the beach. The men there were well nigh invisible now in the shadows, but they would be able to see Kirkham only too clearly if he approached on the cliff-top. Then Gyp dashed off, ears flying. Following his progress through the ruffled undergrowth, Melissa saw him scampering excitedly back along the path towards a tall familiar figure in the far distance.

Melissa's first instinct was to rush towards Kirkham and warn him of Beaucombe's presence, then a sudden stab of alarm brought her to an immediate halt. Between her and Kirkham there was a stretch of relatively bare cliff-top. Long before she reached him she would likely have been seen against the skyline by Beaucombe and his men. What if she was to dodge and weave towards him through the furze, along one of the other minor tracks, as Polly had done? Measuring the distance such a devious path would take, she knew she would never make it. Kirkham would be in full view of Beaucombe's gang long before she reached him.

There was only one alternative. She would somehow have to draw Beaucombe's attention away from Kirkham. Already she had turned and was hurrying in the opposite direction, a plan forming in her brain as she went. The cove below was quite a large crescent in shape, with a small promontory of rocks jutting out half way along. Melissa made her way to just beyond these rocks, no easy matter in her condition, for she had to keep low to avoid detection. With some difficulty she slid and slithered down a narrow track to the beach, confident that the small headland shielded her from the men hiding at the other side. Once she felt her feet touch the shingle she stopped for the briefest moment to compose herself, then, pulling her shawl about her, she moved forward into the full view of Beaucombe and his men, her heart pounding with fear. She hoped she looked like a lady taking a casual evening stroll along the foreshore.

There was a shout of warning, then two men emerged from the shadows. With a dramatic start she felt worthy of Mrs Siddons, Melissa spun round and began to run back along the beach. She was no match for her pursuers, though, and within a few strides she was captured and held tightly.

'Let me go, you brutes!' she exclaimed, as they dragged her along. 'Take your hands off me!'

Was her performance convincing? she wondered, especially since she dared not cry out too loudly for fear of attracting Kirkham's attention. Her hope was that he would pass by on the top of the cliff without noticing that anything was amiss on the beach. After that. . .she preferred not to think of what might happen eventually. All she wanted was to protect Kirkham. Despite her struggles the two men brought her up to the opening of the small cave that was Beaucombe's refuge.

'What are we to do with her, my lord?' asked one of the men, as they released her and pushed her towards Beaucombe.

Melissa held her breath. She, who abhorred gambling, was now playing for the greatest stakes. She was gambling that Beaucombe had one last shred of decency in him and would not harm a pregnant woman. First though she had to give the impression that she did not know why he was there. Maybe that she did not even know he was? Yes, that was the best strategy.

'Sir,' she said. 'I demand to know what this is about. Let me go at once. Are you aware that you are on private property?'

'I am aware that you are a dashed nuisance, madam,' Beaucombe growled. 'Normally I am not averse to a female fairly dropping into my hands. Upon any other occasion I would know well enough how to deal with you. But tonight I have more important fish to fry. A bit of muslin wandering upon the scene just now is the last thing I need, especially one who is obviously with child.'

The incredible thing had happened. In the growing darkness he had not recognised her. Who on earth he imagined her to be, wandering about the shore on Kirkham land at that time of night, she had no idea, but she had to make the most of her advantage.

'I object to your language, sir!' she declared. 'I will have you know I am a respectably married lady. My husband is vicar of this parish.' She breathed a silent apology to the real vicar's wife, who was a cheerfully stout grandmother.

'Is he, now? Then I wish he had kept you at home singing psalms and not let you roam the countryside.'

'But what are we to do with her, my lord?' persisted her captor.

'How the blue devil should I know?' blazed Beaucombe. 'I do not care what happens to her so long as she does not hinder my scheme for tonight. Keep her quiet. For good if you have to. Hit her over the head and drop her in the sea. That would be the simplest way.'

Melissa felt cold terror steal over her. She had gambled and lost. What a fool she had been to expect decent feelings from Beaucombe. But she dared not give up. Maybe she could talk her way out of this predicament — or at least hold Beaucombe's attention caught until help arrived.

'What sort of nonsense is this?' she demanded, hoping her fear did not show in her voice. '"Hit her over the head and drop her in the sea"? I seem to have encountered a pretty despicable specimen of manhood, to threaten such a thing to a defenceless woman!'

From somewhere on the shadowy beach there came a snigger. Beaucombe's men were well trained, but evidently he was not popular. Melissa wondered how he kept control. Money? Fear? Probably both.

'I would threaten you with a deal worse, if I had the time,' Beaucombe snarled. 'Dispatch her, you fool, and have done with it.'

But both of Melissa's captors shuffled uneasily.

'It's unlucky, my lord. Harming a woman who's with child,' explained one. 'Worst ill luck a man can bring on himself.'

'If you two are too lily-livered then let someone else do the deed, only get it over and done with,' snapped Beaucombe.

The other men had remained in their hiding-places during the interchange, and now not one emerged from the shadows.

'Of all of the weak-kneed. . .' Beaucombe flung a curse at his followers. 'Oh, tie her and leave her. When the tide comes in it will do the job for us. And who knows, if I have a few minutes to spare after our little diversion on land I might find time to amuse myself.

She is a quite a taking creature for all her condition. Wasted on a parson.'

A snigger went round the cove. Melissa felt its echo in the shiver that crept down her spine as her hands were grasped and tied tightly behind her with rope. Desperately she struggled to get free, lashing out with her feet, but although she felt her shoe contact skin and bone and heard a grunt of pain, the hands that held her did not release their grip. Only when the rope was bound tightly about both her wrists and ankles did they let her go.

When is help coming? she wondered, swaying precariously. What can be keeping Fraser? Surely he had had ample opportunity to muster the menservants and get here? Her chief consolation was that her initial ploy had worked. All attention was on her. No one had looked towards the cliff-top to discover Kirkham strolling there.

Straining her ears, she hoped to hear the sounds of approaching rescuers above the pounding of the waves. She thought she heard something like a thud followed swiftly by a grunt, but probably she was mistaken. She was convinced that by now Kirkham must be safe. If her calculations were correct he had had sufficient time to be far enough along the path to be beyond any danger, thank goodness. Her one concern now was for her child.

Oh, let help come soon!

'Right, men. . .' began Beaucombe, then he froze as a sudden noise cut through the night air. Brief and high-pitched, it echoed eerily about the rocks.

'W—what was that?' demanded the more superstitious of Melissa's captors.

'It was just a sea-bird or a dog yelping somewhere,' retorted Beaucombe.

'It didn't sound human,' persisted the man nervously.

'Sea-gulls and dogs are not human, you fool,' snapped Beaucombe. 'Forget your old women's fears and prepare to move. It is dark enough now for what we have in mind.'

About the beach the men began to stir, emerging from the shadows.

'And talking of women...' He turned towards Melissa. Even in the gloom she could see the vicious leer on his face. 'If whatever it was should turn out to be a ghostie or a ghoulie, then you, Madam Vicar, can tell us all about it when we get back. It will serve you right for interfering and being where you should not be. Perhaps this will teach you not to get in the way of my plans in future...if you have a future!' With great deliberation he raised his hand and struck Melissa across the face.

Hobbled as she was and precariously balanced, Melissa fell heavily to the damp shingle. Bruised and half stunned, she was aware of a shout of intense rage, of something heavy—a large stone or piece of rock—hurtling through the air to catch Beaucombe a blow on the shoulder. As he spun round at the impact a figure leapt out of the darkness. Befuddled though her wits were she recognised Kirkham at once. Wielding a stout piece of wood as a club and yelling angry insults, he jumped on Beaucombe, belabouring him until he fell to his knees.

'Help! Oh, help me, you dolts!' shrieked Beaucombe.

At first his men had been too astonished by the sudden attack to move. Now their master's cries mobilised them into action. They rushed forward, and Melissa found herself under a mass of pounding feet. Immediately she curled into a ball, instinctively protecting her baby.

Oh, Kirkham, she cried silently, why did you come? You could have got away!

How he came to be there or how he had known she was down in the cove she had no idea. She only knew that his sacrifice had been pointless. He had no chance. The odds against him were too great. The sounds of conflict going on above her head faded swiftly, and she heard Beaucombe call out, 'That will do, you fools. I do not want him killed — yet!'

That one word 'yet', and the sheer malice in Beaucombe's tone made her blood freeze. Then she had fresh cause for fear as he ordered, 'Bring the female here!'

None too gently, she was hauled upright and dragged across the beach to where Beaucombe sat on a rock, clutching at his head and at his shoulder where Kirkham's beating had done the most damage. She would have rejoiced in the sight if the prone figure of Kirkham had not driven all else from her mind.

Twisting away from the hands that held her, she sank unsteadily on to her knees beside him. She longed to touch him, to tend to his hurts, but with her hands tied in such a way this was impossible.

'Kirkham!' she cried. 'Pray God you are not gravely hurt! Say something, for pity's sake!'

To her intense relief he stirred.

'Melissa,' he groaned. 'Melissa. . .'

Not 'madam', nor yet 'my lady', but 'Melissa'! It was ridiculous at such a time and in such a predicament to notice so trivial a detail, yet she could not help the surge of happiness that went through her.

'How very touching.' Beaucombe's voice brought her sharply back to the reality. 'What a fool I was not to make the connection. The Vicar's wife indeed! I thought you looked familiar, but wandering about in the evening in a plain gown and unattended. . . No wonder I did not recognise you as Kirkham's woman!' He broke off to give a moan of pain, his head sinking further in his hands. Kirkham might have only been armed with a piece of wood but he had used it to good effect.

'Shall I have the boat brought round?' suggested one of the men.

'The boat? What for?' demanded Beaucombe, wincing as he spoke.

'Well, my lord, I thought as we've got the fellow you was after, we could leave now, like.'

'What sort of a poxy solution is that?' Beaucombe retorted. 'Where is the sport in dropping him over the side somewhere out at sea? Where is the plunder? Where is the enjoyment? No, we came to burn Kirkham Hall to the ground, complete with its family of resident rats. The only difference is that now we must take the king rat, aye, and his female, with us and throw them on the bonfire. A minor deviation that need not trouble us. My plan stands! We will attack Kirkham Hall!'

But although some of the men gave a muted cheer the others were clearly uneasy.

'My lord ——' began the one who was the spokesman.

He got no further. Suddenly they were invaded by a gang of men who emerged out of the darkness surrounding the cove and launched themselves upon Beaucombe and his thugs. They were not many, but they were well-built fellows who squared up to their opponents most effectively, laying about them with great ferocity. Almost unnoticed in the mêlée a fishing boat rounded the headland, and long before it had been run aground its occupants had leapt into the water and were running up the beach to join in the attack upon Beaucombe.

In order to defend himself, the man holding Melissa was obliged to release her. She fell down again, and again she was in danger of being trampled underfoot. Urgently she struggled to get in a less vulnerable position, but her bound wrists and ankles made it impossible. Then an arm came about her and dragged her away from the fracas.

'Kirkham!' she said, managing to turn to face him.

He did not speak. He could not. All he could manage was the phantom of a smile. The effort of pulling her out of danger had spent the last of his energy. Still suffering from the beating he had received, he was too weak to stand. He must have dragged her along on his knees. There was so much she wanted to say, wanted to ask, but this was not the time. Other more immediate matters had to be resolved.

'Can you free me?' she asked, holding out her bound wrists.

Still beyond speech, he falteringly rummaged in his pocket for his pen-knife. Only then did Melissa notice that he used only one hand. His other arm hung limp and useless by his side.

'But you are badly hurt,' she cried.

'I...will...manage...' he ground out from between clenched teeth.

From the effort it clearly cost him Melissa realised that his injuries must be severe, and she longed to be free in order that she could tend to him. With the battle still raging about them Kirkham sawed doggedly away at the rope on Melissa's wrists. After what seemed an interminable time he finally reached the last few strands, and she was able to snap her way free. Taking the knife from him, she cut the bonds at her ankles, then she turned her attention to Kirkham. He was leaning against a rock, his eyes closed. By chance her hand came upon a piece of cloth. It was her shawl, and she put it tenderly about him, then, tearing off a length of her petticoat, she did her utmost to stem the bleeding from a wound to his head. As she was wondering whether to attempt to strap up his broken arm in the near-darkness might do more harm than good his eyes opened and he smiled.

'I should be tending to you. . .not the other way round. . .' he said in barely audible voice.

'There is no need. I am not hurt,' she replied.

'In that case. . . I will return to. . .the fray. . .'

He would have attempted it, too, if Melissa had not gently pushed him back.

'There is no need,' she said. 'The fight is almost done. You have played your part.'

'Did manage to disable a couple. . .thought to pick them off one by one. . .only chance on my own. . .'

So that accounted for the thud and the eerie cry.

'You took a great risk,' said Melissa. 'Stay back now. Whoever has come to the rescue—I think it's Fox and his companions—seem to be doing a most effective job.'

'Yes, it is Fox. . .and the lads from the village too. . . Don't know how the devil they knew. . . Glad they came. . .' Kirkham's voice faded as his eyes closed.

Fearing he had drifted into unconsciousness, she drew her shawl more closely about him and renewed her efforts to stop the wound on his head from bleeding. Behind her the shouts and yells of the battle continued, but now she scarcely heeded them. All her attention was centred upon Kirkham.

Only vaguely did she become aware of the sounds of fighting dying away. Then someone—Fox, she thought—shouted, 'The day's ours, lads! Lord Beaucombe and his mob've met their match!' This was greeted with a rousing cheer which broke off abruptly in mid-shout.

'Look out! He's getting away!'

The sudden yell, accompanied by frantic footsteps approaching across the beach, made her turn round. She was too late. Beaucombe was upon her. Before she could resist he had grabbed her by the hair and hauled her to her feet. As she began to struggle she felt the coldness of steel against her throat.

'I would keep still, my pretty, if you know what's good for you!' hissed Beaucombe in her ear. Aloud he yelled, 'Take one step forward, any of you, and her ladyship here will breathe her last!'

Immediately the men who had been rushing across the beach froze like so many statues.

'You'd not do that,' said Fox, his great frame heaving with exertion. 'You a lord and a member of the gentry, you'd never hurt a lady.'

'What lady?' demanded Beaucombe. 'This piece of goods was won with a turn of the cards. Or was it the roll of a dice? I forget which. Not that it matters. If one of you moves then her throat gets cut.'

Melissa swallowed hard as the knife pressed firmly against her windpipe made it difficult to breathe.

'There's no need to hurt her ladyship,' Fox insisted. 'Look, we're all standing still. Release Lady Kirkham unharmed and we'll let you go free. We won't pursue you, on our word of honour, eh, lads?'

A roar of assent went round the cove.

'Do you think to take me in? Do I look stupid enough to accept the word of a lot of paid maulers and fishing scum?' As he spat out this insult one of the men took a step forward. 'I said not to move!' Beaucombe yelled, drawing the knife against the skin of Melissa's neck. She gave a scream as she felt the raw line of pain, then the trickle of blood. A gasp of horror came from the men on the beach.

'I didn't move on purpose,' cried the man. 'I fell over. Don't you harm her ladyship no more!'

'That is only a small taste of what I will do if my orders are not obeyed to the letter,' snarled Beaucombe. 'First, any men still on the boat will come ashore. Then all of you will move up the beach, well away from the tide-line. And no tricks, mind, or you know the consequences.' He paused while the Kirkham men reluctantly did his bidding. 'Now, those of my men who are left get aboard and prepare to set sail.'

There were few of Beaucombe's thugs who shuffled their way painfully towards the fishing boat. Some had run away, while others remained where they had fallen on the beach.

'No, leave him you fool!' roared Beaucombe, as one of his men attempted to carry a prone companion down to the boat. 'What use is he to me now? Leave him here and get yourself down to the boat!'

The man looked mutinous but fearful. He did as he was bid.

'Now I am going to take my leave of you,' Beaucombe sneered in the direction of the Kirkham men. 'I did not achieve what I set out to do, but I have done well enough. You can tell your lord and master when he recovers from the thrashing I have given him that I am well satisfied with my night's work. I have taught him a lesson that was well overdue and, besides, I am taking with me his gambler's winnings. Poor man, I almost pity him, to lose his wife as well as his future offspring, *and* to me, of all people.' The laugh Beaucombe gave was the most cruel and vindictive Melissa had ever heard. She almost fainted away with terror at the sound of it, only the agonising pressure of steel at her throat forced her to keep on her feet. 'I wish I could stay to see his face,' Beaucombe went on. 'Unfortunately I have a pressing appointment elsewhere...'

'Oh come, Beaucombe,' broke in a new voice, 'you would not dash away so soon?'

There stood Kirkham confronting them. Knowing the extent of his injuries, Melissa did not know how he had managed to get himself upright, let alone stand there erect and nonchalant. Not even a hint of swaying betrayed the pain he must have been experiencing, nor the weakness he must have been fighting.

'Kirkham!' exclaimed Beaucombe.

'Yes, it is I. You sound surprised. Had you forgotten about me? No, I do not think that can be so, for have I not heard you say you wished you could see my face? Since you are on my land my duties as a host insist upon you getting your wish. You are seeing my face, Beaucombe, as well as any man can on a moonless night. Are you satisfied?'

'Don't come near me!' Beaucombe cried. 'Not unless you want to see your wife and child dispatched with one fell stroke — and I do mean stroke!' He laughed mirthlessly at his own joke.

If he expected Kirkham to be incensed by his words then he was mistaken.

'Your sense of humour is exactly what I would have expected of you,' Kirkham said with scorn. 'It matches your behaviour. The foulest villain from the gutter would be ashamed to acknowledge either.'

Melissa wondered what Kirkham was about, bandying words with this monster. She was sure it was costing him dear simply to stand; she was sure he had some strategy, yet what it was she could not imagine. Then she thought she heard a sound. The merest chink of pebble on pebble, nothing more. It came from behind them.

'Let me go, Lord Beaucombe, I beg of you,' she pleaded loudly in case the sound came again.

'Do you think you can sway me?' scoffed Beaucombe. 'I hold all the cards—a rather apt expression under the circumstances—so stand aside, Kirkham. The boat is waiting for me.'

'Are you really satisfied with tonight's little episode?' persisted Kirkham. 'In future days are you sure you will not regret not having completed the job while you had the opportunity? You hate me enough, therefore I am surprised that you can calmly sail away and leave me here.'

Beaucombe had already begun making his way towards the boat, pushing Melissa in front of him. Now he stopped.

'What are you suggesting?' he demanded.

'Let us finish this thing between us here, once and for all. Just you and me.'

'Oh, no!' protested Melissa in horror. Beaucombe had not escaped the night's battle unscathed but he was nowhere near as badly hurt as Kirkham.

'There, if you doubt the equality of the contest then heed my wife,' said Kirkham. 'She knows how well your men did their job. I could understand you hesitating to take me on under normal circumstances, for you know that I would have beaten you soundly, but after the injuries I have received tonight. . .'

'Kirkham, think what you are about!' Melissa cried. 'Do not do this for my sake! I will be all right! I am not afraid!' None of it was true, of course, but she thought she had detected a tremor of weakness in his voice and she feared his strength could not last much longer.

What chance had he in a fight against Beaucombe when he could barely stand?

But Beaucombe's attention was caught.

'I like your odds, Kirkham,' he said. 'I like them very much indeed. And I would like to beat you into kingdom come even more. Stand aside!' He let go of Melissa and pushed her away. 'Interfere at your peril! Now, Kirkham——!'

He got no further. A shadow seemed to detach itself from the darkness and strike at him from behind with one silent blow. With an almost inaudible grunt Beaucombe collapsed on to the shingle. Hardly had he fallen than Kirkham, too, fell where he stood. Immediately Melissa was with him, holding him to her, sobbing with relief, and by some miracle Polly was there also, trying to hold both her and Kirkham in arms that were woefully inadequate and weeping loudest of all.

Quite what happened next was never clear to Melissa. Everything became a kaleidoscope of bodies and lights and running feet and loud voices. She was conscious of being taken up in strong arms and vaguely aware of protesting, 'No, see to his lordship first.'

From a long way off Fox's voice replied, 'Do not fret, my lady. The lads have got him safe. They are taking him home ahead of you.'

Then everything faded into oblivion.

CHAPTER THIRTEEN

When Melissa awoke she was in her bed at the Hall, with Polly standing by and Dr Adams looking down at her.

'Ah, you are with us again, praise be!' he exclaimed.

'What. . .what happened?' she asked.

'The over-exertion and excitement not unnaturally brought on a swoon, which blessedly turned into a natural sleep. The best remedy you could have had in the circumstances, my lady. Thanks to that, and an exceedingly robust constitution, no serious harm has been done.'

'Thank goodness!' Melissa fell back against the pillows. 'For a terrible moment I thought my baby. . .' Then she remembered. . .'Lord Kirkham!' she cried. 'Where is he?'

'Next door, sleeping off the effects of the laudanum draught I gave him,' said the doctor.

'Is he badly hurt?'

'He certainly knows he has been in a fight,' the doctor said cautiously. 'He has concussion, a broken arm along with a fractured collarbone, and a few cracked ribs, not to mention much severe bruising. . . Oh, and a cut on the head.'

'I must go to him.' Melissa would have jumped out of bed if both Polly and Dr Adams has not prevented her.

'No, you will not, by your leave, my lady,' said Dr Adams sternly. 'You will remain in your bed for two, maybe three days, taking complete rest. And no more excitement! Even robust constitutions have their limits, you know, and in your condition we must take no chances. Think of your baby.'

'Yes, indeed.' Polly plumped up the pillows for her. 'And, besides, it would do no good. I looked in on his lordship not five minutes since and he was sleeping like a babe himself.'

With that Melissa had to be content, but she could not contain her impatience. When the doctor had gone she demanded of Polly, 'Now tell me everything that happened!'

'The doctor said no excitement,' Polly replied.

'Bother the doctor. I shall go into a decline if I am not told!'

'In that case. . .' Polly settled herself comfortably on the edge of the bed. 'When you sent me up to the Hall to get his lordship I only got halfway when I remembered he wouldn't be there. He'd either be at Home Farm or down at the inn with his prize-fighters. Well, the prize-fighters seemed the best bet, so I ran to fetch Mr Fox and the others. They'd have come alone but the local lads weren't going to be done out of a fight, not when Lord Kirkham was threatened. The upshot was that some came by land, and some came by sea, just to cut off any retreat, like. And me, I was told to get back to the Hall—as if I would!' her disgusted expression told what she thought of such an idea. 'I followed on after the men. A good job I did, too, for I was there when that Beaucombe animal grabbed you. Fortunately only Lord Kirkham saw me. I whispered to him that I could deal with Beaucombe if he could create a bit of a diversion. I only meant him to throw stones or something. I didn't expect the poor soul to get up on his hind legs, not the state he was in. But he did, and kept Beaucombe occupied. It was all the chance I needed.'

'But what did you do?'

'I gave the villain a taste of this!' From her boned bodice Polly drew a fearsome-looking stiletto. 'I've always had this by me, from the time before I came to you. I knew it'd come in handy one day.'

'Did you. . .?' asked Melissa in horror.

'Kill him? No, more's the pity. It's not big enough, not unless you strikes real lucky. He'll remember we've met, though!' And she calmly pushed the weapon back into her bodice.

'Where is Lord Beaucombe now?'

Polly gave a chuckle. 'Somewhere in foreign parts, I've been told. And truly foreign parts, not just a few miles up the road from Kirkham Hall. Some of the local lads had an expedition planned across the Channel, and they volunteered to take him along and dump him on French soil somewhere. That should curb his mischief for a spell.'

'I hope the French appreciate the honour,' smiled Melissa. Then she grew serious. 'And Lord Kirkham? You are sure he will be all right?'

'He is not too comfortable at the moment, poor gentleman, but Dr Adams is confident he will make a full recovery.'

'I wish I could see him.'

'Well, you can't! That's doctor's orders and I'm to see they're carried out.' Polly stood up, a no-nonsense expression on her face. 'I am going to get you some breakfast, and then you are going to have a good rest.'

It seemed to Melissa that she did nothing but rest; and it was unnecessary, for she felt fine. She knew better than to defy the twin martinets, Polly and Dr Adams, however. She lay, fuming impotently. How she wanted to be with Kirkham. Time and again she went over the events of the previous evening. He had done so much, taken such risks to defend her. Surely that could mean he had some feelings for her? One incident above all she went over again and again, when he had called her Melissa. That moment she treasured above all others.

Not knowing how Kirkham was faring drove Melissa nearly demented. Then she hit upon the idea of sending him a note. Her first attempt was scribbled swiftly and with enthusiasm. When she read it back to herself she knew she could never send it, it was so full of emotion and betrayed her true feelings too blatantly. After all, he had merely used her Christian name in the heat of the moment, it probably meant nothing. And as for his efforts to protect her, Melissa was uncomfortably aware that he would have exerted himself just as much for some old crone in similar circumstances. Tearing up her letter into tiny pieces, she began to pen a second. It became a model for the carefully formal messages which passed from one bedchamber to the next, Kirkham's replies being in an unfamiliar hand since he was too weak to write.

'Lady Kirkham sends her compliments and hopes that your lordship is not suffering too much discomfort.'

'Lord Kirkham thanks your ladyship for your kind enquiry, and is happy to report that he is tolerable. He is relieved to hear that your ladyship is in such good health after your terrible experience.'

'Lady Kirkham sends her best regards and wonders if your lordship has all the comforts he requires.'

'Lord Kirkham thanks your ladyship for your thoughtfulness. He assures you he has every comfort at his command. He anticipates soon being able to see out of two eyes instead of just one, when the joy of books will be his once more. Until then the Dowager Lady Kirkham is kindly reading aloud to him.'

Reading aloud to him! That was a task Melissa would have delighted in performing for him. Instead she was forced to remain uselessly in bed! Somehow she stuck it for the rest of that day, and half of the next, but by the following afternoon she could bear it no longer. As soon as Polly was out of the way she got out of bed, dressed hastily and went to his room.

To her surprise she found Fox in attendance instead of Wilkins, the new gentleman's gentleman who had come in replacement for Pentecost. Seeing her expression, the prize-fighter grinned.

'Mr Wilkins isn't much of a one for blood and broken bones, my lady,' he said. 'That's why I've come to attend to his lordship until he's on his feet again. I don't mind a bit of gore.'

'But is not his lordship attended by a proper nurse?' asked Melissa in alarm.

'I had one. She barely lasted the morning,' came Kirkham's voice from inside the room. 'She was worse than my old nanny. Kept referring to me as "we" and wanting to feed me gruel. I much prefer Fox. He is good for some decent conversation and does not get the vapours if my language is not up to snuff.'

Still smiling, Fox tactfully withdrew, leaving Melissa alone with Kirkham. Quite what to do next she was not sure. Her first instinct was to hurl herself at him and cover him with kisses; but this would not only have been unseemly it would have been downright uncomfortable for the poor man. There was no denying that he showed his battle scars very plainly. His head was bandaged, his shoulder bound up and his arm in splints. Heavy strapping round his chest was evidence of several broken ribs — as was his laboured speech —

but his face betrayed the aftermath of the fight most of all. Both of his eyes, one of which was still closed, were badly discoloured, his lips were swollen, his cheeks cut and bruised. His nose, that elegant patrician feature, showed the worst signs of damage.

'Your nose,' said Melissa, at an unexpected loss for something to say. 'It is broken. Will it ever be straight again?'

Kirkham squinted at the offending member with his one good eye.

'I doubt it,' he said. 'I shall tell everyone I got it going fifteen rounds with Fox. It will sound better than the truth.'

'There is nothing wrong with the truth!'

'Yes, there is!' Kirkham lay back on his pillows looking disconsolate beneath his injuries. 'It was all caused by my arrogance. We have nothing to fear from Beaucombe! How many times did I say that? Aye, and believed it! I should have known better. But more important things. All goes well with the child?'

'Yes, Dr Adams is very satisfied.'

'Thank heavens! If anything had happened to the babe—and to you, of course—I would have blamed myself to the end of my days.'

He put the child first, and rightly so, but Melissa noticed how she came a very belated second, almost an afterthought.

'That is being silly,' she said crisply to cover her sudden hurt. 'How could you possibly have known he would attack?'

'Knowing Beaucombe, I should have guessed. It was all right in London. Polly saw to that.'

'Polly? What has she to do with it?'

'She kept me informed about Beaucombe's moves. I thought you knew that. Where she got her information from I never asked. It was always accurate, though. The information reaching me here was not so good. Oh, within the environs of Kirkham things were secure enough, but I should have allowed for Beaucombe residing some distance up the coast and coming here by boat. Because of my stupidity I put you and everything I hold dear in jeopardy.'

For a hopeful moment Melissa considered his words. Was he saying he held her dear? In that case would he not have said 'Everything *else* I hold dear'? No, it was useless looking for endearments that were not there. She would not torment herself.

'You were very brave,' she said. 'You have nothing to reproach yourself with.' There were many things she wished to say to him, and ask, yet somehow she could not think of one. To cover the awkward pause she said, 'I can see it pains you to speak. You have been disturbed for long enough. I will leave you to get some sleep.'

'I thank you for your visit. I appreciate how distasteful it must be for you to look upon me. My injuries make me no fit sight for any lady.'

'You really are talking nonsense,' said Melissa angrily, completely forgetting to maintain the peace of the sick-room. 'How you look has nothing to do with anything. I came because I was concerned for you, and I am leaving for the same reason. You need your rest.'

'You were concerned for me?' he sounded surprised.

'Naturally. What else did you expect?'

'I do not know. . . You will come back again?'

'Of course I will — if you want me to.' But she was talking to herself. Kirkham had fallen asleep.

The next day there was no argument. She flatly refused to lie in bed.

'I promise not to over-exert myself,' she assured Dr

Adams. 'I will not set out on long route-marches, but I cannot — will not — remain in bed any longer.'

'As your ladyship pleases,' said Dr Adams with resignation.

The reason for her determination was Kirkham. She felt she had to be with him, to care for him. He had wanted her to go back, too. Had he not said so? She did not even try to put any loving inferences into this; the truth was too painfully obvious. She was his only diversion apart from Lady Kirkham.

'His lordship has had a very poor night,' whispered Fox as they passed in the doorway. 'Do not trouble if his temper is short.'

The instant she entered his room Kirkham greeted her with a sharp, 'Oh, it is you!'

'Yes, I said I would come back. Are you in pain?'

'No, madam. With a broken head, a shoulder and arm likewise afflicted, and goodness knows how many ribs stove in, I can honestly say I never felt better in my life.'

Melissa knew then that she would have her work cut out giving any comfort at all.

'Would you like me to read to you or shall we talk?' she asked.

'Talk!' The response was brusque and uncompromising. 'There are things I must know. They kept me tossing and turning last night. You have some explaining to do.'

'I have?'

'Yes, you, madam.' There was no calling her Melissa this morning. 'Why did you go down to the beach? That question has troubled me much. You knew Beaucombe was there, for Fox tells me you sent Polly to raise the alarm. Surely a woman of your intelligence knew better than to confront him?'

'It seemed a good idea at the time.' In his present mood, albeit the result of his discomfort, he was quite likely to scoff at the idea of her risking herself for him. She could bear many things, but not that.

'How typical of your responses, madam. What were you about? Did you think to persuade him to go away?'

'I suppose some such thought may have been in my head.'

'And you gave no thought to the child? Do you *never* give thought to the child?'

'Of course I did, but I thought even Beaucombe would not harm a pregnant woman.'

'What? You knew Beaucombe's character, yet you try to tell me that? I fear it is another of your Banbury tales, madam. It would have been sensible — nay, it was your duty — to have got away from that place immediately. Yet you tarried about, taking foolhardy risks. Tell me why, madam. I would have the truth.'

He was growing agitated and had begun to toss about the bed. He seemed hot, too, yet when Melissa attempted to cool his brow with a damp cloth he pushed her hand aside irritably.

'Tell me the truth, just for once in your life,' he demanded.

'Very well, I will,' she retorted, worried by his increasing restlessness. 'If the truth will make you calm then you shall have it. I was about to go back to the Hall, as you said I should, but Gyp came upon me. I knew then that you must be in the vicinity. Sure enough, I saw you in the distance heading straight for the stretch of cliff where the furze is lowest, where Beaucombe was bound to see you. There was no way I could warn you without being seen myself. I decided the only alternative was to divert Beaucombe's attention away from you. That was why I went down into the cove.'

'You did that? In your condition?' His voice was sceptical.

'As I said, I did not think Beaucombe would harm me.'

'What did you think he would do? Offer you his arm and escort you home? Madam, you have told me some rare stories in our time together, but never have you devised such a flight of fancy for my amusement. Forgive me if I do not laugh, for it is painful.'

'You asked for the truth and that is it,' she protested.

'I beg of you, madam, not to try me further. Merely leave me, if you please, and send Fox to me as you go.'

One look at his face, already flushed and feverish, and she knew she could not argue. Without a word she left the room, pausing only to summon Fox before she sought sanctuary in her own chamber. She almost wished Kirkham had scoffed at the truth; it might have been better than his blank disbelief. He was far from well, and she knew that his state of health would have coloured his reasoning, yet in some ways this only made things worse. He was in no state to think rationally, in which case would not his immediate reaction be his true one?

For the rest of the morning she nursed this uncomfortable idea to her. Any hope that the fracas with Beaucombe might have made any difference to them disappeared. Nothing had changed. Kirkham was as indifferent to her as ever.

It was about noon that Polly came to her, looking anxious.

'Mr Fox sends his apologies for disturbing you, but he begs permission to call Dr Adams,' she said.

'Kirkham is worse?'

'He's got a nasty fever on him,' was the reply, but Melissa was already hurrying up the stairs.

'I fear it's been brought on by his injuries, my lady,' said Fox, his large battered face looking even more crumpled with concern. 'I've seen it before after a man's had a bad beating, and I've tried all the remedies I know, but nothing has worked. I hope I did right to call you.'

'You did exactly right.' Melissa looked down with alarm on Kirkham's face streaked with perspiration. The bruises looked painfully livid when enhanced by the flush of his fever. 'Send down to the stables. The swiftest horse is to be saddled and Dr Adams sent for. If he is not at home then scour the neighbourhood until he is found, even if every servant in the place has to be sent out.'

Although the doctor was actually up at the Hall within the half-hour to Melissa it seemed like an eternity. With Fox in attendance she sat beside Kirkham's bed as he tossed and turned. All their attempts to help him were useless. In his delirium he thrust away tepid sponges, refused to take cooling drinks, and spat out Fox's remedies. She watched him thrashing about and feared for his broken bones. Particularly his ribs. Stirring violently the way he was he was liable to puncture a lung. Fox, too, shared her fears.

'We've got to keep him still somehow, my lady,' he said.

Melissa racked her brains. 'Bolsters!' she exclaimed. 'Lots of them!'

The bolsters were brought, and seeing them packed tightly round him she was reminded ironically of the single bolster that had occupied their marriage-bed in the early months.

'An excellent idea,' said Dr Adams approvingly when

he arrived. 'They will prevent his lordship from hurting himself through too much movement.' Then his face grew grave as he examined his patient. 'You do not need me to tell you this fever is severe. I can give you a draught to bring down the fever, if he will take it in his state. Also, his lordship must take lots of liquid, barley-water for preference. Apart from that I fear we must let nature take its course.'

Melissa felt terribly helpless. The doctor's recommendations had been near useless, he had suggested nothing they had not tried already.

'Let nature take its course indeed!' she snorted, suddenly angry at her own impotence. 'We will do no such thing, unless it be for Lord Kirkham to get well again.' The dreadful alternative she refused even to consider.

Patiently, one by one, she began slipping spoonfuls of barley-water between Kirkham's cracked lips, along with the fever-breaking draught left by the doctor. Frequently there were spillages, often he refused to swallow; it was a painstaking, long-drawn-out affair, but it proved worth it. Kirkham swallowed far more liquid than when it was offered in a cup. How long she would have continued alone there was no knowing if Lady Kirkham, Fox and Polly, along with half the servants, had not voiced their protest and begged to be allowed to help. Reluctantly she gave up the spoon to Lady Kirkham, only to be confronted by another problem. The bolsters, while effective, made Kirkham hot and she feared they might aggravate his fever. Aided by the housekeeper, Mrs Cobb, she turned out the linen store. The result was that the bolsters were swathed in cool linen sheets regularly every half-hour, aiding Kirkham's comfort. Then, and only then did she consent to rest. It was a long, long day.

When next the doctor called, just before dinner, he was able to pronounce that Kirkham was at least no worse.

Although there were more than enough people willing to help with the nursing, Melissa insisted upon doing the lion's share. She wanted to be with Kirkham, even though he was not aware of her presence. And would not approve of my being here if he were, she told herself wryly.

That did not matter. She was with him, and could tend to his needs, and look down upon his poor battered face with all the love that was in her—and which he did not want.

'He's been calling out a great deal,' whispered Fox, when she took over from him. 'Almost as if something was troubling the poor gentleman, though no doubt it's the fever talking.'

'No doubt,' agreed Melissa, settling down by the bedside.

Almost at once Kirkham began muttering.

'Shouldn't!' he mumbled, tossing fretfully. 'Didn't mean. . . Shouldn't. . .' Then there was much that Melissa could not understand. 'Shouldn't!' he yelled suddenly. 'Too cruel! Too wicked!'

'Hush, my darling,' whispered Melissa softly. 'Hush, there is nothing to be disturbed about, my love. I am here.' She wished she could say such things to him when he was conscious.

Strangely enough the sound of her voice seemed to have a soothing effect, for he grew more quiet. Encouraged, she reached out and took his unbandaged hand in hers. Then the miracle happened. He opened both of his bruised and swollen eyes and looked at her quite clearly.

'Melissa,' he croaked. 'You are here. . . Good. . .' Then he closed his eyes again.

After his delirious mumblings and the rasping of his breath the sudden silence in the room alarmed Melissa. Fearing the worst she leaned forward and put her ear close to his mouth. He was breathing peacefully and normally. He was asleep. Mercifully the fever had broken.

When Melissa awoke she was lying on the bed beside Kirkham, her fingers still entwined with his. She had a hazy recollection of being overcome by fatigue. . .yet being reluctant to release his hand. . .and the bed looking so inviting. . .

'Strange how bolsters play such an important part in our marriage.' Kirkham was gazing at her, a faint smile on his face. He still looked wan — his bruises apart — but his eyes had lost the unnatural brilliance of the fever and his skin was cool.

'How long have you been awake?' she demanded, then added hurriedly, 'I should not have fallen asleep. It was very remiss of me.'

'No, it was not. You were exhausted. That was why you sensibly dispossessed the bolsters and took their place.'

Awkward at being found in such a situation, Melissa tried to pull away.

'Nay, lie still,' Kirkham insisted, holding on to her hand. For a man who had been at death's door only hours since he had remarkable strength.

'I presume you are feeling better,' she said.

'Yes, much thanks to you.'

'I was only one of several who nursed you — your grandmother, Fox, Polly, Mrs Cobb.'

'But it was you who was most frequently by my bedside. Delirious as I was, my wits were not completely to let. I was conscious of your presence hour after hour. I am grateful to you.'

'There is no need.'

'Yes, there is. As there is a need for me to apologise to you, something at which I am well practised.' He paused, his thumb gently caressing her fingers. 'At the start of my fever I could hear myself accusing you of lying. I was horrified that I should be saying such things, yet somehow I could not halt my tongue. You risked your life for me down on the beach and all I did was to revile you.'

'Things said during a fever are best discounted. Besides, you exaggerate. My life was in no danger.'

'I beg to disagree. Beaucombe would have dispatched you without a second thought if it had suited him.'

'Then why did you have to ruin my plans and come down to the cove after me?' demanded Melissa. She knew she was going to have to justify her actions. How could she do that without admitting her love for him? 'I hoped you would not even know that I was there.'

'You can blame Gyp for that. He was frantic to get down to you. I had to tie him up so he would not come dashing down to the beach with me and give my presence away. Thank goodness someone found him afterwards and brought him home.'

'But why did you come at all? One man against Beaucombe's mob! I at least had some chance. You must have known you had no chance at all with him. You were mad to come down.'

'Is that what you really think of me?' He regarded her with distress. 'Do you honestly imagine I would walk away and desert you, knowing the danger you were in? You have never made any secret of the fact that you have a very low opinion of me, but I had no idea you considered me to be so utterly despicable.'

Melissa was shaken by the stricken look in his eyes.

'I think no such thing!' she protested. 'Low opinion of you? Utterly despicable? Whatever gives you such stupid notions?'

'Your behaviour. The way you look at me. Only a fool or a blind man would have failed to notice the utter contempt you have for me.'

Now Melissa was truly appalled. What had she done? She had tried so hard to assume a mask of indifference in his presence. It had never occurred to her that he might interpret her offhand manner as contempt.

'I confess that in the early days I did not approve of either you or your way of life,' she admitted. 'All that changed a long time ago. Once I got to know you better. . .' Her voice faded. That was as far as she was prepared to go in confessing her true feelings.

'Changed? You gave little hint of it.'

Suddenly all of Melissa's past anxieties and hurts welled up in her. 'Yes, I did!' she retorted. 'Time and again I tried to show that I cared but you were never interested. Sometimes you fooled me into thinking you felt some fondness for me, but it never lasted long.'

'I never fooled you,' he protested. 'Of course I had some fondness for you. . . Far more than that, in fact.'

'Then why did you seem to prefer to think of me as some sort of lying monster?'

'It was myself I was fooling. You despised me. I had to try to despise you in return.'

'Enough to regard me as someone who would give up her own child in exchange for a paltry allowance and a chance to live in some seaside town along with all the other deserted wives?'

'Of course not!' he cried, raising himself on his good elbow. 'I knew you would never leave the babe. Never in a hundred years! I was depending on it.' The effort proved too much for him and he collapsed on to the bed with a groan of pain.

'Now see what you have done,' declared Melissa, too concerned at his relapse to take note of his words. Gradually, as his face lost its ashen look and she made him comfortable once more, the full significance of what he had said sank in.

'You were depending on my staying?' she said.

'How else could I prevent you from leaving me?'

'Prevent me from leaving you?' she repeated.

'Yes. . . I could not bear the thought of losing you. It was cruel, I know. But desperate men use desperate measures. . . The hardest thing to bear in this world is to love someone yet be convinced that they despise you.'

'To love someone?' Try as she might she could not prevent herself from repeating everything.

'Yes, of course I love you. You look surprised. You should not — I think I fell in love with you that very first moment when I awoke and found you in bed beside me. You were everything I had ever wanted in a wife, but with spirit and an intelligence I had never dared to hope for. At first pride would never let me admit my feelings, then when you showed me nothing but contempt. . . But you deliberately walked across that beach to draw Beaucombe's attention away from me. It was a magnificent gesture and a brave one. . . For the first time I am really beginning to hope. . . It was not the action of an indifferent heart?'

'No,' whispered Melissa, close to tears. 'Far from it.'

She had heard his words, listened to him declare his love, yet she could still scarcely believe her ears.

'I have loved you for so long,' she stated, her voice suddenly strong. 'What a fool I was to hide my feelings. I was afraid you would scorn me, you see. At first I was convinced that you disliked me for ruining your life. Then, lately, I was sure it was only the child you wanted, not me.'

'I am greedy. I want both.' He was beginning to sound faint with weariness. 'In my fever I thought I heard you calling me "my love" and "my darling" but I was not sure.'

'Then be sure, for that is how I have thought of you these many, many months,' she cried. 'We have wasted so much time. Oh, how I wish I could put my arms about you and hold you close and show you how much I love you. But with your injuries I dare not.'

'Did ever a man have a better reason for recovering?' His voice was the merest whisper. 'What a future! I have the woman I love, and soon there will be the child. Boy or girl, it does not matter. For me my happiness will be complete.'

'It will be a boy, I promise you,' Melissa assured him.

'You are certain?'

'Yes, so certain that I will. . . I will wager upon it!'

Kirkham's eyes were closed now, but at her words a delighted smile crossed his face, and his free hand grasped hers as if he would never let it go.

'Just as I will wager on our future happiness,' breathed Melissa. 'Now, and for always.' She hoped he could still hear her, but if not it did not matter. She had many, many years ahead in which to prove that her words were true.

LEGACY of LOVE

Coming next month

BEAU'S STRATAGEM
Louisa Gray
Regency 1814

Lady Allegra Ashley was banished to Bath to stay with her Aunt Lydia, but on arrival there was no aunt; instead a strange gentleman was attempting burglary. Luc Fleetwood was looking for clues to the whereabouts of his brother, the Earl of Hawkhurst, but, on learning Lydia had disappeared too, Luc lost no time in transporting Allegra, her young brother, his tutor, the parrot and the dog to stay with his grandmother! Certain it was somehow a French plot, Allegra let her vivid imagination take over, and even Luc was not to be trusted—whatever her growing feelings for him...

ESCAPE TO DESTINY
Sarah Westleigh
Sark 1571/2

Rescuing a naked man from the sea took all Judith Le Grand's strength and her fortitude when sheltering him from the Spanish cost her brother Edward's life.

Part privateer, part spy, Oliver Burnett had to get back to London to report his knowledge of the Ridolfi plot to assassinate Elizabeth I, though a little dalliance as he recovered his strength wouldn't go amiss—but marriage, to save Judith's reputation? Yes, for the right to bed her! He could always go back to Sark later, when he was ready to settle down. Judith had other ideas!

LEGACY of LOVE

Coming next month

RANSOM OF THE HEART
Kate Kingsley

New Orleans/Morocco 1824

Her late brother's debts had left Danielle Valmont penniless, homeless and forsaken by the New Orleans élite whose conventions she had previously flouted. Still, Danielle was prepared to pick up the pieces—until that scoundrel De Leon came crashing back into her life, wreaking all manner of havoc...

Erstwhile pirate Arturo De Leon felt obligated to rescue Danielle from the danger she unwittingly faced—even if that meant kidnapping her aboard his brigantine. When Danielle showed her gratitude by stabbing him, the privateer steeled himself for what promised to be a long—and intriguing—voyage!

SILVER LINK
Patricia Potter

New Mexico 1846

Antonia Ramirez knew that the tall, blond American was not to be trusted. Yet Tristan Hampton had awakened something deep inside her that would not be denied.

Since the moment he had first laid eyes on Antonia, Tris Hampton had been lost. He was haunted by her dark beauty. She made him feel he had finally found the completeness he had been searching for. But her father clearly hated him, and someone wanted to see him dead. Of Antonia's love he was certain. The question of her loyalty was still to be answered.

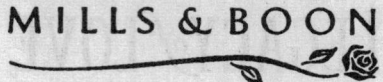

Proudly present...

This is a remarkable achievement for a writer who had her first Mills & Boon novel published in 1973. Some six million words later and with sales around the world, her novels continue to be popular with romance fans everywhere.

Her centenary romance *'VAMPIRE LOVER'* is a suspense-filled story of dark desires and tangled emotions—Charlotte Lamb at her very best.

Published: June 1994   **Price:**   £1.90

*Available from WH Smith, John Menzies, Volume One, Forbuoys, Martins, Woolworths, Tesco, Asda, Safeway and other paperback stockists.
Also available from Mills & Boon Reader Service, FREEPOST,
PO Box 236, Croydon, Surrey CR9 9EL (UK Postage & Packing free).*